# The Cat and the Corpse in the Old Barn

## Kate High

CONSTABLE

CONSTABLE

First published in Great Britain in 2020 by Constable

1 3 5 7 9 10 8 6 4 2

Typeset in Caslon Pro by SX Composing DTP, Rayleigh, Essex
Printed and bound in Great Britain by Clays Ltd, Elcograf S.p.A.

Papers used by Constable are from well-managed forests
and other responsible sources.

Constable
An imprint of
Little, Brown Book Group
Carmelite House
50 Victoria Embankment
London EC4Y 0DZ

An Hachette UK Company
www.hachette.co.uk

www.littlebrown.co.uk

# The Cat and the Corpse
## in the Old Barn

*For Ted*

# Chapter 1

The first dog burst out like fizzy lemonade from a shaken bottle before the door to the cottage was fully open. It was followed closely by a second much larger dog, and then, at a more sedate pace, by Clarice.

The garden was still white at 6.30 a.m., after a night temperature of minus four. The frosty ground cracked underfoot as Clarice walked the two-acre boundary.

The first dog, Jazz, was brown and white, a long-haired bitch unidentifiable as belonging to a single breed. Her legs were short, her ears big, and her tail, going around in circles of excitement, appeared to be far too long for her body. Behind her, Blue, a thickset black Labrador cross, with a splash of white on her chest, tried to keep up, determined not to drop the red rubber bone clamped between her teeth.

Trailing behind them, Clarice, slim and over six feet tall, strode forward purposefully. Her long glove-covered fingers were pushed deep into her jacket pockets, her auburn hair tucked up inside a tan-brown woollen hat that matched in colour her calf-length fur-lined boots. The muffler around her neck and face did not hide the exhale of her breath, showing as a moving cloud of white.

The property, enlarged over the years by various incumbents, dated back to 1855. Much of the garden was now given over to a wildlife meadow, trees and hedging, with a vegetable patch and herb garden nestling close to the cottage. Beyond lay the outbuildings: Clarice's workshop, which looked like a small bungalow; a barn converted to a garage; another old semi-derelict barn; and a long, low building surrounded by an outside enclosure, a temporary home to feral cats.

A year ago, she had walked the boundaries of the garden with Rick. They'd been seeing each other for three weeks when he came to visit for a weekend and, getting married along the way, stayed for thirteen years. He was her confidante, husband and lover. Conversations started as soon as one walked into a room occupied by the other, the picking-up of an endless, unbroken thread, neither wanting to put space between them. And then a year ago, it had changed. That she, who was known for her awareness and intuition, did not immediately recognise what was happening, and the speed at which it happened, astonished her. They became as an evolving species, one living organism that, having become toxic and in order to survive, had split in two. They had been estranged for six months.

The dogs ran back and forth exuberantly. After doing three circuits of the boundary, Clarice went into her workshop to turn up the heating, before going back out, leaving the dogs inside, to walk to the enclosure.

She stopped, reaching a point halfway, to look at the willow. It stood as a lone presence, stripped by the god of winter, throwing upwards beseechingly its frost-white naked arms. Its beauty deepened her sense of sorrow. Her face contorted for a fraction of a second. She pulled the heavy rainproof jacket tighter to her body, as if, by keeping the warmth in, the sadness might be driven out.

Reaching the enclosure, she unlocked and removed the Yale lock to go through the first gate, a wooden frame with mesh infill, then, less than five feet away, the second. The two-door double-lock system created a barrier so that none of the feral cats within could escape. The low brick building was about thirty feet from the second gate, the enclosure resembling a small wired-in garden. As she opened the door, she was greeted by a hiss.

'Good morning, Lucy.'

The ginger tortoiseshell cat strolled slowly past her to go outside. The relationship between woman and cat was one of compromise: Clarice fed Lucy and her litter, and Lucy in return had stopped growling and allowed her kittens to be handled. Clarice waited for Lucy to do a U-turn and go back inside, aware that the cat's protective instincts would not yet allow anyone to remain alone with her brood.

Standing in the centre of the room, she looked around. The bare brick walls accommodated cupboards and cabinets, a sink with a drainer, a kettle next to a jar of instant coffee, and a small fridge. On the tiled floor stood wooden hiding boxes, each with a circular hole cut out on one side for the kittens to enter and feel safe. A radio, an important part of the kittens' learning process, familiarising them with different noises, was fixed to a wall so it could not be knocked over. She pressed the switch and it came to life with the pips that preceded Radio 4's 7 a.m. news.

As she sat down on a plastic chair near the table, she was immediately pounced upon. The four kittens were five weeks old, and, having been socialised by handling and play, all but one were confident, doing well in their progress towards adoption.

'Hello, Lula, you are the pushiest girl,' she said to the small creature, while running her fingers down its back. Noise from the nearest cat box alerted her to activity as one ginger body rushed out pursued by another – Larry and Lenny, indistinguishable from each other. Although she was aware that new owners would rename them, it was her habit to christen members of each family group by working through the letters of the alphabet. This particular family comprised mother Lucy and her kittens Lula, Larry, Lenny and Liza – also known as Miss Shy Boots.

Clarice spent half an hour talking to and playing with the three youngsters before going to look for the missing kitten. Finding her hiding behind a box, she scooped her up, to return to sit holding and stroking her until her silence was replaced by a purr. Throughout, she had been stalked by Lucy, who, sitting nearby, watched intently. Lucy had been captured by use of a cat trap, and left with Jonathan Royal at the town's veterinary practice. Clarice liked Jonathan; he had a good sense of humour and enjoyed a gossip, generally putting a witty spin on rumours or tales as he passed them on. A squat man, small but broad, his most notable feature was his abundance of snow-white hair. He had a self-conscious habit of talking to Clarice from behind his hand, as if fearful of being overheard. 'I know your reputation as a sleuth,' he would say after telling her what he considered to be a juicy piece of gossip. 'Get to the bottom of that!'

When he had asked Clarice to take Lucy, he'd described the cat as 'a tad feisty'. She knew him well enough to interpret his words. Feisty meant she was antisocial and grumpy. The pre-attachment of 'tad', while folding his arms and raising his eyebrows for dramatic effect, meant that she scared the shit out of him: she was a full-on feral. Over the weeks, Clarice had made progress with her, but though no longer the hissy, spitting creature taken from Jonathan's surgery, she would never make a pet. After being neutered, she would begin a new life as a farm and barn cat.

Clarice sat down on the floor in the centre of a circle of kittens. While she absent-mindedly knocked table tennis balls for them to chase, she looked at the boxes, remembering the weekend that Rick had made them. It was the weekend she had realised the relationship was in trouble. There had been an atmosphere of animosity, and rather than staying to help him, she'd withdrawn to her workshop. Later in the evening, they'd argued, the underlying problems of their relationship like a festering wound, raw and visible. They'd picked over the minutiae of their lives: Clarice criticising his unpredictability due to work, the time he spent with his friends and playing sport; Rick expressing annoyance at the prioritisation of her work as a ceramicist and caring for the rescue animals above spending quality time with him – he was, he said, 'at the very bottom of the food chain'. She'd said things that were exaggerated and mean, and he had reciprocated in kind.

The relationship had limped on for several more months, but they were both guarded and critical of one another. They talked less, both being overly polite in order to avoid conflict, the physical side of the relationship diminishing over the weeks, until it ceased altogether. The marriage had died slowly of a thousand tiny pinpricks of complaint and neglect. Rick now rented a small modern house in Castlewick. Having taken it on a six-month lease, she imagined that he must be at the point of renewing it or finding another property. Some kind of decision must be on the horizon.

She considered now with guilt the sudden awareness after his departure of how much he had supported her in caring for the fostered animals. She'd sought more help from volunteers over the last six months, allowing her to relinquish and delegate many of her roles. Why had she ever imagined that she could do it all herself? And, she chastised herself, Rick had been a police officer from the beginning of their relationship; she'd known the hours his work entailed, and she knew about the number of officers whose relationships had failed due to the unsocial hours and heavy workload. So what had changed?

A table tennis ball being knocked around the floor alerted her to the fact that Liza had joined her siblings' hooligan gang and was running amok about the room.

Returning to her workshop, Clarice let the dogs out and they accompanied her back to the cottage. Her old friends Sandra and Bob would take on the role of kitten-handling in the afternoon. Until then, she was alone.

It was late morning when she received a call from Rex, an acquaintance who lived near the town.

'Hi, Rex,' she said, her voice lifting. 'Are you OK?'

'I'm fine,' he said. 'Some news for you – good, I think.'

Clarice stayed silent, waiting for him to continue.

'Your cat, the three-legged ginger . . .'

'Yes.' She said the word slowly, suddenly filled with hope.

'I spotted him late last night; drove past him on my way home.'

'It's a shame you didn't call earlier. He might be gone now.'

'Sorry, Clarice, meant to; the morning just slipped away.'

She guessed immediately that he had been out drinking until

late the previous evening. She imagined he would have taken the back roads home, in the hope of not being stopped and breathalysed. Now, having just woken, he was phoning with the expectation that the information might be rewarded with a pint. Rex never gave anything away for free.

'Are you sure it was him?'

'Yeah, full moon, ginger cat, three legs. How long has he been on walkabout?'

'Three weeks. He belongs to Vita at Winterby Hall.'

'Lady Vita! You do move in posh circles. He was one of yours, though, wasn't he?'

'Yes, she adopted him years ago. Where did you see him?'

'It was outside the Hanging Barn; you know where that is?'

'I do. I'll go there now – and thanks, Rex, I owe you a pint.'

'Great – sound like good news for both of us.' He laughed.

Walter had been given a home by Lord Roland Fayrepoynt and his wife. Clarice and Lady Vita shared a common interest in ceramics, and Vita had a number of Clarice's pieces within her vast collection.

Clarice put the phone down and wrote a note for Sandra and Bob.

*In case I'm not back when you arrive, Rex Cook spotted Walter near the Hanging Barn – YIPPEEEE! I'm going over to get him while he's still there. Cherry cake in the cake box, see you later. Clarice xx*

# Chapter 2

Having climbed the rickety ladder, Clarice pressed down hard with her hands to test the strength of the beam that stretched between the two platforms. It felt firm, but would be impossible to walk across, either standing or in a crouched position. What remained of the roof was only three feet higher than the beam. Swinging her leg over to straddle it, she began to heave herself along before looking down: a fifteen-foot drop.

The ruined building on the edge of the Lincolnshire Wolds known locally as the Hanging Barn had last been used for that purpose in August 1752, when William Thomas was hanged for stealing a horse. Before that, it had hosted only two other hangings within the same decade: one man convicted of sheep-stealing and another of burglary.

There was an overpowering smell. It was not just the stink of ordinary decay. She had noticed it when she first came in, but up here, it was worse. It made her think of a damaged animal. One that had come to this quiet place to die, and was decomposing somewhere below in the hay.

The barn had three remaining walls. Where the fourth should have been there was an empty space; that and half of the roof had long gone. The place was filthy and decaying. Rotting wooden pallets, once possibly in a neat stack, had imploded downwards in a corner, resembling, thought Clarice, a sculpture, an unsung homage to the inevitability of the passage of time.

Icy rain flew in through the gap in the roof and the space where the wall had once been. Sufficient to make the open area saturated, it did nothing to eradicate the stench. Branches from an overgrown willow trailed downwards, making a clicking noise as they moved with the wind to hit against the structure.

On the climb to reach the beam, a jagged piece of metal protruding from the ladder had torn Clarice's jeans. A throb of pain alerted her that it had cut into her thigh. Resting for a moment, she stared at the cat, which gazed back, unblinking.

'Walter, do you really want me to get splinters in my arse?' Although she was annoyed, the voice she used was soothing.

The scrawny ginger tom regarded her, body posture unchanged, attitude defiant. He had come to Clarice ten years earlier as a stray, damaged after being hit by a car. Where his left back leg had been amputated was now a small stump. He moved well on the remaining three legs, but at sixteen years old and toothless at the front of his mouth, his disappearance three weeks earlier had caused concern about his ability to survive. His unblinking stare, however, suggested that he considered himself to be neither lost nor in need of rescue.

Clarice edged forward along the beam, hand over hand, getting nearer to the cat. Suddenly she heard a groaning sound beneath her. As she squeezed the cheeks of her buttocks, an image came into her mind of two large soft oranges trying to hold a solid piece of wood, and failing. For a moment she was poised in mid-air, before she and the beam went crashing downwards.

*

Later, at the hospital, each doctor asked the same question. Had she been knocked unconscious? If so, for how long? She gave each the same answer: she didn't know. One moment she had been up there talking to the cat; the next thing she remembered was being flat on her back in the hay below.

The stink on the ground had been vile, overpowering. Even half conscious, she'd found herself gagging with each breath. Someone was prodding her in the chest, and there was a rumble of distant thunder. She lay, eyes closed, trying to remember where she was. Moving her fingers in the hay, she worked out that it was not her bed.

She opened her eyes to find Walter sitting on her chest. A silver thread travelled downwards from the cat's mouth, and she realised that while he was gleefully purring and paddling, he was also drooling through toothless gums.

Looking past the cat, she followed the direction in which a raised hand was pointing. The hand was grey, with long red fingernails, two of which were broken – snapped but still attached.

Could it be a discarded tailor's dummy?

Her head throbbed with pain, as did her back and left ankle. She made an effort to focus on her surroundings.

The hand, although a strange grey colour, was realistic.

It had taken several minutes for her to understand. The smell was coming from beneath her. The hand was attached to an arm, which was attached to a body. She was lying on top of a rotting corpse.

# Chapter 3

Clarice lay on a trolley in a curtained cubicle. Her ankle, which had been strapped, rested upon a support pillow. She awaited her relocation to a ward, when a space could be found. She felt like an unattractive parcel waiting to be moved on.

Feet scurrying, the babble of voices, telephones, the wheels of trolleys, the crying of a small child all assaulted her senses. Most injurious to her peace of mind was the smell of the hospital, a combination of disinfectant, urine, sweat, handwash and fear, which, for her, always had an association with death.

At the barn, after the fall, when the fog in her brain had cleared sufficiently, she had used her mobile phone. Unable to reach Sandra and Bob, she'd called Georgie Lowe, friend and neighbour. Her second call was to the police. Georgie had gone to Clarice's home and grabbed a cat basket, plus a pair of jogging pants, a T-shirt and a sweater for her to change into. She had been insistent that she wanted to go with Clarice to the hospital, but Clarice, knowing that her friend had to get back to collect her children from school, was adamant. As she was assisted into the ambulance, she assured Georgie she would be all right on her own. Georgie left reluctantly with Walter, promising to feed him if Sandra and Bob had not yet arrived.

Clarice tried to resist the temptation to flatten her hair. It was shoulder length, a deep auburn, always well cut and usually shiny. It now looked like a tangled bush. She had attempted to wash it, but had been hampered by her inability to bend over the sink in the A & E bathroom, or even to stand upright. The nurse who had been with her, blonde, small and brisk, with an air of superiority, had chided her to deal with the health issues first. A small terrier capable of delivering a nasty nip, Clarice thought. A & E was too busy for staff to assist her, but perhaps, the nurse suggested, when they found a space on a ward, one of the staff there might help. She was aware that she had brought with her the foul smell of the barn and the decomposing corpse, part of which, she realised, was still in her hair. Minuscule scraps of another woman's flesh, blood and bone. She shuddered, trying to remove the image of the remains of the destroyed face from her mind.

Her head throbbed. Thinking again about the dead flesh, the grey hand with its long red claw-like nails, how could she have imagined it was anything other than human, and why had she not freaked immediately? Was what she now considered to be her idiotic reaction all down to the fall and the bang to her head?

'Bloody Walter!' she whispered with a smile.

'You could have killed yourself!'

Clarice looked up. Her husband, Rick, stood over her, his face flushed. Glowering, he immediately launched into a ranting tirade.

'What an utterly stupid, ridiculous thing to do! You are not in your prime, not agile, not especially fit. And what's to say that even if you had reached Walter, he wouldn't have scarpered down, out of your reach? He might only have three legs, but he knows how to make good use of them. What were you thinking?'

He was tall, over six feet four, a good three inches taller than her. An ex-rugby player for the county and police force, his height and bulk made his presence imposing. It was one of the things that had attracted her to him. He was the tallest man she had dated. She admitted her own true height to few people, only conceding to five feet eleven.

Her first thought, as always, was to correct herself. Rick was not her husband; he was her estranged husband.

'I'm OK,' she said, seeking to placate him.

'Don't talk to me as if I'm one of your bloody cats!' he snapped. 'It's one of those buggers that got you here, and you are not all right: a busted ankle and concussion!'

'Calm down and sit down,' Clarice said. 'I'm not seriously hurt. They thought I might have had a bleed on the brain, but it doesn't show that I have. I've still got a cracking headache, and I'm pissed off I've got to stay in overnight, but that's only a precaution.'

'You were knocked out.' He spoke more calmly, a deflated balloon that had lost its air, as he followed her instruction to sit on the chair next to the bed. 'That is serious, *and*,' he added, 'you sorted out that bloody cat before you even phoned the police.'

'I had to phone Georgie to come and collect Walter after going to all that trouble to get to him. Bet that's your buddy Sergeant "the Snitch" Daisy telling tales.'

'Daisy likes you. Enough to tell me when you've fallen from a great height onto your head.' Rick spoke quietly.

'And I like Daisy.' Clarice smiled at him. 'Detective Inspector

Beech, anyone would think you were still my husband,' she teased.

He leaned towards her. 'I am, as it happens, even if it's in name only.'

Bet he's thinking the same as me, Clarice thought, looking at him; both of them deciding not to go in that circle of your fault, my fault, your job, my cats, we could still be together, we're better apart – around and around.

'So,' she said, '*was* it Rose Miller?'

'Daisy told me that's who you told her it was – after you'd buggered up the crime scene. Good guess. Her face was a mess, and you hardly knew the woman.'

'I didn't deliberately land on top of her. It was an accident.' Clarice moved the conversation back to the identity of the dead woman. 'I'd know those nails anywhere.'

'There must have been something else.'

'So I *am* right.'

He didn't respond.

'They were more talons than nails,' she said thoughtfully. 'That shape isn't fashionable now. The current trend is more squared. She was the only person I knew who still had that style. She was in her late forties, but she loved the fifties. People often wore their nails long and pointy then. She liked fifties clothes too. I don't know why – boring decade, style-wise. The sixties are much more interesting.'

Still he said nothing.

'You're right, her face was a mess, but that blue fitted skirt was another giveaway. They sometimes called them "hobble" skirts because they restricted your walk, to give the wiggle effect. Very sophisticated for the more mature woman.'

'You still have the ability to amaze me. What normal person would notice the shape of someone's fingernails?' He smiled for the first time since his arrival. 'Someone she's only met, what, once or twice?'

'Four times.' She matched his smile. 'But I'll take that as a compliment.'

'Rose Miller has not been officially named as the victim yet. She needs to be identified and next of kin informed before any details are released,' he said. 'Daisy went to her house with Rob. Someone had been there, trashed the place.'

'DC Rob Stanley?'

'Yes, he's on the team.'

'Do you know what was taken?'

'We don't know yet, but it wasn't a regular robbery. There was a lot of jewellery untouched.'

'Was she killed there or at the barn?'

Rick raised his eyes towards the ceiling. 'That's not information being put into the public domain, and it's too early to say exactly.'

'I'm not the public domain, I'm your wife.'

'My estranged, soon-to-be ex-wife.'

She flinched at his use of the ex-word, but continued, 'You're a professional, Rick. You always have a good idea by this point, even though it needs to be confirmed. There wasn't much blood in the barn, so I don't think she died there. And—'

'All right.' He lifted his hands to cut off her words. 'Remember, not to be repeated.'

'It goes without saying.' It was her turn to cut in.

'I know you'll witter and witter until I tell you.'

She was offended. 'I never witter!'

'Yes, sorry. I agree: you don't.'

She moved her head in acknowledgement of the apology. How had they become like this? she wondered. They had been good friends, and now they were adversaries, intimate ones, each knowing the other's strengths and weaknesses.

'She wasn't killed in the barn or in her home. Somewhere else. We're working on it.'

Clarice thought about this.

'You can't get involved, you know that?' He looked at her intently.

'Yes, of course,' she said, knowing she didn't mean it. And that he was aware she didn't.

'What did you make of her? Did you like her?' Folding his arms, he leant back on the hard plastic chair.

'No.' She spoke decisively. 'She was not especially likeable. A difficult person. I doubt she would have had any really close friends. Rose was one of those people that if I'd seen her every week for years, I wouldn't have known her any better. And I wouldn't have ever warmed to her. When I was young, with people like that, I thought it was a lack of communication on either their part or my own. Now that I'm older, I realise that there isn't anything more to them, nothing more to get to know!'

'No friends in town, then?'

Clarice thought about Castlewick. It was a small country town. She often thought it had locked down into the 1940s. Her mother had talked to her about what it had been like when she had been a child. Clarice recognised the descriptions of that past in the present. It seemed that everyone knew practically everybody else and took an overactive interest in the business and private lives of their neighbours. On the positive side, there were still many small independent shops, including a fish shop and two old-fashioned ironmongers where it was possible to buy just a couple of nails or screws rather than a pack of twenty. And when she walked through the Saturday or Wednesday market at the centre of the town, even vague acquaintances nodded or said hello.

'I would say no real friends,' she replied. 'She'd been in Castlewick for maybe two years. She came to the first two sessions of one of my six-week ceramics courses. I could tell it wasn't her thing, but she had just moved to the town and had joined everything. It's what people do when they want to get to know new people. She didn't produce any work, just talked to the others in the group.'

'Stopping them working.' He smiled.

'That's it.' Clarice nodded. 'I also met her at Jane Mason's coffee morning, and when Clare Robbins invited a crowd for lunch. On both of those occasions, and at the classes, I heard her telling people that she lived at the Old Vicarage. It was in a showy way. It's a big house, and she'd had it fully modernised. Kept moaning about the time and cost of the builders, electricians, workmen. I felt it was her way of letting people know she could afford it, that she was rich and important. People who've always had money don't do that, and I assumed she was newly wealthy. The word was that her husband had died and left her well provided for. Having said that, she always accepted offers of lunch or a day out and never repaid the hospitality.'

'Anything else?'

'She always reminded me of Brenda Prescott. Can you remember her?'

'Vaguely. Moved to Norfolk?'

'That's the one. Brenda was competitive, in a mean sort of way.'
He nodded.

'She told me once that someone had asked her for a recipe
– a date and walnut cake she'd put on the charity cake stall for
the church. She was known to be a good baker. I said that it was
a nice compliment, and she told me, in a skittish, girly way, that
she didn't *ever* give anyone complete recipes. She always left out
or added a couple of ingredients, or altered the weight of the
flour or sugar, because she didn't want anyone else's cakes to be
as good as hers.'

Rick snorted. 'What did you say to that?'

'I told her it might be better just to say that she didn't pass
on old family recipes, rather than giving out false ones. And,'
Clarice went on, 'I could imagine Rose doing that. She told
lies. They were small and rather silly, but it did alter the way I
thought about her. She wore a perfume, lily of the valley, at the
second class. Another lady complimented her on it and asked
what it was called. Rose waffled in a childish voice, saying she
couldn't remember but thought it was by Estée Lauder.'

'And?'

'It was Diorissimo, a Dior perfume that was introduced in
the 1950s. My mother used it for a while. I knew Rose was lying.'

'Did you say anything?'

'No. I try not to get too involved in student chat. The classes
are always busy. Then, at the lunch at Clare's, Rose said she had
lived in St Albans, in Hertfordshire, she and her late husband.'

'You know that area well, don't you, with visits to your aunt?'

'Right.' Clarice nodded. 'That's what I told Rose. I asked her
what she thought of various well-known places. Just making
small talk.'

'She hadn't lived there?'

'Didn't have a clue.' She paused. 'Rick, can I ask you something?'

'What?'

'Do I smell?' she whispered.

'Ah ...'

'That's a yes, then?'

'You smell of the barn. I noticed it when I arrived. Think I preferred the cat piss.' He laughed at his joke. Then, seeing the look of distress on Clarice's face, verging on tearful, he stopped.

'I'm sorry. That was mean, silly. You never smell.'

She looked at him, her eyes glassy with unshed tears.

'I know, I know.' He repeated the words. 'Point-scoring, any chance for a dig.'

She nodded. 'My bloody rescue cats, your bloody job.'

They exchanged limp smiles, each of them aware that they still had the power to inflict pain on one another.

'I wanted to wash my hair, but I kept wobbling,' she said. 'The nurse told me they're too busy here to help. I can't imagine they'll have any more time on the ward.'

He took her hand and squeezed it.

'Don't be kind,' she pulled away, 'or I'll cry. I keep thinking I've got bits of Rose's corpse in my hair. It makes me want to throw up.'

'Be about an hour, Clarry.' A voice made her jump. 'We're moving you to a bed on Ward 3.' This nurse was small, dark-haired and rotund. She referred to notes on a clipboard.

'Clarice,' Rick said as he stood up, looming over her.

'What?'

'My wife's name is Clarice, not Clarry. Clarice Beech.'

She looked down at the paperwork. 'Sorry, yes. Clarice, that's a name to remember. There was a Clarice in that film, *Hannibal Lecter*, about a mad murderer.'

'*The Silence of the Lambs*,' he corrected her. 'Nineteen ninety-one.'

'Yes, that's the one.'

'Clarice was the name of my wife's mother's favourite potter. Have you heard of her, Clarice Cliff? That's where she gets her name from.' He spoke in a friendly tone. Clarice watched the woman beam up at him. He's charming her, she thought.

'Do you know, I thought it was Clarence – a bloke. I've seen cups and saucers on that antiques programme. That's me not listening properly. I shall remember the next time they come up.' The nurse laughed. 'Now I've met a real Clarice.'

'My wife is also a potter, a ceramicist, but her work is contemporary, very modern.'

'Lovely.' She turned her smile to Clarice.

'Could you do me a little favour?' Rick spoke in a conspiratorial whisper, and the nurse's expression changed to curious. 'If it's going to be an hour, could you find a wheelchair and direct me to a bathroom,' he bent down towards the small woman, 'and somewhere I can get decent soap, shampoo and towels?'

The nurse opened her mouth to speak. Rick got there first.

'I know it's a bit irregular, and how busy you all are. We wouldn't want to take staff away from the really serious work, but my wife does need to be cleaned up. It won't take long. It's distressing for her after the accident, not to feel clean. If you can help me find the necessary kit, between us we can sort things out.' He smiled engagingly.

Clarice looked at him, at his height and bulk. His

close-cropped dark hair had speckles of grey and was thinning at the back. He had a permanent five o'clock shadow, and his rugby player's nose was flattened to an odd shape. His accent was south London. He was a cliché from a crime novel and could only be a villain or a copper. Whichever of the two people imagined, if he so chose, he could charm them.

'I'm not supposed to,' the nurse said, folding her arms across her chest and striking a pose. She smiled. 'It's meant to be the staff on the ward who do all that.'

Rick pressed his finger to his lips and laughed. The nurse chuckled, as if in the company of an old buddy.

She directed him to the hospital shop, where he bought a citrus soap, shampoo, a hairbrush, toothpaste and a toothbrush. A different nurse awaited his return ten minutes later. A young man with a nice smile was leaning on a wheelchair, chatting amiably to Clarice. On its seat were two towels, well used and coarse, but both large. Also a fresh hospital gown.

They were taken in the lift to the third floor, which was made up of three separate sections, each dealing with different medical problems. The nurse, leaving them outside a bathroom, instructed them to return to wait in Ward 3 reception when they were finished.

Entering the bathroom, Clarice felt a wave of utter helplessness, followed by embarrassment. Ten minutes later, she was sitting naked on the plastic seat in the invalid shower, her damaged ankle wrapped in the waterproof bag the toiletries had come in, the leg protruding out to rest on a chair. Rick took off his tie, folding it to put into his jacket pocket, then removed the jacket, hung it behind the door and rolled up his shirtsleeves. With the shower turned on, warm water running gently down, he dropped shampoo on her hair from above, and as she massaged it in, perhaps to distract her from her self-consciousness, he started to talk to her about blood splatters.

Some of it she already knew, having had similar conversations before, but much of it she didn't. He told her about pattern analysis, the examination of size, shape and distribution. The principles of biology, the behaviour of the blood. The use of physics with regard to cohesion, capillary action and velocity. How mathematics was used – geometry, for the distance and angle – to work out the direction the blood splatter had come from, the direction the wound was inflicted. Then how the splatter could indicate how the victim and perpetrator were positioned and what movements were made after the blood was shed. He had just started to talk about the three basic types of stain – passive, transfer, and projected or impact – when she realised she had gone onto autopilot. With Rick's assistance, she had washed and dried herself. He had helped to get the clean hospital gown in place before removing the plastic carrier bag tied to her foot and guiding her back into the wheelchair.

There had been no sexual content in the encounter. They had been, for a short time as he talked, as they once had always been together, relaxed and the best of friends. He had not commented on the cuts to her legs and back, or the bruises on her body. She had seen the compression of his lips, the eyes unable to meet her own, the self-control she imagined he was using to stay silent. She was grateful he had made no comment; he had already expressed his opinion when he arrived in A & E. But she empathised with what she guessed he was feeling. In turn, she had had to restrain herself from remarking on his obvious tiredness, or enquiring about his diet. She imagined him eating a burger and chips for most meals. His shirt looked creased, his trousers as if they needed a wash. But they were no longer a couple; it was not her place to comment.

Having replaced his jacket and tie, he crouched to her eye level.

'Thanks, Rick.' She spoke shyly. 'Above and beyond the call of duty.'

'We used to be a good team, you and me,' he said. 'Didn't we?'

'Yes,' she said. 'Yes, we did.'

# Chapter 4

Evening visiting time had started at six. Each of the three women occupying the other beds in the four-bed bay had one or more visitors, the many people making the space seem small. As they entered, the room fell silent. The nurse led the way, followed by Clarice pushed in the wheelchair by Rick. All heads turned to look at the new arrivals. Each nodded or smiled to acknowledge them before turning back to their own conversations.

Once Clarice was settled on the bed, Rick came to sit next to her. 'I'll call in tomorrow,' he said.

'I trust I'm going home tomorrow!' She hoped she wouldn't be kept in for very long. She had things to do.

'We'll have to see. Speak in the morning.' He bent to kiss her cheek.

'There is just one thing I was thinking about.'

'Yes?'

'It's Walter.' She looked furtively at the others in the room, keeping her voice low. 'He's scrawny because of his age, but he looked pretty good considering he would have had to scavenge for food for about three weeks. He's a bit gummy at the front, but has teeth at the sides and back.'

'I had thought of that.' Rick twisted his lips into a sardonic grimace. 'His own larder, with a plentiful supply of raw meat.'

She nodded.

'Don't worry about it. Try to sleep.' He kissed her cheek again and then was gone.

Settling into the pillow, Clarice realised that he had been with her for over two hours, a big chunk of time while on a murder investigation. She had not heard his mobile ringing, and the thought came to her that he must have turned it off, something he rarely normally did.

Twenty minutes later, Georgina Louise Lowe, Georgie to her friends, arrived.

'It took me ages to find you. I know, I know – you told me not to come.' She sat on the bottom of the bed, holding up an overnight bag that Clarice recognised as being her own. 'Toiletries, jeans, tops, dressing gown, pyjamas. I couldn't find slippers. You don't wear them, do you? You're always barefoot in the house.'

Georgie, as was her way, talked without a pause. Forty-five years old, but looking much younger, small, with brown urchin-cut hair and enough freckles to beat Clarice's count, she was petite, with a pretty heart-shaped face.

Eventually running out of words, she said, 'Well, you look better than you did earlier. I was worried.'

'I am better – much.'

'I can't really stop, but I'll be back tomorrow if you're still here.'

'It's so good of you to come.'

'In fairness, Alan wasn't his usual grouchy self, even sent you a get-well-soon message, and was OK looking after the kids.'

She smiled. 'Perhaps the pub burned down and nobody's told me.' She put her head back and laughed, a loud and unexpected noise in a room of quiet conversations and silences. 'I saw Rick in the car park. He didn't spot me. Has he been with you long?'

'About two hours.'

'Ooh, two hours!' She gave Clarice a knowing look.

Clarice acted mock-surprised. 'Now go home.' She wagged her finger.

'OK, OK, I'm out of here.' Georgie leaned over to kiss her, putting an arm around her. 'Take care of yourself. Speak tomorrow. I told Bob what had happened. He and Sandra are at yours until late, with the beasties. They'll telephone Lady Vita to tell her the good news about finding Walter. They're taking the dogs home with them overnight. And they'll be back in again early in the morning to feed the cats. They both send love.'

'Thank you, thank you so much.' Clarice returned the hug.

When she was sure Georgie had gone, she slid downward into the bed, curling on her side into a foetal position. She had observed glances from the other occupants, looking to engage her in conversation. Even if it could only be managed for a short time, she would attempt to avoid the inevitable questions about what had happened to bring her here.

Later, when she'd changed into the pyjamas Georgie had brought in, the lights had been dimmed and her room-mates had gone to sleep, she lay still on her back, listening to the low voices of the two nurses at the desk outside the ward, the intermittent swish of doors closing as the night staff moved around. Occasionally a beeper sounded where a drip bag needed replacing, then there was the noise of feet, followed by the beeper being silenced. The woman in the bed opposite was snoring, the noise she made one drawn-out word, followed by a stutter – caaaaar-ic, ic, ic . . . caaaaar-ic, ic, ic.

The gentle but unfamiliar sound made Clarice feel disoriented, alien. The single blanket on her bed was light; she was used to the weight of her duvet. There was only one pillow and the room was too hot. She had been given medication for her headache, but had refused a pill to help her sleep, thinking it might make her confused and twitchy. She did desperately want to fall into oblivion, to get the night over, but she knew sleep would not come easily.

She burrowed down once more into the bed, turning onto her side again. By way of distraction, she filled her mind with thoughts.

She could speak two other languages: French and Italian. She could bake her own bread. She could change a fuse and a plug. She could build and fit her own shelves. She could plaster a wall, paint it or hang wallpaper. She could create, in clay, abstract pieces large and small; the glazes on porcelain or stoneware were her signature. She could play the fiddle, not well, but well enough to amuse. She could trap abandoned and feral cats and with kindness turn the hissing, claw-slashing creatures into loving, unique beings, with longer, better-quality lives. She could take a dog that had been scarred by a bad experience and make it whole.

As well as animal behaviour, she understood human nature. It fascinated and repelled her in equal measure. An observer of the human animal, she could work out the mindset of an individual as easily as she could a four-legged creature. She was usually accurate in her assessments. The big difference between the two- and four-legged beings was that those with four legs did not kill for pleasure. She had often heard the argument that the domestic cat playing with its prey was cruel, but it was part of the instinct that was required for it to survive. The fact that the domesticated cat had a full belly did not remove that instinct.

And then there was what she couldn't do: she couldn't mend her marriage. On a shelf in her workshop was a Clarice Cliff vase that had belonged to her mother. It had been broken, an accident caused not, as most people imagined, by a cat, but by a friend's child. She'd had it professionally repaired, and from a distance it looked acceptable; but it wasn't. The cracks would always be there; the damage done could never be undone. Looking at that vase now made her think about grief and the death of her marriage. That thought, like a maggot in an apple, had lodged itself in her brain, where it continued to fester.

She tried to shift her thoughts away into another direction. She thought instead of Rose. That foolish woman with her petty lies. Why had she been murdered? It could be random, but that was unlikely. She hadn't had children. Her husband had died. Or had he? Back to the beginning – Rose had lied. Clarice mentally went over the woman's small, pointless fibs. If there was a husband, he might not be dead. And Rose might have children. Could she have upset someone locally? The fallout would have to be significant for them to have murdered her.

She realised that after her miserable day, her thinking and judgements were not sound. If she couldn't sleep at home, she imagined the sea, the waves coming back and forth, the sound, smell and salty taste. She thought of Rick, walking with him as newlyweds, hand in hand. It was Christmas Day, eleven years ago. The deserted beach, an hour's drive from home. Gulls screeched above them, the sky was white, as was the foam from the waves as they moved in and out, in and out.

*'Woman much missed, how you call to me, call to me,*
*Saying that now you are not as you were.'*

The voice was Rick's, the words by Thomas Hardy. It was an elegiac poem written, in grief, after the death of his wife.

No, no – Emma, Hardy's wife, was dead. I'm not dead. Distress moved like the waves to engulf her. Why, she thought, why am I thinking this?

*'When you had changed from the one who was all to me,*
*But as at first, when our day was fair.'*

The image of herself and Rick was from behind. She saw herself stop and turn, but the face was not her own. It was damaged beyond recognition. It was Rose Miller.

'No, that's not me. I'm not dead.' As she spoke, she woke up.

It was still night. The nurses had gone from outside the room. The snoring continued. Clarice was damp, her pyjamas clinging to her with perspiration.

She fell asleep again almost immediately, waking at six with the sounds of movement around her.

# Chapter 5

Over ten hours later, at 4.45 in the afternoon, she was sitting in her own kitchen, a mug of tea before her on the table.

Rick, as promised, had taken her home. Having already called earlier to enquire from the nursing staff what sort of night she had passed, he called her mobile just after 9 a.m. to ask her the same question. He would, he told her, confirm with the staff what time she might be able to leave. She was examined by a doctor in the morning, who shone the light from a small torch into her eyes before asking questions relating to her vision, memory and balance. In the afternoon, Mr Dixon, a consultant, arrived. He was attired in a smart and, Clarice thought, expensive bespoke brown suit, and advanced to her bedside within a fluid circle of students, all wearing identical white coats and expressions of rapt attention focused on the great man. After asking Clarice the same questions as the junior doctor in the earlier visit, he talked about her, rather than to her.

'Concussion is a traumatic brain injury, and the loss of consciousness, even for a short period, is the body's way of protecting itself, switching off. You.' He pointed his pen at a short man with wispy hair and large silver-framed glasses. 'Symptoms?'

'Well,' the student said, 'nausea, sickness, dizziness, loss of balance, blurred vision.'

'What else?'

'Slurred speech.'

'Thank you, Mr Grey. I think we can all agree this patient does not currently display these symptoms. What else?'

'Emotional outbursts, mood swings.' A pretty Asian woman spoke up.

'In all cases?'

'No,' she responded. 'The symptoms of concussion vary from patient to patient. There may be more problems over the days or weeks after the initial incident.'

He nodded, looking around the group.

'Has anyone anything to add?'

'Pupil dilation.' It was the man with the wispy hair again. 'Pupil dilation is an indicator of the concussion.'

'Right,' said Mr Dixon. 'Now tell me about Mrs Beech's other injuries.'

Clarice listened intently as they discussed fractures. The tibia and fibula in the leg, joining the talus in the foot. She had sprained her ankle but also had a proximal fracture, the fifth metatarsal, the one attached to the little toe, which was the most commonly broken bone in the mid foot. She thought the students were knowledgeable, and looking at each as they talked, she tried to work out their ages.

Before leaving, Mr Dixon spoke to the attendant nurse about an elastic bandage, a flat-bottomed boot and crutches. He agreed with the diagnosis of the junior doctor. Clarice could be allowed to go home. After nodding at her, as if in acknowledgement that he had not been unaware of her presence, he walked away, followed as gulls in the fields behind the tractor by the white-coated students.

Eventually, at 4 p.m., after all the formalities of form-filling, expressions of thanks to the staff and a visit to the hospital pharmacy for medication, she and Rick had left.

Clarice felt stiff. The places where she was bruised were painful. She'd slept at an odd angle in the unfamiliar bed and her neck ached, adding to her physical difficulties. Discharged with crutches and told to bend her knee, not to put weight on her damaged foot, she felt unbalanced. Her usual habit of striding forward purposefully was completely at odds with her new circumstances. It was only when she'd left the hospital building, going outside to a dark sky that hinted at rain, that her spirits soared. Bring it on, she thought; rain could not dampen her mood, the relief she felt in getting away from the hospital.

Rick walked slowly beside her, carrying the bag Georgie had brought in the previous day.

'So what's new on the murder?' she asked as soon as he pulled away from the car park.

He gave a wry smile. 'No small talk, no foreplay?'

Ignoring the question she said, 'Are the post-mortem results back?'

'Not officially; they like to be thorough.'

'But what did Steve tell you?'

'Is there any point in my saying that we should talk about you? How are you feeling?'

'Crap, actually.' She pushed her fingers through her hair, feeling where her head was still sore.

'You look tons better than yesterday.'

'Thanks for that; I couldn't look worse. Stop hedging, what

32

did Steve tell you – unofficially? I know the games the two of you play.'

'He said she had been punched, hard; the blow broke her jaw. Then her skull was shattered with a blow intended to finish her.'

'With?'

'Steve thinks something like a mallet.'

'Was the blow to the back or front of the head?'

'The front.'

'Interesting. You said *intended* to finish her?'

'She died of asphyxiation.'

'I suppose, if she had been knocked out by the punch, at least she wouldn't have known what came next.'

'If.'

Clarice fell silent to consider the hell Rose might have suffered, seeing her murderer swinging the heavy implement intended to finish her off – and then when it didn't, what?

'Steve tells me there's some sort of grain dust in her lungs.' His words cut into her thoughts.

'So she was still alive in the barn?'

'No, not necessarily. That place hasn't had grain in it for years, and she definitely wasn't killed there.'

'Was there anything else?'

'One or two small matters.'

'How small?' She waited for him to continue.

'Rose Miller was not Rose Miller, she was Sharon Cocker. Changed her name by deed poll over two years ago.'

'How did you find out?'

'Her prints were in the system. She was once accused of blackmail, another time extortion and threats. Neither went anywhere. A few years after that, she did time for a scam. She was involved in it with her sister and brother-in-law, Jackie and Pete Smith. It seems, from the number of potential prosecutions on file, that she always got away with it – nothing could stand up to take her to court. But finally her luck ran out. There's another sister – Maggie – who we haven't found yet.'

'What was the scam?'

'Selling holidays that didn't exist. People turned up at a property they'd paid to rent for the week and found the owner knew nothing about it.'

Clarice was silent.

'You're not surprised?'

'No,' she said. 'People who tell small pointless lies become desensitised to telling bigger lies. It's easy to work up the scale to bigger ones. Anything else?'

'We haven't found out where she was killed.'

'Or why. What about her house, anything new there?'

'They're still in there, going through the place an inch at a time; won't be finished until tomorrow evening at the very earliest. We found almost three thousand pounds, in twenty-pound notes, in a drawer in the bedroom, and her bank statements show large amounts paid in cash into the account over the last couple of years – but she had no form of employment.'

'So it's blackmail again?'

'It would seem so,' he replied. 'And we were both right about that other thing.'

'Walter?' She spoke with hesitation, still appalled by the thought.

'Her face was eaten by animals, but that could include rats and foxes.'

'And cats?'

He nodded.

It took them thirty-five minutes to get to the cottage from Lincoln hospital. Driving along the track to reach the isolated property, Clarice felt a sense of relief as her home came into sight, the slope of the red tiled roof sweeping down on one side, the washed-out white of the painted brickwork, the green window frames. There was a thin trail of smoke spiralling upwards, and she smiled, thinking of Bob and Sandra sitting in front of the open fireplace, and the smell of the burning logs.

She had used the insurance money paid to her after her mother's death to modernise the cottage. It was four miles from Castlewick, where the uncompromising flatness of the Lincolnshire landscape softened to undulate into the Wolds. She thought, as she often did coming down the gentle incline, that the property and the two acres surrounding it resembled an island. Encircled not by water but by the green and brown of fields of mud and crops.

As they got nearer, she noticed her own dark blue Range Rover parked next to Bob and Sandra's silver Mazda. 'You got my car home?' She spoke with surprise.

'Of course. Couldn't leave it at the Hanging Barn, with all the cars and activity from our lot, and the press sniffing around. And when our mob have gone, the army of rubberneckers who are sure to turn up.'

'Thank you, Rick.' She spoke formally. 'I really do appreciate it.'

'Well if that's so, do something for me.'

She waited to hear what she already knew he would say.

'Please don't get involved. I know you're good at sleuthing and you find it hard not to become drawn in, but Rose – or Sharon – is dead, and I am serious about this: whoever killed her wouldn't worry about breaking your jaw and smacking you over the head with a mallet as well if you poke your nose in and get too near. You've been through a shit time in the last forty-eight hours.'

He had pulled over to halt next to the other cars, turning off the engine, looking at her directly as he spoke.

'It has been a bit weird and scary,' she admitted.

'One to ten, how weird and scary?'

'Think I'd rather have cartwheeled naked down Steep Hill on the busiest Saturday of the year – Lincoln Christmas market – with a rose sticking out of my bum.'

'So that's an eleven, then?'

'Might even be a twelve.'

'Phew.' He raised his eyes while drawing his hand across his brow as if wiping away perspiration. 'So you'll listen to me, take it easy?'

'Look . . .' She paused and gave a thumbs-up to the elderly man who had come out of the cottage to welcome her home.

'Did you hear me?'

'Yes.' She turned back to Rick. 'I did – and thanks again for bringing the car back.'

He drew in his breath sharply. She imagined him silently counting to ten.

As Bob Todd neared the car, he called to Clarice, 'At last! Sandra and I were getting concerned that they might want to keep you for another night.'

Short and rotund, with a ruddy complexion and a sprightly step, Bob looked at seventy-two like a retired farmer, though he'd been an office-bound social worker for most of his working life. He'd met Sandra almost fifty years earlier, working in the same department, and as Sandra told it, if love had not arrived at first sight, it had followed quickly after a couple of dates.

'Come on, Sandra wants to hear everything – every minute gory detail.'

Bob opened the car door for Clarice, helping her out. Rick followed them. The insistent barking of dogs greeted them as they approached the back door.

As Clarice walked in, Jazz as always reached her first to jump up and down demanding attention. Behind, awaiting her turn, stood Blue. She carried in her mouth a lone brown sock, which Clarice recognised as one of her own, probably stolen from the laundry basket, to be offered as a gift. Her tail moved back and forth, rocking her body as she made a low murmuring noise.

'Jazz, good girl, good girl.' Clarice sat on the floor, allowing the dog to greet her, which she did by wiggling and rubbing her head against that of her mistress.

Cats started to come into the room, until two black-and-whites, one ginger, two tabbies and one grey had formed a semi-circle around the pair.

'And Blue, my beautiful girl.' The larger dog advanced with her present, dropping it into Clarice's lap as Clarice put her arms around her.

Rick, standing in the doorway, looked on.

'She's been waiting for you,' Sandra said as Clarice got up awkwardly from the floor. The long and the short – Sandra at just over five feet, a foot shorter than Clarice, hugged her, her head fitting under Clarice's chin. She held her close for a minute, to give a gentle squeeze.

With Clarice on her feet, both dogs rushed to Rick in excitement. He, in turn, made a fuss of each.

'Just need Ena and it'll be a full house,' said Bob.

The kitchen was large, the dominant shade red, with its brick walls and the red oil-fired stove that heated the room. On top of the many pine kitchen cupboards were varying sizes of pots, different shapes and colours, evidence of Clarice's journey as a designer-maker ceramicist. On the walls were framed posters of exhibitions in different parts of the UK and abroad. In the corner, the metal spiral staircase had been painted bright red to match the cooker. A double butler sink stood at one end of the room, at the other a Victorian dresser, bought in the first year of their marriage from one of the many junk-cum-antique shops Castlewick was renowned for. It bore shelf after shelf of photographs: Clarice with her mother, she and Rick on their wedding day, friends and rescue cats and dogs that had been found new homes.

Clarice saw Rick's eyes go to them briefly, before he diverted his gaze elsewhere.

'Nice to see you, Rick,' Sandra smiled.

'I saw him yesterday,' Bob said. 'He came with Daisy – Detective Sergeant Bodey, I should say, lovely girl – to get your spare car keys.' He looked at Clarice.

'I saw the car was back.'

'And Lady Vita called by to collect Walter.'

'Good. I bet she was pleased to see him.'

'Over the moon.' Sandra spoke for both of them.

Clarice smiled, looking around at the small gathering of people and animals, all those she loved most in the world. The awkwardness was agonising. Bob and Sandra had been friends of her mother; she'd known them most of her life, and they were always the first to volunteer their help in caring for the animals, her own and the rescues. In dog terms, Bob was a sturdy, friendly springer spaniel, Sandra a small, busy whippet. The relationship between the two couples had been easy, the best of friends. They had sat around the table in this kitchen over the years for a chat, a cuppa or a glass of wine, for celebrations, birthdays, Christmas dinner and anniversaries. Since her separation from Rick, they'd all tried to keep the friendships as they had been, but it was impossible. Bob and Sandra saw much of Clarice and little of Rick. Where their loyalties would eventually rest was an inevitability.

'I'd better get back.' Rick went to Sandra, to kiss her cheek. He and Bob gave each other a matey pat as he passed, Bob turning to follow him. Finally he came to Clarice. He briefly hugged her, Jazz resting her head against his leg.

'Speak soon.'

'Yes,' she replied. 'Speak soon.'

# Chapter 6

'You look bleedin' terrible,' Sandra said once they were alone, peering closely into Clarice's face.

'Should have seen me yesterday!' Clarice laughed, but Sandra looked away as she went to fill the kettle.

Hobbling to the table, Clarice lowered herself onto one of the pine chairs. Jazz followed, jumping onto her lap, looking up to focus her button-like brown eyes on Clarice's. Blue came over to lean against her legs.

'I wanted to go to the hospital,' Sandra spoke rapidly, her East Ender's ex-smoker's voice near breaking, 'but Bob said that Rick and Georgie would be there and you'd be all right, so best to be here with the animals.' She turned her head away from Clarice, as if concentrating hard on the tea-making.

'Bob was right. And I'm so grateful to you for taking care of all the beasties.'

Clarice noticed guiltily that Sandra looked tired. Her accident had clearly inflicted stress on her friend. Sandra, at seventy-three, was a year older than her 'toy boy' Bob and was determined never to give in gracefully to old age. Her hair was dyed black and her eyes were darkly mascaraed to stand out from her perfectly made-up face; she always kept her deep-pink lipstick in the back pocket of the trousers she wore when helping Clarice with the animals. She had a habit, when sunk in thought, of reapplying it without a mirror. Clarice smiled, watching Sandra as she used her left hand to put tea bags into the pot while haphazardly replenishing her lipstick with her right.

Bob returned, closing the solid pine stable door behind him, cutting off the blast of cold air that followed him in. They took their mugs of tea into the living room to sit in front of the fire he'd built earlier. Rather than her usual robust wedges, Sandra had made delicate smoked salmon sandwiches, white bread with no crusts, a squeeze of lemon and a grind from the black peppermill: Clarice's favourite. She realised Sandra had produced them as a treat, and smiled appreciatively.

As she ran through the details of the accident and a little of what the doctors had told her, she pecked at the edges of the bread, trying to hide her lack of appetite. She didn't mention the turmoil she had felt at taking the smell of death from the barn to the hospital, or the help Rick had given her in cleaning herself. Neither did she talk in detail about the murder, or the information she had gleaned from Rick.

'I never had much time for her,' Sandra said, finishing the last of the sandwiches.

'Rose?' asked Clarice. 'You didn't know her.'

'We met at the Castlewick Animal Welfare charity fundraisers.'

'She'd come over to the tombola and look at the prizes, but she never bought a ticket,' added Bob.

'Don't think she thought the prizes were up to much. I don't know what she expected for a pound a strip.' Sandra gathered the plates into a pile. 'Still, poor cow didn't deserve that, not what happened to her.'

'Don't forget, it's a week on Sunday, the next CAW tabletop at the town hall.' Clarice changed the subject.

'We know, darlin', we've not forgotten, but one thing . . .'

'What?'

'Don't stick us next to that Paula, will you, she does my bleedin' head in. She's only the housekeeper at Winterby Hall, but you'd think she was the lady of the manor, with her la-di-da airs and graces.'

'It's not down to me,' Clarice said reasonably. 'Georgie organises everything, which stall goes where. Paula's always done the cake stall.'

'You're being a right mardy cow, Sandra!' Bob spoke sharply. 'First you didn't like poor Rose, now you're having a crack at Paula!'

'I do understand,' Clarice cut in. 'Paula can be hard work.'

'She tries to copy Lady Vita,' said Sandra in a huffy voice, looking at her husband. 'And she pisses you off as well, you've said so.'

'Yes, that's true.' Bob nodded meekly. 'She always has to tell everyone how much she does for charity.' He sounded contrite.

'Yeah, *and* how she makes every bleedin' cake by hand herself, with no help. *And* she has to go around at the end asking how much each stall has made compared to hers. We all know Georgie does a phone-around the next day when she's counted the money, to tell us what the final amount is.'

'She's not a team player, very competitive,' Bob added sagely. 'Although her children, Laura and Jack, are the opposite.'

'Georgie will be in for a cuppa in a couple of days,' Clarice said. 'I'll discreetly ask if she can put you nearer the main door, tell her it's to catch the punters on their way in and out. Paula likes the stall in the corner, so it's easier to move you. She might say no, but I'll ask – how does that sound?'

'Thanks, darlin', that's great.' Sandra bent down to plant a pink kiss on Clarice's cheek.

'We ought to go,' Bob said. 'Let Clarice rest.'

As Clarice thanked them for all they had done to help her, she sensed that if encouraged, Sandra would have stayed all night, out of concern for her. But she was glad, after waving from the kitchen doorway to the departing couple, shutting the door and hobbling back to the fire, that she was finally alone. Ten minutes after they left, she had a cheery call from Georgie, after which she unplugged the telephone jack from its socket, knowing that if it rang again, she might not be able to ignore it.

She went to the spiral staircase, knowing it was going to be a challenge. As she climbed the stairs slowly, getting used to holding onto the metal banister, avoiding putting weight on the injured foot, she heard a low clicking noise. 'It's me, Ena,' she called as she pushed open her bedroom door, and was rewarded by the appearance of a gnarled black paw with terrifyingly long nails, a foot from her face. Its owner's head appeared, and Ena, perched on the shoulder-height chest of drawers behind the door, began nonchalantly washing the paw, rather than using it to swipe at an intruder. The rattlesnake clicking noise of her tongue against the roof of her mouth was her battle cry.

Ena, whose age was unknown, had come to Clarice from Jonathan fifteen years earlier, having been left with the vet by an owner who couldn't live with her aggression. Jonathan

43

named all his cats after characters from his childhood viewing of *Coronation Street*. Once sleek and shiny, Ena's fur was now a dull black and grey with a sprinkle of white, her muzzle and ear tips completely white. Clarice had realised that the cat would be impossible to re-home, and somehow she and Ena had bonded. The scrawny old moggy could often be observed stalking around the garden a few feet behind her. Jazz, Blue and the rest of the animals gave her a wide berth, for although Ena was elderly, she was still undoubtedly top cat.

Clarice changed into an old, favourite floppy sweater that came down to her knees, rolling the sleeves back to her elbows, before going back out of the bedroom to the large landing area, its four doors leading to two bedrooms, a study and the bathroom. She stood for a moment looking down the open well of the staircase, and decided to try another method of descent. Using one crutch and leaning her weight against the banister rail, she hopped down step by step on her undamaged foot.

Downstairs, she turned the main lights off so that the glow of the fire softly lit up the living room, which, when she was a child, had been two small rooms. Knocked into one, it was long and rectangular with a large window at one end currently hidden by the heavy blue and white wool curtains. There was a mahogany tallboy near the door that had belonged to her maternal grandmother, and framed prints on the walls associated with jazz artists. She slid a disc into the CD player and the sweet sound of Bill Withers' 'Ain't No Sunshine' filled the space.

Two of the cats – diabetic BB, a large black-and-white, and asthmatic Ella, a dainty tabby, named like all her adopted cats except for Ena after jazz or blues artists – came to join her.

She and Rick had sat like this together, she on the long brown fabric sofa opposite the fireplace, legs tucked up under her bottom, surrounded by brightly coloured cushions; Rick in the armchair to her left, his long legs stretching out. They would discuss her latest ceramic creations and the work in progress, or the cats and dogs. Then the case he was currently involved in. He knew she was discreet and fascinated and useful, more often than not coming at the problems that needed resolving from a different angle from his.

'Work around the edges,' she would say, after first letting him run dry of words, and then she did just that herself. He'd told her she was a good listener and observer. Combined with her sharp mind, she picked up details others wouldn't. Sometimes he called her a good woman, a phrase she found strangely old-fashioned.

Clarice had first met Rick on a cold and wet November day, when she had been returning two men to an open prison. Darren Wren and his cellmate had been considered suitable to be rehabilitated into the community before their release, and were allowed to leave the prison and return at a prearranged time. On this particular day, they had been helping to move furniture at a charity auction. With so many animals to feed – not only those she cared for, but many more looked after by foster carers – not to mention veterinary costs, such events were an important means of raising funds for Clarice's charity Castlewick Animal Welfare, known locally as CAW.

As they'd entered the prison office, the officer on duty had told Darren there was someone to see him. A man she hadn't noticed stepped out from the shadows behind them. Tall, with close-cropped hair, a five o'clock shadow and a nose that had obviously been broken.

'Hello, Darren.' He'd delivered the words with a hint of humour and a south London accent. 'We need to talk.' Clarice had realised immediately that he was a police officer.

Dragging her mind back to the present, she reminded herself not to live in the past, instead letting the immense sense of relief at being in her own home infuse her being. Although her body was exhausted, her brain was wired.

Considering what Rick had told her about the way Rose had been killed, it must have been a terrible death. She still thought of her as Rose, not Sharon. She recalled the woman's inappropriate clothes when she'd attended the ceramics classes; everybody else in jeans, T-shirts and tatty trainers, Rose in high heels, a 1950s-style dress or suit, trying not to get covered in clay dust and endeavouring not to break one of her precious nails. Rose and ceramics had been a non-starter.

From the little Clarice knew, it seemed highly likely Rose had been a blackmailer in Castlewick just as she had been a blackmailer elsewhere. But her murder had not been a simple one. Having had her jaw broken, she was then hit with a heavy implement before being smothered. The interesting fact that she had been hit from the front rather than the back led Clarice to assume the killer had no fear of looking his victim in the eye while inflicting what he presumably thought would be her death blow. Perhaps even enjoying it.

Suddenly she knew what she would really like to do – have a good look around Rose's house to find out more about her hidden life. There had to be something – a clue, a strand from the past that she might be able to recognise and others might miss – that could lead to Rose's murderer.

# Chapter 7

Despite her protestations, as they were leaving the previous evening, Sandra and Bob had insisted they come back early to help in the morning.

'I'll be OK,' Clarice had told them. 'I have to get on with things.'

'Yes, but not straight away,' said Bob. 'Let us come over first thing, around seven for a couple of mornings, then I promise we'll leave you in peace and go back to the afternoon routine.'

She remembered what they'd agreed as the car tyres clicking over the gravel in the driveway the next morning woke her and she realised that she'd forgotten to set the alarm. Once inside the cottage, the couple were insistent that she go back to bed for a couple of hours. Although she attempted to resist the suggestion, to please them she took the mug of tea offered and returned to her bed to drink it. After which she immediately fell back to sleep.

Over two hours later, in the bathroom, Clarice placed a plastic stool in the shower and, having removed the elasticated bandage from her foot, sat under the running water. Although her head felt clearer than it had yesterday, she still felt jaded, but she was pleased to find that washing her hair and body and drying herself while standing on one leg was less complicated than she'd envisaged.

Before dressing, she looked at her body in the long wall-mounted mirror, shocked at the reflection of extensive areas of black. She grabbed her clothes, dressing as hurriedly as her injuries would allow, keen to conceal the image both physically and mentally. Blue, who always went into the bathroom with her, sat upright, her head to one side, looking quizzical, a lone blue sock dangling from her mouth. A creature of habit and routines, she watched this new one in fascination. Anything that varied in the minutest way needed to be absorbed and analysed. She had come to Clarice aged two, a hairless wimp terrified of people and unusual or loud sounds. Now five, and having known nothing in this home but affection, she had filled out and grown a thick coat, becoming robust and confident. Blue was selective about whom she trusted – men were sometimes a problem – and she hated Bonfire Night. But she was a good guard dog, especially protective of Clarice and Jazz.

Clarice smiled, watching Blue watching her. She wondered distractedly about Rick helping her in the hospital bathroom. It hadn't felt embarrassing once they got started with the shower, maybe due to the blow on the head, and it still didn't, but struggling with the awkward memory, she mused that Rick might, in hindsight, find it so.

In the kitchen, Sandra was at the round pine table with a cup of coffee, the newspaper they'd brought with them and an upside-down Jazz resting on her lap enjoying her chest being scratched. As Clarice and Blue came in, Jazz turned to jump down and ran to them, her long tail doing skipping-rope loops.

'Did you put something in my tea?' Clarice laughed. 'I went spark out.'

'That's great, darlin'.' Sandra smiled. 'You should always listen to your Auntie Sandra.' Getting up and walking to the coffee percolator, she picked up a mug and looked questioningly at Clarice.

'Yes, please,' Clarice smiled. 'Has Bob gone home?'

'No.' Sandra poured the coffee. 'He's off for another cuddle with Miss Shy Boots. She's really come on; we'll have to change her name to Pushy Pants.'

Clarice nodded her response.

'Do you need anything from the shops, apart from milk and bread?' Sandra asked. 'We're going to do a bits-and-pieces shop in a while.'

'I can't think of anything else, but there is cash; I topped up the housekeeping tin before the accident.'

'Lady Vita called, about half an hour ago.'

'I didn't hear the phone!'

'She said she wanted to come over and collect you. She'll bring you back later; she's going to give you lunch.'

'Sounds like it's already arranged. Did she tell you how Walter is?'

'You can probably see Walter for yourself, if he's around – you know cats . . .' Sandra brought the coffee to her.

Clarice nodded. 'I did want to catch up. Vita only got back from Italy a few days ago, and she wasn't here when Walter went walkabout.'

'You gonna get stuck with Paula?' Picking up her own mug, Sandra stuck her little finger in the air, a mischievous look in her eyes.

'She might be difficult to avoid; she does work there.'

'You just need to give her ladyship a quick call to fix a time,' Sandra said as Bob came in wearing a large overcoat, a scarf wrapped around him like a shawl.

'Are you talking about Lady Vita, and is there any coffee left?'

Clarice looked at Sandra. 'Yes, and yes,' they said in unison.

Vita collected her later that morning.

'So I want to know all about the holiday. Did you have a great time with your sister and the family?' Clarice asked as they set off in the Land Rover.

'Brilliant, I had a lovely time. But bugger my holiday – that's so boring in comparison with your news. Dead bodies, broken bones ...'

'Only one dead body. I'll tell you all about it.'

'Tell me over lunch. Nothing better than talk about a rotting cadaver to get the juices flowing.'

'Yuck.' Clarice screwed up her face. 'Italy hasn't improved your macabre sense of humour.'

They both smiled.

'How many boys has your sister got?' Clarice asked.

'Five – she kept on thinking that the next one might be a girl, but reckoned five was her limit.'

'Sounds more than reasonable.'

Vita nodded. 'We're happy with our Harry. Did I ever tell you his real name is Horace, after his grandfather, but much to Roland's annoyance, he prefers to be called Harry? Sarah's boys are Stephen, Matthew, Robert, Donald and Michael. I think it was a bit like you trying to think of names for the cats and dogs.

She had loads of girls' names lined up to choose from, and gave up when she ran out of boys' names she liked.'

'At Harry's age, I think winding up your father comes with the territory,' Clarice said. 'Can you imagine it – five boys in the same house? Imagine if she'd done what I did with naming the cats.'

Vita thought for a moment. 'Matthew, Michael, Martin, Max, Marvin.'

'I can beat you in that game,' Clarice said. 'Stephen, Shane, Saul, Simon and Santa. I've had a lot of practice with all the beasties.'

'*Santa!*' Vita threw her head back and let out a roar.

Looking at her, Clarice could not help but feel that even with her mouth open, guffawing, Vita never looked anything less than stunning. She was slim and fine-boned, with beautiful blue eyes and delicate pale skin, her dark hair styled into a bob similar to Clarice's, though Vita's beautiful monthly cut by a well-known Knightsbridge hairdresser was far superior to Jake of Lincoln's.

'Harry will be back at St Andrews for his final year now,' Clarice said.

'Ah.'

'He's not?'

'He should've been, but much to our consternation, he's dropped out. He says that he knows what his future holds and university is a waste of time.'

'But uni isn't just about getting a degree – it's a rite of passage, becoming self-sufficient and being a part of the larger world!' Clarice spoke with passion. Part of her fervour was disgust at Harry's discarding of something precious. He'd taken a place that someone else would have valued.

'I've used that argument and a thousand others.' Vita sounded exasperated. 'Harry is strong-willed – he gets that from me. Once he's made up his mind, he won't be turned.'

Vita drove on in silence for a few minutes before saying, 'I'm sorry about Walter. You trust me to adopt cats and then I lose them.'

'You don't lose them – both times previously he was a stowaway in someone's car. And it is only one cat.'

'At least on those two occasions he was back within an hour. We were lucky his kidnappers were people we know who live locally. As soon as they arrived home, they found him and brought him straight back.'

'Do you think he was coming to visit me?'

'What?' Vita thought for a minute. 'You're five miles from Winterby Hall, so he got more than halfway.'

'You think he did the car trick again?' Clarice asked in a serious voice. 'Someone left a door open and this time he wasn't noticed? A delivery driver, maybe?'

'I don't know.' Vita sounded pensive. 'We all know what he's like, so we try to keep an eye on him. But of course I was in Italy with Sarah and the family. Roland didn't tell me until I got home.'

'He probably did the right thing. What could you have done? It would have spoiled the holiday.'

'Yes, I suppose that's true.'

'Who noticed him missing? Was it Roland?'

'No, Tom.'

'Roland's brother?'

'Yes. Well,' Vita spoke in a measured tone to clarify the point, 'people always say brother, but you know he is actually Roland's half-brother?'

'Yes, of course.' Clarice didn't say any more. She was aware, as everybody in the area must have been, that Vita's deceased father-in-law Lord Horace Fayrepoynt had had three children. His firstborn was a daughter, Miranda, Vita's sister-in-law, who now lived in New York. Thomas Lyme, known as Tom, was his second child. His mother had been a housekeeper at Snarebrook Hall, the Fayrepoynt family weekend retreat near Hunstanton in Norfolk. Although the boy was illegitimate, Horace had never made a secret of the relationship and had financially supported Tom and his mother. Roland, the longed-for legitimate son and heir, had been born five years after Tom. Vita rarely spoke of the connection between her husband and his half-brother.

Looking out at the rolling parkland that surrounded the Fayrepoynt estate, Clarice thought how difficult the situation must be for Tom. Roland had his father's title and the wealth that came with it, and although Tom managed the estate, he was an employee and would never be more. If Horace hadn't produced a legitimate male heir, the title and estate would have passed to his eldest male cousin. Despite that, the relationships within the family appeared to the outside world to be good: all seemed content with their position. Although Clarice felt she knew Tom's wife Paula better, meeting her at the fundraisers, she saw Tom frequently when visiting Vita and always found him to be helpful, friendly and courteous. But even if his house was on fire, he'd still wear his professional face, never showing his feelings. It was, she imagined, a quality imbibed from birth.

She changed the subject. 'How are Tom's children? I know Laura's getting a divorce.'

'Fine,' said Vita. 'Jack is still working for the estate; he's managing the fishing lakes and lodges now. His thirtieth birthday wasn't long ago. Laura's back home with her mum and dad, and at college in Castlewick. A mature student, making a new start after the failed marriage.'

'What's she studying?'

'Floristry,' Vita said. 'It had to be that or hairdressing; not much choice in the town.'

'Floristry, that could be useful,' Clarice mused. 'I do know Laura from the Castlewick book club, but I've missed a couple of meetings and she has too, so our paths haven't crossed for a while.'

'She's started to produce small arrangements for the house.' Vita wrinkled her pert nose. 'Her mother suggested it, but I'm afraid poor Laura hasn't much in the way of artistic interpretation.'

'Ah,' Clarice mumbled to the windscreen.

'I'll give it six months, see if she improves.' Vita smiled absent-mindedly as she turned to drive through the woodlands that were part of the Winterby estate.

After half a mile, a signpost indicated a turning to the first of eight man-made lakes, home to carp, barbel, bream, tench and roach. Guests could come for a single day's fishing, but the majority stayed a week in one of the thirty-five lodges scattered amongst the woodland. There was a shop selling rods, bait and tackle, with a nearby restaurant that also acted as a coffee shop, popular with the inhabitants of Castlewick as well as visitors.

Clarice knew that the lakes were the estate's main source of income, though it also hosted shooting parties, Roland and Harry's favourite activity. The Orangery, situated behind the main house, had also recently become available for summer weddings, the formal gardens a perfect backdrop for photographs. Vita had once told Clarice that the income from all these activities was sufficient for them not to have to open the house to members of the public, something she implied would be beyond the pale.

Soon the woods merged with Winterby House's wide sweeping drive. Beech trees formed a guard of honour, bringing into view the magnificent house with its column doorway and sash windows. Built in the late eighteenth century, it played on the best of Georgian architecture, the details of design and craftsmanship outstanding. Inside, Clarice knew, the rooms were elegant and, with their large windows, well lit.

'Did I tell you Tom had had an accident? The two of you – what a pair!' Vita said, pointing to Clarice's foot encased in its flat-bottomed shoe.

'No, I didn't know. What happened to him?'

'The rug in his office had a tear. He caught his foot in it, landed on the fender and fractured his arm.'

'Poor man, when was this?'

'While I was away – the day after I left, I think. He was in A & E all day. He might have realised Walter was missing sooner but for the accident. He's very good at keeping an eye on things. Roland wouldn't have noticed. He's not sentimental about animals.'

'And Tom is?'

'I wouldn't say he's sentimental, but he is diligent – if he said he'd keep an eye on them for me, I would trust him without question. Look, there he is!'

As the Land Rover approached the gravelled area reserved for cars, they saw Tom looking towards them smiling. His bearing was upright, as befitted someone in service, and everything about him was spick and span: neat hair, black jacket, white shirt and grey slacks. His black shoes were highly polished. Clarice's mind went to the family portraits in the drawing room. Like Roland, Tom had the Fayrepoynt chin, or lack of it, inherited from their father. It had also been passed down to the grandsons, Harry and Jack, an aristocratic cliché they had not managed to avoid. The crêpe bandage sling on his right arm looked incongruous against the perfection of his attire.

He'd been in conversation with a small, pale woman Clarice recognised as his wife, Paula, the housekeeper. She dressed as smartly as her husband, everything about her faultless. Clarice had witnessed her remonstrating with the staff under her control on a number of occasions. A little power went a long way with Paula. Even when being accommodating to guests and visitors, a peevishness lurked not far below the surface. Remembering Bob and Sandra's words, though she had no personal experience of the competitive side of Paula's personality, Clarice was sure that their assessment was spot-on.

As they neared, Paula lifted her hand in welcome before turning to make her way back to the house.

'Put paid to his croquet on the lawn,' Vita smirked.

'Does he enjoy croquet?' Clarice asked, turning her head to look at the grass stretching away from the parking area.

'Not on my lawn,' Vita snapped. 'I'm not having him bashing hoops in here with his ruddy great mallet. He does it in his own garden.'

Tom started to walk towards the car, but before he reached it, Vita stopped, leapt out and marched briskly around to Clarice's side.

'Hello, Clarice, good to see you again.'

'And you, Tom. You've been in the wars.' Clarice swung her legs out carefully.

'So have you,' he said. 'Vita told me you'd had a fall, you poor thing.'

'It's all the rage at present,' Clarice smiled.

'Well, then we are both at the very pinnacle of fashion.'

'I don't suppose you're left-handed?' Clarice looked at the sling on his right arm as she spoke.'

'No, afraid not.'

'Bad luck.'

Vita, who had opened the back door behind Clarice, brought out her crutches and passed them to her.

'Thanks.' Clarice positioned them to move forward, keeping her left leg bent at the knee.

'Do you need anything?' Tom asked Vita.

'No, it's sorted. We're going to have lunch in my private sitting room. Mrs Ray is doing us a warm meal; she'll put it in the heated trolley.'

Tom nodded.

'Look!' Vita pointed. 'It's the boy who went walkabout.'

Walter, whose thin, bony body and lack of a back leg were proving no impediment to the arrogance of his swagger, walked slowly towards them.

'Walter!' Clarice moved forward. 'Let's have a look at you.'

The cat came to a halt, lifting his tail almost straight, its end a question mark hook. He looked purposefully at Clarice and her crutches, then, raising his head in disdain, turned and walked slowly in the opposite direction.

'That told me,' laughed Clarice.

'Ha – maybe he preferred the barn,' said Vita before turning to Tom. 'Where's Roland?'

'With a police sergeant – I think they're in the drawing room.'

Vita looked at Clarice.

'It's about Walter,' Tom continued.

'My God!' Vita exclaimed. 'What's he done now?'

'I expect it's Daisy Bodey,' Clarice said. 'It'll be routine, don't worry, because he was at the Hanging Barn . . . you know, where I found the body.'

'So he's not a suspect?' Vita said, wearing what Clarice knew to be her teasing face. 'Come on, let's go and help poor Rolly out. You know how hopeless he is with anything out of the ordinary. And he knows nothing about my domestic arrangements – or Walter.'

Moving forward on her crutches as quickly as her injury allowed, Clarice found herself suddenly progressing at a brisk pace into the house. Tom went ahead to hold open the magnificently carved great door. She imagined, as often before, the royalty and politicians who over the centuries must have entered through the arch within an arch to walk across the key-patterned marble floor. High above the L-shaped hallway was an Adam-style plaster ceiling with cornice and panelled splays, and in front of them the staircase, with its mahogany rail and decorative iron balusters, led to the upper floors.

Tom slipped behind Clarice as Vita's stride quickened, heading towards the drawing room to the left of the stairs.

# Chapter 8

As she stepped across the threshold, Clarice was reminded how far her world was from Vita's. The smell of beeswax and almond permeated every part of the elegant room, with its perfect proportions and carefully balanced colours. On the pale yellow walls hung portraits of family members, a line going back centuries. Above the focal point of the room, an antique Siena marble fireplace, was an eighteenth-century Chippendale gilt-wood overmantle mirror. The armchairs used by Roland and Vita were a pair of carved mahogany library bergères, well used and cracked with wear; what Vita referred to – turning a popular phrase with her dry humour – as shabby-shit. Clarice's favourite piece was a period chinoiserie bureau bookcase.

'Where have you been?' Roland asked his wife. 'This lady is a police officer, Vita. She wants to know when that three-legged ginger cat disappeared.'

'You mean Walter. You know his name, Roland.'

Roland looked perplexed. Although only eight years older than his wife, the gap appeared wider; they were not an obvious match. He was of medium height, with a large girth and wispy strands of hair brushed forward over his skull, which matched in colour his red-blotched fleshy face. The only resemblance to his spruce half-brother was the receding chin. He wore his habitual uniform of green cord trousers, checked shirt and brown waistcoat.

Looking at him, Clarice thought that if she had seen Roland from a distance, she might have judged him to be either a vagrant or a clown.

Detective Sergeant Daisy Bodey, a pretty woman with a slim, athletic build, her light brown hair cut unfussily short, nodded to Clarice.

'Can't remember names for cats,' Roland said, scratching his chest thoughtfully. 'I remember the names of all the girls well enough.'

'He means his gun dogs; they're all springers,' Vita told Daisy.

'Yes, he told me that before you came in, Lady Fayrepoynt.' Daisy addressed Vita with formality.

'The cat belongs to my wife. Tom might know something; he keeps an eye on most things that go on.'

'It is true, my husband wouldn't be able to help you. And I'm not going to be much better.' Vita glanced at Tom as she spoke. 'I was away, visiting my sister in Italy. Tom was keeping an eye on Walter, making sure that he had food and water.'

All eyes turned to Tom.

'Walter, the cat in question,' Tom spoke directly to Daisy, 'does have rather an unfortunate habit. If someone leaves their car door open, he might well get in and go for a drive; he's been brought back a couple of times. He's not fussy whose car it is – he just enjoys the ride. It is possible that he got into a car, and when the door was opened at the end of the journey, he got out without being seen.'

'Yes, DI Beech mentioned it, and Lady Fayrepoynt was away?' Daisy asked.

'Lady Fayrepoynt left on the seventeenth,' said Tom. 'I drove her to Stansted airport. Mrs Ray, the cook, had been delegated to look after Walter. She told me she fed him on the seventeenth but couldn't find him the next day, the eighteenth.'

'And you didn't see him that day?'

'Unfortunately, it was on the eighteenth that I had a fall and had to go to A & E. I wasn't about at all and I'm afraid I didn't realise he was missing until the following day.'

'I got back from a three-week break with family in Italy to be told he'd gone walkabout,' Vita added, 'but then the day after that, Clarice found him – though you know more about that than I do.'

'Yes.' Daisy nodded before turning to Tom. 'Do you have a list of people who came that day in cars or delivery vans?'

'That might be difficult.' Tom looked at Roland.

'Had a shoot over at the north end of the estate. Lots of cars, lots of people. The cat's supposed to be locked in when that happens.'

'You never left him out when the shoot was on!' Vita exclaimed.

'I neither left it out nor took it in,' he replied. 'It's only a ruddy cat.'

Vita looked piercingly at him, elegant eyebrows raised.

'It wasn't as smooth as usual that day, with Tom out of action – bloody inconvenient,' Roland blustered, the redness of his face spreading down his neck.

'Right.' Vita spoke decisively. 'Tom, where's the list of people invited to the shoot?'

'It's in the record cupboard, in the office.'

'Trust it to be there – you'll never open that door one-handed.' She turned to Daisy. 'I'll just pop up to the office with Tom to find the book. Roland can go and get himself a small drink. Poached salmon for lunch, darling!' She addressed her husband. 'And remember the word *small* when pouring the whisky!'

'Am I having lunch with you two beauties?' He looked hopefully at Clarice, who rewarded him with a smile.

'You are joining us for lunch, after which you can bugger off to give me and Clarice the opportunity for a girly catch-up.'

Roland beamed broadly, his gloom lifting. 'Right you are.' He turned to leave, followed by Tom and Vita.

'Bring the police lady with you, Clarice, to wait in the hall,' Vita called over her shoulder. A command, thought Clarice, not a request. 'Tom can photocopy the list and bring it to her there.'

After they'd gone, Clarice walked slowly across the large room to the door, Daisy following her carefully. They knew each other well. While working with Rick, Daisy Bodey had been first a constable before being promoted to sergeant. She was divorced, often remarking that she was married to the job. After the break-up of her marriage and before Rick and Clarice had parted, she had been a few times to supper with the two of them, and had sometimes visited Clarice on her own, when she had provided a sympathetic ear to tales of Jerry, Daisy's philandering spouse.

'How are you now?' Daisy gently touched Clarice's shoulder.

'I'm fine – well, not fine exactly, but much better.'

'You had one hell of a fall.'

'Thank you for looking after me at the barn – the ambulance and everything. I was lucky it wasn't much worse.'

'I'll second that. When Rick heard what'd happened to you, he left at about ninety miles an hour!'

They had stopped at the large mahogany drawing room door, which had swung closed. 'Yes, I'm sure he told you, he came to the hospital.'

Daisy nodded.

'I've been thinking about Walter,' Clarice said. 'The barn is five miles from here. He looks doddery, but he was always a wanderer, and it is possible he could have walked there. But then if he did get in a car ...'

'Thanks for mentioning that, but we'll need to check all the people who came and left in a vehicle anyway.'

'Of course. Did you manage to find anything in Rose's house?' Clarice said.

Daisy gave her a long look.

'Rick told me that Rob found the house had been trashed. He said you were going through it an inch at a time.' Clarice spoke casually.

'Ah,' Daisy said. 'I didn't realise he had told you.'

'We still talk,' said Clarice. Then, looking at Daisy's doubtful expression, she added, 'Sometimes.'

They both laughed.

'We've found nothing of consequence,' Daisy said. 'We finished this morning; they should be out properly by this afternoon. Just that woman – you know her – making a fuss at the station.'

'Who?' said Clarice.

'Apparently came to your classes when Rose did – Jean Whittle?'

'Yes, I know Jean, nice woman. I wasn't aware that she had any connection to Rose.'

'Just a recent one, apparently.' Daisy turned her lips downward. 'It seems Rose latched onto Jean's social circle, got invited to lunches, girls' days out – that sort of thing. She borrowed money from Jean, two thousand pounds, and became evasive when Jean asked for it back. Jean wanted to know how she'd get her money now that Rose – everyone still calls her that – is dead.'

'Jean's soft, probably too kind. And two thousand pounds is a lot of money for her to lose. Has she got any proof that Rose borrowed the money?'

'Nope.'

Clarice made a mental note to phone Jean later.

'Have you found the sisters?'

'One of them.' Daisy spoke warily. 'Jackie Smith and her husband Pete are being questioned tomorrow morning, but there's still no trace of the youngest, Maggie.' She looked at Clarice as she stepped towards the door. 'And you didn't hear that from me.'

'Hear what?' said Clarice, in a tone that mustered incredulity. As she put her hand out, the door swung open.

'Hello, Clarice.'

'Jack, what a nice surprise,' Clarice said.

Jack moved forward to push the door wide, holding it to allow Clarice, followed by Daisy, to leave the room. Good-looking, with long, floppy blonde hair and a clear blue gaze, he was a match for Clarice in height so their eyes met on a level. A beard disguised the lack of chin that would have marked him out as a Fayrepoynt, his voice slow and melodious, his smile sincere. He seemed unaware of his attractiveness, giving no indication of vanity, but he spoke with self-assured confidence and there was a hint of steel behind the eyes. He was a man who would stand his ground.

'I've just taken my break with Ginny,' he said as Clarice entered the corridor to find the young woman standing a few feet away.

'Ginny.' Clarice's voice lifted with pleasure. 'I haven't seen you for ages.' Ginny Blake and her best friend Lucy Marriot, both in their twenties, were live-in staff employed at the hall. Looking at Ginny's perfect creamy skin, large brown eyes and long dark hair falling in a neat plait down her back, she was reminded of a young deer.

'Still here,' Ginny said. 'Lucy's in the kitchen on biscuit-making duty; you might bump into her. We're getting ready for Art at Winterby on Saturday; it's one of Lady Vita's events to support artists.'

'Yes, I know,' Clarice said. 'It's contemporary makers – jewellery, glass and ceramics – putting their work on display to an invited audience. With luck, they may sell some pieces. I've been asked by Vita to help. What duty are you on? I thought you worked in the fisheries with Jack?'

'I do normally,' Ginny said. 'I've been packing up everything in the Orangery that's not needed for Saturday. Mainly stuff used for weddings. And I'm trying to find the glassware Lady Vita says we can't do without. It's by two different makers; the styles apparently complement one another.'

'What are their names?' Clarice asked, intrigued. 'The glass makers?'

'Sorry, I can't remember, it's on my pad upstairs,' Ginny said. 'Nobody is going to drink from them; she wants them displayed in a case.'

'The pad with a list of a dozen more jobs.' Jack sounded sympathetic.

Ginny nodded. 'Any new dogs for me and Lucy to walk yet?'

'No, sorry,' Clarice said. 'We have dogs with other foster

carers but I've none needing walkers at the moment. Although that could change.'

'Let me know if it does. We love doing it.'

'Yes, I will.'

'Guess I'd better get back to work.' Ginny looked cautiously over her shoulder towards the stairs.

'We'd both better,' Jack said, picking up on the implication of Ginny's furtive glance. He moved away with a nod to Daisy. 'We'll be in trouble with the boss if we exceed our official break time.'

'Roland's gone,' Clarice said, 'with your dad.'

He looked at Ginny and smiled. 'Roland's not the one to look out for.'

'And,' Ginny added, giving Jack a sly look back, 'it's not just Vita either – Paula's my boss.'

'Yeah,' Jack said, 'my mum can equal Vita for scary!'

'Lovely to see you both,' Clarice said before watching them walk away. When they reached the stairs, Ginny went up and Jack headed outside.

'He's gorgeous!' Daisy muttered.

'And so is his girlfriend.'

'Mmm,' Daisy said. 'I had noticed.'

Walking into Vita's private sitting room, Clarice always found it impossible not to be drawn immediately by the chandelier. A contemporary piece that hung from the centre of the ceiling, it was made up of hundreds of individual pieces of brass, copper and silver, soldered and curled, dangling down to catch the light. There was always a smell of lemons in the room; a deep porcelain bowl sitting in the centre of a low table was filled with them, their bright yellow peel a contrast against the deep swirling blue of the glaze. The display was one of Vita's minor eccentricities, Mrs Ray delegated to the daily checking and replacement of the fruit. There were tall bookcases in silver- and white-painted wood, as well as contemporary glass showcases that melted into the background, not overpowering the work they displayed. The items exhibited were part of Vita's own personal collection, work from makers still struggling to establish their reputations, as well as many established artists. Clarice had been privileged to be invited into this room on several occasions to admire a newly acquired piece. Her eyes, as usual, went to a Grayson Perry vase, then a David Burnham Smith plate, before finally resting on a tall red vase with flashes of minimal silver, one of her own creations.

Walter and the police visit forgotten, Roland poured drinks and began to regale his wife and Clarice with anecdotes from his misspent youth. Vita, who must have heard the tales hundreds of times, appeared to be playing the role of dutiful wife, smiling and nodding encouragingly. The performance, Clarice realised, was for her benefit.

It was the first time she had lunched in this room. A table had been placed in an alcove by a window, and even for a casual meal, Mrs Ray had set it with a crisp white linen tablecloth and silver cutlery, the old-fashioned heated trolley standing by ready with their salmon in white wine, potatoes and broccoli.

'Apple pie for pud,' Roland told Clarice. 'Yum yum, my favourite,' he added, filling his glass with white wine.

Previously at Winterby House, Clarice had been invited to what Vita referred to as her 'girls' lunches'. They were held in the dining room with up to eight ladies in attendance, all with some connection, such as the charity Vita was currently supporting, or the tennis crowd. Clarice's invitations had fallen into the arts category. Her work as a ceramicist was well established in Lincolnshire, and the fact that she exhibited throughout the UK and abroad gave her extra kudos, welcomed by Vita's artistic cronies.

She was aware, though, that for some she was an oddity, and they didn't know quite where to place her. She looked at Vita and Roland, imagining that doubtless they must think that too. She was an artist, which gave her a certain status, but the animal rescue side was not sympathetic to Roland's hunting, shooting and fishing fraternity. And Vita had hinted that the interest and ability Clarice displayed as a sleuth was decidedly strange.

Her friend enjoyed being at the centre of an artistic hub. She was establishing a reputation as a collector, not only of ceramics but of contemporary painting, and she encouraged young writers. She relished, Clarice thought, playing the role of the titled lady patroness. Fortunately she also loved cats, and that, along with their shared quirky sense of humour, was the two women's real meeting point.

'. . . So Pa said . . .' Clarice's thoughts returned to Roland just as he reached the punchline in a protracted tale about a shooting party he had attended as an innocent youth, '"Get your backside into gear and bloody well move them yourself."'

Clarice obligingly joined in Vita's laughter.

'How long ago did you lose your father, Roland?' she asked when the hilarity had died down.

'About . . . What was I? Twenty? So thirty years ago.'

'You were young?'

'Bloody right.' He seemed to expand as he talked. 'All that responsibility, but I didn't shirk.' He paused for a moment. 'Born to it, I suppose – goes with the territory.'

Clarice nodded sympathetically.

'Married Vita when I was twenty-nine. She was the making of me.' He beamed at his wife.

'Roland's mother had died of cancer, then only a year later his father died in a road accident, so it was all very sudden and unexpected. He hadn't imagined having to take on all the responsibility of the estate so soon.'

'It must have been difficult,' Clarice said.

'What about you, Clarice?' Vita spoke kindly. 'Your mother was your sole carer after your father's death, and she died of cancer while you were still young.'

'Yes,' Clarice agreed, 'but not as young as Roland. After I'd taken my A levels, I wanted to travel. I was in Italy for a year, then on to France for two years. When I came back, I did evening classes in Lincoln in metals, textiles and then ceramics while I worked full time. I knew I wanted to do something in the arts, but it took a while to decide what.'

'What sort of work did you do?' Vita asked.

'All sorts, anything from being an au pair and a fruit picker in France and Italy to office work when I came back. I was twenty-three when I started college in London, and I was in my final year when I found out Mum had cancer.'

'You dropped out?' Vita said.

Clarice hoped she was not making a comparison between her and Harry. 'Yes, when I found out Mum's illness was terminal. I looked after her for seven months, until she died. I always meant to go back to college, but my life here moved on.'

'So very sad.' Vita put her hand on Clarice's, which was resting on the table, and patted it.

'Taking on the estate made a man of me,' said Roland,

moving the conversation briskly back to himself, 'and I soon found who my true friends were. Miranda, my big sister, was wonderful. We never got on much as children – her being older – but she rallied round.'

'You must miss her, what with her living in America,' Clarice said.

'Married a Yank and that was that. I've got Vita now.' Roland spoke philosophically. 'And Tom to run the estate. He lived in Norfolk with Paula and their brood before that; worked for a big company.'

'He came back after Horace died?' asked Clarice.

'He did – good man. He'd done a degree in business studies, paid for by Pa, of course, so he owed me. Did the right thing repaying his debt.'

Clarice smiled. It occurred to her that in Roland Land, everything was about himself. Tragic circumstances for others were only important in relation to how they affected his life.

Finishing his apple pie, Roland drained his glass, the wine bottle empty. The door opened quietly.

'All right, Pa, anything left for me?'

Clarice turned to find Harry coming into the room.

'Harry,' Vita said. 'Your lunch's in the kitchen. We didn't know what time you'd be back.'

Harry at twenty was lanky and fluid, and with his combination of acne and a weak chin not conventionally good-looking. His hair was thin and stood up, but not in a fashionable way. It was his assurance that made him attractive, something that Roland, Clarice presumed, would also have had at his age, and probably what had attracted Vita to marry him: that and a title.

Harry carried with him the intuitive ease that came with wealth and privilege. Clarice had realised on previous meetings that she could find little about him to admire. She had observed his capricious nature: an ability to appear charmed and interested, before, within the blink of an eye, becoming bored, and moving on without care or consequence to being curt and dismissive. Perhaps it was because he was just twenty and an only child. As he matured, might he have less conceit? But no, honesty prevailed. Harry's internal world was not dissimilar to Roland's, though he showed an intelligence not obvious in his father.

'Hello, Clarice.' He came over to her politely.

'How are you, Harry?'

'I'm good.' He beamed as he spoke. 'You found a dead body at the Hanging Barn?'

'It sort of found me!' she retorted, pulling a sour face.

'Poor you, what a bugger – and rotting and stinky, Ma told me.'

'Harry,' Vita cut in, 'please take your pa and *go away.*'

'Girl time, yay,' Harry laughed. 'OK, I'm going, but I want a catch-up – all the horrid grisly bits.' He spoke directly to his mother, and Clarice laughed.

'I don't know where he gets it from.' Vita joined in Clarice's laughter as her husband obediently eased himself out of the chair to follow his lanky son out of the door.

'I wonder,' said Clarice.

As Vita pulled up to Clarice's cottage, Sandra came out to greet them.

'Hiya!' she shouted, and waved before disappearing back inside.

'Such a funny little woman!' Vita spoke in an undertone, although it would have been impossible for Sandra to hear her.

71

'In what way?' Clarice asked.

'Voice like a foghorn, and all that make-up.' She turned her lips downward into a grimace. 'And the dyed black hair – it puts ten years on her!'

'Sandra is lovely, a gem,' Clarice said briskly. 'It's just her way.'

Sandra was replaced by Bob, smiling affably as he walked to the car.

'I'm sure she is.' Vita turned to look at Clarice, perhaps sensing she had not been sufficiently aware of the strong bond her friend shared with Sandra. 'She's such a good volunteer for your cause; devoted to the animals, I imagine.'

Clarice smiled in response as Bob opened her door.

'Had a good day?' he asked.

'Brilliant,' said Clarice. 'I've been thoroughly spoilt. I'm going back on Saturday for Vita's arts day.'

'Hello!' Vita leant forward to speak to Bob. 'Crutches in the back.'

As she levered herself out of the car, the thought crossed Clarice's mind that despite enjoying Vita's generous company and having a lot in common with her, they would never be close, though they were useful to one another in the context of cats and ceramics. And she had known her long enough to recognise that Vita's adroit social skills would ensure, after Clarice's response to her less than flattering comment about Sandra, that she would never again make similar remarks. If nothing else, she was a fast learner.

# Chapter 9

As Bob and Sandra were about to depart, Clarice steeled herself to ask Bob for a special favour.

'When you say *special*,' Bob said, 'I'm thinking it's something illegal, or else not something you want Rick to find out about.'

Sandra listened, pulling on her jacket.

'You know me too well,' Clarice said ruefully.

'So which is it?'

'A bit of both. Although I don't know why I worry about what Rick thinks.'

Bob and Sandra exchanged quizzical glances.

'I need to look in Rose's house. The Old Vicarage.'

'Whoa, stop there,' Bob huffed. 'Rick would go ballistic, probably have you arrested, and me too.'

Sandra nodded.

'Sleep on it,' Clarice said. 'It's a big ask, so I'm not going to be offended if you say no. But I'm sure I'll find something there that might give me a clue as to what happened to Rose.'

'If there was anything to be found, the police would have got it,' Bob said doubtfully.

'Not necessarily. I didn't know her well, but at least I did know her. That gives me an edge. Getting there is the problem. It's a sod not being able to drive, though I've phoned Jim at the garage and he has an automatic he's going to lend me.' She paused, looking at the expressions of disbelief on both their faces. 'I don't want you to go in with me. You could wait around the corner in the car. Jim can't let me have the automatic until tomorrow afternoon. It's the morning that I need to go in. They're interviewing Jackie and Pete Smith – Rose's sister and brother-in-law – so I know they won't be at the house.'

'But whether I help you or not,' Bob said, 'you'll still do it?'

Clarice nodded.

'How will you get in without a key?' Sandra asked.

There was silence for a few seconds, long enough for a smirk to spread over Bob's face.

'*Bloody Darren Wren!*' He spoke in what he imagined to be a south London drawl, in imitation of Rick.

'You've got it,' laughed Clarice.

'Ah.' Sandra's face showed comprehension. 'The geezer from the prison who worked with you at CAW.'

Clarice nodded.

Sandra thought for a moment. 'Darren Wren taught you how to pick locks?'

'He did.' Clarice smiled. 'When I told Rick, he was amused.'

'Not so amused now?' Bob said knowingly.

'Noooo,' said Clarice. 'He found it funny then – endearing even.'

'That's men for you, darlin'.' Sandra crossed her arms as she spoke, looking thoughtful. 'When our Michelle started going out with Ron, he thought it was sweet how she got lost in the car – no sense of direction. That was over twenty years ago. What he says now is that the silly cow could get lost trying to find her way out of her own drive!'

Clarice nodded. Sandra and Bob's daughters Michelle and Susan both looked like their mother – short, with Sandra's colouring and pert features – but their personalities were different from either parent. In their forties, each with two children, their domestic lives, according to Sandra, revolved around packaged ready meals and watching television. 'They ain't got no sparkle,' she had confided to Clarice. 'Their get-up and go has bleedin' got up and gone.' But Clarice was aware that Sandra's real worry was their weight-related health issues, since Michelle was a Type 2 diabetic and Susan, having knee problems, had been advised by her GP to lose three stone.

'Some things don't change.' Sandra looked at Clarice as if reading her mind. 'Michelle's never going to have no sense of direction, and no matter how much I nag, neither of my girls will learn to look after their health.'

In the morning, Clarice phoned Jean Whittle to arrange to call in on her the next day. Jim had agreed to drop the car off that afternoon, so she would not need to ask Bob to take her there. As she put the phone down, she wondered what pretext Rose had used to get two thousand pounds out of Jean – she was a sensible woman and wouldn't have been easily duped.

She felt a twinge of guilt when Rick phoned.

'How are you getting on?' he asked.

'I'm fine.'

'You always say that.'

'And you never believe me. I'm going out with Sandra and Bob this morning.'

'You're meant to be resting!'

'You've got more interviews this morning?' she said, ignoring him.

There was a silence.

'Jackie and Pete Smith?'

'Not for half an hour. Daisy talks too much.'

'My fault, not Daisy's, I ask too many questions.'

'Going back to you resting . . .'

'Supermarket shopping with Sandra and Bob, then I'll rest.' Clarice felt a momentary pang of guilt, but consoled herself with the thought that they would be dropping Sandra at the supermarket to do the shopping while Bob took her on to the Old Vicarage, so it was at least partly true.

'I was going to come by later, early evening. Is that OK?'

'Yes,' Clarice reassured him, 'you don't need to ask.'

There was a moment of quiet in which Clarice thought he might say that actually he *did* need to ask, but instead he said, 'See you this evening,' before hanging up.

Bob and Sandra arrived half an hour later, and after Bob had visited the barn to make a fuss of the kittens, they set off. Wrapped up in her dog-walking jacket and hat, Clarice sat in the back of the car while Bob talked over his shoulder, laying down the rules for the expedition.

'I won't wait outside; I'll be around the corner. I'll come in to get you if you're not out within twenty minutes.'

When they pulled up outside the supermarket, Sandra got out of the car.

'Wait in the coffee shop; we should be back within the hour,' Bob said.

'Be careful,' she hissed, looking around furtively, as if the passing shoppers pushing trolleys might be aware that her husband was about to assist their friend in breaking into a dead woman's house.

Bob parked in a small lane next to the vicarage. 'Are you sure you don't want me to come in?'

Clarice shook her head, not wanting to talk, mentally concentrating on her goal.

'What about fingerprints?' Bob asked urgently as she got out.

'You watch too much TV,' she replied.

She moved purposefully away from the car, the noise of the crutches tapping on the road going unheard in the uninhabited lane. On her left, the fenced field normally occupied by beasts was empty, the cows having been moved to barns for winter shelter. The field on the opposite side looked barren, devoid of crops. Low grey-black clouds hung just above the land, giving the appearance of distant hills. The frost of the morning had long cleared, and as she turned the corner, she felt the start of a fine drizzle of rain.

Reaching the entrance porch of the vicarage, Clarice dipped under the plastic tape emblazoned with the words *POLICE DO NOT ENTER*, then stopped to listen. The only sound was the rain as it picked up pace. She put on a pair of plastic gloves she had taken from a supply in the cat outhouse.

She was inside within three minutes, and as she moved quietly within the silent house, she took a small camera from her pocket, a present to herself on her last birthday. It had been horrifyingly expensive but took photographs accurately, in the smallest detail, something she found useful for recording stages of construction in her work with ceramics.

The house felt cold, and the decor in the living room didn't help. The rooms in the Victorian building were large, with high ceilings, the walls painted a pale green – always, she thought, an emotionless colour. The living room's wooden parquet flooring was laid with four large woollen rugs in different shades of green, and on chairs, shelves and windowsills sat hundreds of dolls in assorted lacy dresses.

On a table was evidence of the break-in: piles of paperwork and broken items – a vase, lamp, picture frame. She assumed the police had put them there, having taken them from the floor, before leaving.

The house had a strange musty smell, as if it had been empty and unloved for a long time. Three weeks she reminded herself, only three weeks. Her mind jumped from Rose inappropriately dressed for classes, to the person described by Sandra, snooty and offhand at charity events, then to the woman in the barn with the ruined face. And now a new image formed, of Rose on her own, filling her time by wandering listlessly from room to room in this big house. Clarice shuddered before mentally forcing herself to start to work around the room with the camera.

She did the same in all the downstairs rooms before going upstairs. Her crutch made a clearly audible clonk on each step, making her look cautiously about, as if someone might at any moment suddenly burst out of one of the bedrooms and run down the stairs to challenge her.

'How can one woman have so many dolls?' she wondered out loud to herself as she looked in what she thought must be the main bedroom. The collection here was of dolls in costumes from across the world. The wallpaper was a blue William Morris design. On the walls, framed collections of teaspoons vied for space with prints of places in England, Scotland and South

Africa, and reproductions of works by famous artists: *The Ballet Class* by Degas and Renoir's *The Theatre Box*. Knowing the police would have been thorough with the dolls, she photographed each quickly.

She paused for a moment, puzzled, and then realised what was missing: it was books. There were plenty of magazines throughout the house, mainly about celebrity gossip, clothes and make-up, as well as style and decor, but she had not seen one book.

Pulling out a drawer of an antique chest, she was surprised to find it contained more, smaller drawers, layer upon layer of them, blue velvet trays filled with jewellery. The rest of the chest's drawers were the same. She looked in astonishment at the sheer volume of items. It certainly hadn't been a regular break-in. As with everything in the house, the taste was diverse. Modern mass-produced items lay side by side with designer and antique pieces, freshwater pearls next to plastic beads. Switching on a small torch to light them from behind, she began taking each piece of jewellery out to photograph it from different angles, placing rings at a tilt to record hallmarks or inscriptions.

Looking at her watch, she realised she'd been there for forty-five minutes; Bob would be getting fretful.

It was as she closed the final drawer that she heard the noise: the lightest tread. Pushing her camera into her jacket pocket, she stood still to listen.

The sound had been indistinct. Perhaps she had been wrong?

Then she heard it again, a slow, stealthy sound. Someone was coming up the stairs.

Rick's words about Rose's murderer came back to her with a horrible sense of prescience. *Whoever killed her wouldn't worry about breaking your jaw and smacking you over the head.*

Perhaps it was Bob. He'd said he'd come in if she wasn't done in twenty minutes. But it wouldn't be him; he would have called her name.

Her body tensed, and she hobbled to the side of the door, balancing on one leg to lift one of the crutches, poised like a tennis player ready to deliver a slam.

Standing still, she listened. Silence; the sounds had stopped.

Then, with the smallest of movements, the closed door gave an infinitesimal sigh. She had an image of the murderer standing on the other side of it, much like her; a large man with enormous red hands, the palms of which were now spread flat against the wood, his features twisting in anticipation of the kill.

Remembering Rose's destroyed face, she realised that despite the cold, her back was damp with sweat.

Suddenly the door flew open. Clarice swung the crutch, but the man was ready, sidestepping to put himself behind her. As the momentum of the swing caused her body to continue forward, slamming against the wall, the fear entering her became a hook, dragging her guts downwards.

She pushed hard against the wall to turn, only to feel hands gripping her shoulders to pull her upright. At the same time, the man spoke.

'Bloody Darren Wren!'

# Chapter 10

Rick turned Clarice around to face him before letting her go, detaching his hands with a sharp flick. His infuriation seeped out with every gesture.

'Go.' He spat the word.

'Don't talk to me like that!' she hissed. But she did as she was told, going down the stairs as quickly as she could manage, not wanting to give him an excuse to complain.

They went outside. As Rick turned to lock the door, she saw a silent, woeful Bob waiting.

'Why didn't you let Bob come in?' she muttered. 'You scared the shit out of me.' Rick put his face on a level with hers.

'Good.'

They glowered at one another, silently antagonistic.

'Halfway through the interview with Jackie Smith and the bloody penny dropped. *You've got more interviews this morning?*' he mimicked, moving his head as he spoke. 'How slow am I?' He smacked the palm of his hand against the side of his head. 'Do you want to get me fired?'

'No . . . that's a completely ridiculous thing to say.'

'You are still my wife and this is an official crime scene.'

'I'm genuinely sorry that I've upset you, but—'

'The least that might happen is that I'll be taken off the case, my reputation in ruins. Do you hate me that much?'

'Now you're being silly,' she snapped. 'I'd never harm you, but I won't be bullied by anyone; that includes you.'

Bob looked at the ground studiously as he walked away.

Rick glared at his departing back.

'Don't blame Bob,' Clarice said.

'I do not blame Bob.' He stretched out his words. 'The blame is reserved exclusively for you.' He stared at her unblinking.

'I'm beginning to remember why we split up.' Clarice held his gaze with her own, throwing the words at him. 'It's always my-way-or-no-way with you.'

'Do you really want to go down that route?' His expression had hardened further, his voice cold. 'I'm going back to try to finish an interview I was forced to walk out of. I'll see you later.'

Clarice opened her mouth to respond, then, knowing the words would be spoken in anger, closed it. Instead she turned to follow Bob. She zipped her jacket, pulling up the hood, before ducking under the police tape and stepping out of the shelter of the porch into the squall. The sky had changed to an all-over dull grey, the rain coming in waves, pushed by a sharp wind. Sensing Rick's vitriol-infused gaze boring into her back, she tilted her nose in the air in what she hoped was a *do I look as if I give a damn* posture. It was difficult to make a nonchalant and dignified exit hobbling on crutches while battling the elements. Once she was through the gate, she glanced back. He had gone.

The return journey to the supermarket was silent. Sandra stood waiting outside the main entrance with a trolley loaded with bulging carrier bags. As Bob got out to help her put the bags into the boot, Clarice watched them surreptitiously, hearing their hushed whispers.

On the way home, Sandra sat in the back of the car. Halfway there, Clarice felt a small gloved hand come from behind to rest on her shoulder. Wordlessly she rested her own on Sandra's.

Later they sat silently around the kitchen table, mugs of tea and an untouched Victoria sponge in front of them. Sensing the sombre mood, the two dogs sat motionless, one on either side of Clarice, their eyes moving from one face to another.

'Enough of this bleedin' hangdog crap,' said Sandra finally. 'You went in, you did the business. That's all there is to it.'

Four pairs of remorseful eyes turned to her.

'You got caught, move on. Now, tell us, did you find anything worthwhile? A nest egg, a stash of cash, what?'

Clarice put her head to one side pensively.

Blue, sensing the change of mood, slipped the tea towel unnoticed from Sandra's lap and sat with it dangling from her mouth.

'Well, yes.' Clarice was thoughtful. 'No stash, but she did collect jewellery. I've never seen so much belonging to one person; she was obsessed. Some nice pieces – contemporary and antique – but also a huge amount of crap.'

Bob picked up the knife and cut into the cake while Sandra moved three small plates in front of him.

'She had some lovely antique furniture,' Clarice went on, 'but a lot of rubbish there as well. I think her style came from magazines. Perhaps she saw something she liked so she bought it on impulse. She threw good pieces and trashy ones together. There was no emotion – the house didn't feel at all like a home, and the jewellery wasn't personal, just a collection of *things* picked up by someone with an acquisitive nature. I thought there'd be more pieces from the 1950s, since she wore so many fifties clothes. There *was* some fifties jewellery, but apart from her clothes and a couple of vases, there was nothing around the house furniture-wise that shouted 1950s.'

Sandra and Bob ate their cake, listening.

'I do wonder what sort of childhood she had. It would be interesting to talk to the sisters. I wonder if they were always having to make do. I got the feeling she was awash with money but didn't know what to spend it on.'

'Other people's money?' Bob asked.

'Most likely. What was really peculiar was that there were so many dolls.'

'Dolls?' Sandra's face twisted derisively.

'In every room. She obviously collected them. I can understand why people enjoy collecting, but they had no artistic, financial or intrinsic value as far as I could see.' Clarice paused. 'I think she was someone who wanted to be part of something that she'd looked at from the outside – with envy. Rich people who had lovely homes, who owned beautiful things: antiques that they'd inherited, modern pieces they put together with proper taste. People who had something she knew she hadn't.'

'Are you talking about *old* money?' Bob asked.

'Yes,' Clarice thought again, 'I suppose I am. So where did that come from? Had she visited a lot of people with those sorts of homes – people with really significant wealth?'

Bob and Sandra looked at her quizzically, waiting for her to continue.

'I don't think so.' She answered her own question. 'I can't see the Rose I knew mixing in that social circle. So perhaps she was employed by people who had the things she admired, people she envied.' She lifted her hands apart expansively. 'And now there she was, she'd got it made; she had the big house and the financial resources to make her into *that* person, the one she'd always dreamed of becoming. The antiques I imagine were bought, not inherited, and then the rest ...'

'Be careful what you wish for,' said Bob.

Clarice nodded. 'I suspect that Rose, having achieved her dream, wasn't necessarily happy.'

'What now?' he asked.

'I need to download everything from the camera to the computer. There's something to be found there, I'm sure of it.'

Hearing a car arriving, Sandra went to the window. 'Two cars. Jim from the garage, with Fred following him.'

'He'll be dropping the automatic,' Clarice said. 'Fred'll be there to drive him back.'

Later, on her own, after a session of kitten handling, she went to the study and switched on the computer. The dogs, following her upstairs, made themselves comfortable on an old chaise.

Tomorrow, she thought, after sorting the animals, she must have a morning in the pottery. She had pieces to fire, already loaded in the kiln. She wrote *kiln timer* on her things-to-remember pad. It would start to warm up from 5 a.m., while she was still in bed.

Jean Whittle was expecting her at 2 p.m. tomorrow, and then on to Jonathan the vet before he began his afternoon appointments. She needed medication for two of the old cats, and he allowed her to collect items out of surgery hours. Not having spoken to him since her accident, she was looking forward to a catch-up.

As soon as she sat at the computer, Toots, a long grey cat, climbed up, flopping his body elegantly across her lap. She scratched his head absent-mindedly as she moved from one photograph to another, enlarging each to look in close detail. But what was she looking for? A link between Rose and the murderer? It had to be here, but the cliché about haystacks and needles kept popping into her head as she scoured the shadowy images.

An hour later, as it was starting to get dark, she saw car lights sweep the driveway.

Downstairs, she opened the front door to step out. The rain had stopped but the ground was sodden. The air smelled of a mixture of damp and the woodsmoke that drifted from the chimney, a strange but pleasant combination. She watched Rick walk across the yard, then turned back into the kitchen as he neared the door.

Once inside, they stared at one another.

He looked, she thought, dishevelled and tired. She was desperate to put her arms around him, not as a lover but as a friend.

'I'm so sorry.' She spoke first.

He shrugged his shoulders and gave his slanted half-smile.

'It's done,' he said, 'and for what it's worth, I'm sorry too. I still don't agree with what you did, but I was shitty. I should have called out going up the stairs. I shouldn't have scared you.'

He bent down to Jazz and Blue, who were both vying for his attention.

'There's a fire going,' Clarice said. 'Do you want a drink or something to eat?'

'A coffee would be good.' He came past her, walking to the coffee machine. 'Is the jug still dribbling?'

She nodded. 'There's cream if you want it.'

They exchanged a knowing flicker of a smile, both aware that she never bought cream for herself; a peace offering. 'It's from the freezer,' she said.

'Ah.' A look of recollection lit his face. 'From the bottomless black hole!'

She nodded. Rick had never accompanied her to the super-market. He had had no idea, when they were a couple, what might be in the freezer. His joke was that, like a magician's bag, it had an endless supply of secret goodies waiting to be revealed.

Half an hour later, he sat in the armchair to one side of the fireplace, while Clarice perched on the sofa, her injured foot out in front. The dogs had joined them on the hearth.

He'd drunk a coffee and had also, after saying that he wasn't hungry, taken a plate with a large slice of cheese and tomato quiche, wolfing it down before going back for a second slice, which he had eaten more slowly. Squashed beside him, purring while rubbing her face back and forth across his arm, was the five-year-old tabby, Muddy, his favourite.

Clarice repeated what she had told Sandra and Bob about her thoughts on Rose's home.

'Have you looked at the photographs yet?'

Although she hadn't told him she had taken photographs, she'd known he would ask the question.

'I've downloaded them onto the computer. I was going through them when you arrived.'

'Any links?'

'Do you want to come up and see them?'

'No, I've looked through probably identical ones at the office and I've seen everything in the house.'

'There were a couple of things ...'

He nodded, listening.

'In terms of places, there were the framed prints. One related to the south-west of Scotland, two to Norfolk, near King's Lynn. Four were located around the Whitby area and four more had connections to South Africa. It may be she just bought the lot in a junk shop, of course.'

'Anything else?'

'A number of the rings were interesting, as well as two of the brooches.'

'Why?'

'Two rings had initials engraved on the inside; both looked like wedding rings.'

'I saw those. There were eleven wedding or band-type rings; why were those two special?'

'The hallmarks indicate they were made within the last four decades.'

'You think that's relevant?'

'Possibly, and one brooch was in the shape of an M – very eighties, not Rose's era.'

'Why is that one interesting?'

'The sister is called Maggie.'

'So are a lot of people. Their aunt was called Margaret, too, although she was known as Peggy – she lived in Norfolk.'

Clarice nodded thoughtfully. 'It might be her brooch. Is she still around?'

'No, she died two or three years ago; the family liaison officer is checking.'

'Who is the FLO?'

'Julie Buckley.'

Clarice nodded. 'The other brooch contains human hair.'

'It's an antique?'

'Yes, Victorian mourning jewellery, containing the hair of a loved one. But what if it was a way of hiding hair that related to somebody alive, for the purpose of blackmail? A good place to hide it?'

Rick shrugged non-committally. 'I'll get someone to collect it tomorrow to have it looked at.'

'Have you had all the dolls checked out?'

'Yes,' he said sarcastically, 'funnily enough, we did think of doing that. The ones you saw have already been checked by a PC. There's another lot that need taking apart, which will be time-consuming, so they've been taken to the office. She'll drop them back to the house after they've been checked.'

Clarice went on, ignoring his tone. 'I haven't had that long to look at the photographs. I might get a couple more hours tomorrow.'

Drinking his second coffee, Rick didn't reply immediately.

'Did you work out how the housebreaker got into the vicarage?' she asked.

'No.' His attention came back to her. 'Assuming it wasn't Darren Wren.' When Clarice didn't respond, he continued, 'I'm guessing she used a regular handbag, with the usual crap ladies have in them. There was no handbag, no keys.'

'So the murderer took the bag and used her key?'

'It looks that way. What are you doing tomorrow, when you're supposed to be resting? I see you've got another car.'

'It's Jim's, an automatic.'

'So,' he smiled, 'the plan is to avoid getting Sandra and Bob involved in what you've got planned next?'

'I'll be in the workshop in the morning, and in the afternoon I'm seeing friends for a cuppa,' she said primly. They had both relaxed, but she sensed the game was on between them.

'Are the *friends*,' he said, 'connected in any way to this case?'

'Jonathan,' she said, before adding, as if an afterthought, 'and Jean Whittle. You might remember her; she used to come to my classes.'

'Yes, I remember her. Is that the same lady who lent money to Rose Miller?' He lifted his eyebrow cynically.

'Yes, that's her,' Clarice said cheerfully.

He frowned. 'We are going to have to come to an agreement.'

She nodded.

'I can't stop you seeing people, talking to them, nosing around.'

She nodded again.

'The rules are—'

'Your rules?' she asked.

'The rules are,' he repeated, 'rule one, you do not do anything illegal that might get me sacked; rule two, you do not put yourself in danger.' He held up three fingers. 'And rule three, you don't keep things secret; you pass on anything important.'

Clarice sat gazing at the fire for a few minutes, considering.

'I'll agree,' she said, 'but rule three has to work both ways. *You* must share with me.' She put up her hands to stop him as he started to speak. 'I know you're going to say you can't tell me certain things that would breach the rules of your job, but you can tell me other things.'

'Such as?'

'Such as, what was your impression of Pete and Jackie Smith, as individuals? I can search out people who know them to find out more, but I trust your judgement, and it would be a shortcut for me, avoid me having to do a lot of digging.'

Rick gave a deep sigh. 'All right, just as long as you stick to your side of the bargain.'

She nodded encouragingly.

'Pete Smith is a nasty piece of work, a thief, a swindler and a borderline alcoholic. His record includes GBH; he'd smack you because he thought you'd looked at him the wrong way. A man to be avoided.' He paused as if checking that she was taking in what he said. 'Don't go anywhere near him. His wife, Jackie, is as thick as they come – no brain cells, not even one. She'll do as he tells her. She says Maggie, her younger sister, got pregnant as a teenager, married and moved to Scotland with her husband. They heard no more after that, but I guessed by the way she talked that she didn't much get on with either of her sisters.'

Clarice nodded.

'Pete Smith's keen to know what happened to his sister-in-law, but not, I suspect, out of any sentiment. He strikes me as being the type to live hand to mouth, and I imagine that he must be itching to get hold of all that jewellery. He wants to strip the house and sell the stuff, but I've told him he can't remove anything yet.'

'Didn't go down well?'

'That would be an understatement.'

'If he's that desperate for money, he's going to push the boundaries.'

'He'll keep out until I say otherwise, which will be when the case has been resolved.'

'That makes sense.' Clarice looked at him thoughtfully. 'And thanks for the insight. He sounds like a nightmare.'

# Chapter 11

The following afternoon, driving to Jean Whittle's house, Clarice considered what Rick had told her about the Smiths. She had enjoyed a less than productive morning in her workshop. Having intended to work on new ideas for a touring exhibition, the planning of which was currently taking shape, she had instead found her thoughts drifting to the youngest sister, Maggie.

As a child, she had never considered what it must be like to have a brother or a sister. She'd seen how Rick was with his three brothers; the feelings between siblings must, she decided, be like the sentiment between friends, but perhaps deeper, more intuitive. What had the falling-out between the sisters been about, to cause such animosity? Money, perhaps, or boyfriends? They'd clearly had no interest in keeping in touch with one another; the only reason the Smiths had now turned their attentions to Rose – or Sharon, as Rick told her Jackie still called her – was because the police had contacted them and there was financial gain to be had. Jackie had told Rick she had not seen Rose for over two years, and the last she had heard of Maggie was about thirty years ago.

Clarice momentarily moved her reflections to her friend

Georgie. She knew Georgie hadn't spoken to her own sister for over five years; perhaps it was, after all, normal sibling behaviour.

Could the blackmailing have also involved one or both of the sisters? As the youngest hadn't been around for three decades and the middle sister's only intent was to get her hands on any possessions of value belonging to the eldest, it seemed unlikely, but couldn't be ruled out. Or could Rose have been married? The initials inside the rings did not fit with her names, neither did they fit with either of her sisters'. One was the childlike *MM loves RP*, the sort of thing teenage lovers might carve on a tree. If it was a wedding ring, the initials and a date would have been more appropriate. The other had the initials MP and RB engraved on the inside. And was there any connection to South Africa, Norfolk, Scotland or Yorkshire?

The drive into Castlewick was often slow, dependent upon the time of year. In the autumn, the roads might be clogged with tractors bringing produce from the fields; in summer, it was the main route to Skegness, Saturday being the busiest day with the changeover for rented caravans and chalets. Today, being neither tourist nor harvest season, the traffic flowed without problems. It was cold, the sky a clear vanilla beige with watery sunshine. She'd quickly got the hang of driving the automatic, an eight-year-old silver five-door Citroën estate, lower in the seating than her own Range Rover, but comfortable.

Still immersed in her thoughts, she drove through the town to get to the quiet 1960s housing estate on its outer fringe. Set in a cul-de-sac, with no through traffic, Jean's pebbledash white bungalow, with its neatly cut area of grass to the front, was identical to all the others. Almost all the properties were owned by older or retired people. The cars, Clarice noted, were universally small and spotlessly clean, as were the net curtains that fronted the windows, neat and bleached, pure white. It was, she imagined, a place of boredom, watchers from behind those impeccable nets, in their dust-free boxes, measuring time by when they ate or watched the evening soap on TV.

She pulled up on the road next to Jean's driveway. Her friend was waiting at the door holding one of her two cats, a large, handsome tabby called Nigel, who, not having been neutered until he was well over four, had a body that merged with his head by way of a thick, bull-like neck.

Inside, Clarice sat in the living room with Nigel on her lap as Jean went back and forth to the kitchen. They made small talk about people they knew in the classes and the town's book club, which met at the library once a month and whose new reading choice Clarice intended to track down later in town.

'Have you spotted Nicola?' Jean called.

'I've seen her tail,' Clarice shouted back. Nicola was the last of a litter of kittens and Nigel a friendly older stray; Jean had adopted them from Clarice as a pair. Clarice had been on the letter N with that group and was surprised that Jean had not changed the names. Nicola, a shy tortoiseshell tabby, was currently lurking behind a curtain; her huge bushy tail, the longest Clarice had ever seen on a cat, always gave away her hiding place.

The living room was traditional, with two comfortable armchairs and a sofa. Shelved ornaments, mainly cats, including some of Jean's own creations made in Clarice's classes, lined the room. Photographs showed Jean and her husband Bill, both in their late sixties and retired. They looked so alike, both white-haired, medium height and solidly built, that Clarice wondered if they had started out like that or grown into a matching pair over the years. Other photographs included them with their son Tim and the grandchildren.

'Where's Bill?' Clarice asked.

'He's gone over to Tim's to help with the decorating.'

'Lucky Tim,' Clarice said, 'having a dad who enjoys that sort of thing.'

'It's the doing it together that Bill enjoys,' Jean said, 'the father-and-son thing.' She brought her own coffee to sit opposite Clarice. 'I can guess why you're here. Did Rick tell you about the money?'

'No,' Clarice said, 'but somebody else did mention it.'

'Oh . . .' Jean sounded distressed. 'Does everyone know?'

'I honestly have no idea.'

When Jean remained silent, Clarice went on, 'Is it really so bad you're ashamed of people finding out? I can't see that you've done anything wrong.'

Jean looked down into her coffee mug. 'I feel such a fool; the others do too. Who told you? Was it Clare?'

'Clare Robbins?' said Clarice, remembering that she and Jean had been friends while attending her classes.

Jean looked up at her attentively.

'No,' said Clarice.

'You're not going to tell me, are you?'

'I would prefer not to,' said Clarice. She wondered how many people had given money to Rose. 'What does Bill think?'

Jean put her cup down on the coffee table, her hands going up to her face, her bottom lip suddenly trembling.

'Jean,' Clarice said, leaning over to rest her hand on her friend's arm. 'I'm so sorry I've upset you.'

'It's not you.' Jean pulled a tissue from a pocket in her skirt. 'Bill's hardly spoken to me since he found out.'

Clarice nodded.

'He says it's illegal.'

'In what way?'

'Rose called it a friendship club, with us all putting the money in, but Bill said it's a form of pyramid selling. He said it's something called bottom-loaded: the people who join later have no chance of getting their money back or making anything out of it.'

'He might be right.'

'He told her to give me the money back.'

'Did he?'

'Yes.' Jean nodded. 'He went to the vicarage to confront her, but she laughed at him, said that's not how it works.' Leaning forward, she began to cry, wave upon wave of anguish suddenly rippling up through her sturdy body.

'What's done is done,' Clarice said, gently stroking her arm. 'Have the others admitted that they gave Rose money?'

'I'm the only one to complain to the police. Bill said if I told them I had lent it to her, I might have a chance of getting it back.'

'Not without any proof.'

'That's what the police said.' Jean sniffed, her sobs under control now.

'You must *all* tell the truth,' Clarice said. 'It's a murder investigation. Please do be honest, and ask the others to do the same.'

'That might be difficult,' Jean answered quietly.

'Why?' Clarice asked.

'Because,' the tears started again, 'none of us is speaking to one another. We were such good friends, and now everyone is blaming each other.'

'What the hell are you blubbing about?' Bill stood in the doorway, having come in through the back door without being heard.

'Nothing.' Getting up quickly, Jean bent to pick up her cup, hiding her face.

'I'll get you some tea,' she mumbled, moving past him.

'All right, Clarice?' Bill asked, nodding to her.

'Yes, I'm good, Bill,' Clarice smiled. Despite their always having got on well in the past, she could hear a flinty distrust in his voice.

'You don't look that good to me.' He glanced at her crutches on the floor next to her.

'I had a fall.'

'I heard about it,' he said. 'Are you making me that tea or not?' he shot at Jean, who was standing behind him, listening. Nodding to Clarice, he turned to follow his wife as she shuffled into the kitchen, his lips still pressed together into a sullen straight line.

Their voices drifted through, just too far away for Clarice to hear the words distinctly. Picking up her crutches, she worked her way to the door to bend and make a fuss of Nicola, who had sidled behind it.

'They may be divorced, but she's still his wife.' Bill spoke abruptly.

'They're not divorced, they're separated; it's six months now.'

'All I'm saying is, it's illegal, so don't think she won't tell him, husband or not. And who's the mug who'll end up in court? *You.* It's you who lied – you told the police you'd *lent* the money.'

'But,' Jean's voice wobbled, 'it was you who told me what to say. And you were the one who said to go to the police in the first place!'

Clarice worked her way back to where she had been sitting, grateful for the silence gained from a fitted carpet.

'Jean.' She smiled at the older woman's return a few minutes later. 'I'm afraid I must go. I've got to collect medication from Jonathan.'

Jean followed her to her car. 'Don't tell anyone,' she pleaded, as Clarice manoeuvred herself into the driver's seat.

'You are innocent in this,' Clarice said quietly, looking up at Jean's tear-blotched face. 'Rose was at fault, not you.'

Jean nodded.

Glancing at the door as she pulled out, Clarice saw Bill waiting, his arms folded, his mouth again set in a grim line.

As she drove into the town centre, Clarice decided that instead of pottering around the book shop as she'd planned originally, she'd drive directly to Jonathan's home, next to his veterinary practice.

The house, in one of the side streets leading from the market square, was tall with a white façade, one of many in the town built at the turn of the twentieth century. The surgery itself was a squat 1940s building, formerly a chemist's. Both the house and the surgery had been modernised by Jonathan and his partner Keith Banner when they'd come to Castlewick over two decades earlier. The number of customers requiring a vet had multiplied over the years, and Jonathan now employed two further vets within the practice. Keith, a solicitor, was a partner in Baines and Banner, one of the town's two legal firms.

'Hi, Jonathan,' Clarice called through the half-open back door of the house.

'Clarice, my lovely!' Jonathan came out to give her a hug.

'You caught me putting the bin out. I'm *so* pleased to see you,' he said. 'I've been getting Clarice withdrawal symptoms.' He watched her using her crutches to make her way to the kitchen. 'My goodness, you've certainly got the hang of those.'

'No choice,' she laughed, her mood lightening after the encounter with Jean and Bill. Jonathan was always so upbeat, it was hard to feel otherwise. He was like an exuberant Labrador, affectionate and trustworthy. Clarice knew he was also an outrageous gossip, but he had an ability to bounce between kindness and wicked humour that never failed to lift her spirits.

'How are you, and Keith? I'm sorry I haven't called earlier – it's been a bit manic since the accident.'

'Do you want a cuppa?' He picked up the tin containing tea bags, in anticipation of her response.

'Yes, please.'

'We're both great,' he said. 'You know about Keith's hip, he might need a replacement . . . yes, I told you about that a while ago.'

Clarice smiled as Jonathan talked about health and family matters before moving on to local issues, and filling her in on developments.

The small, low-ceilinged kitchen was cosy. Two Windsor chairs, each with a plump orange cushion, stood next to a small square oak table. A dark floor-to-ceiling chest with over thirty small brass-handled drawers, salvaged from the chemist's shop, fitted perfectly into the space allocated to it. In contrast, a large shiny orange Italian cooker took up almost one whole wall. Above was a row of bright copper pans and to one side steel knives. Jonathan and Keith enjoyed cooking, Clarice having been invited on many occasions with Rick and recently on her own to join them for meals. They were both accomplished and competitive, never shy of expounding the delights and merits of each dish they produced.

'And have you heard about the pyramid-selling scam?' Jonathan asked eagerly.

'What?'

'Here, in a small town – you wouldn't believe it.'

'Tell me,' said Clarice, 'is it this friendship scheme?'

'You've already heard.' Jonathan sounded disappointed that somebody had beaten him with the gossip.

'I don't think I've heard it all, just bits and pieces.'

'Well,' he said, crossing his arms, all thoughts of tea gone. 'It was that woman, the dead one, Rose.'

'Yes, I know.'

'Well you would,' he said with a deep chuckle. 'It was you who found her. Now, let me think, who else was in it?' He counted the names on his fingers as he spoke. 'Jean Whittle, Lydia Pembroke, Clare Robbins, Martha Dickson and Pat Leach.'

'Pat Leach?'

'Yes, she's a small white mouse of a woman, hardly ever leaves home; you'd never believe she had that sort of money. It all went along hunky-dory for a couple of months. Then, from what I've been told, the doubts set in. The fact finally dawned on them that none of them would make money from it and they'd also lost their original investment. That was when everything went pear-shaped. Hitting, shit, fan, rearrange those three words.' He stopped momentarily to prolong the tale. 'Bill Whittle went ape, marched off to visit Rose to demand their money back, and said that he was going to wring her neck. Shortly followed by Frank Pembroke attempting to attack her in the market.'

Clarice was surprised. 'Frank Pembroke, I didn't know about that.'

'He waved his walking stick in her face, calling her a thief, and guess her response?'

Clarice shook her head.

'"Wave that in my face again, old man, and I'll stick it where the sun don't shine!" Finishing triumphantly, he leant back against the table, awaiting a reaction.

'I'd expect Lydia to retaliate verbally, but Frank is so easy-going,' Clarice responded. 'The more I hear about Rose's behaviour, the more I think there's still a lot more to come out. It's all pretty depressing.'

'Do you know,' Jonathan asked, looking crafty, 'if she might have done something like this before, in another town perhaps?'

'I couldn't say, Jonathan,' Clarice said sternly, 'but she must have been *very* persuasive. The five ladies involved are not silly; they're all sensible types. And they hadn't known her for very long.'

'About two years.' Jonathan spoke with an air of innocence.

Good try, my friend, she thought. She knew Jonathan's methods well, and couldn't help thinking he'd hoped to get something new from her. He'd failed this time, although he would probably still feel it had been worth a shot. She contemplated the irony of a friendship club that had destroyed friendships going back over twenty years. She would phone Rick when she got home, relieved that it was Jonathan who had given her the names, rather than poor Jean. She could keep her promise to Rick to share information with a clear conscience. But what she really needed now was that cup of tea.

# Chapter 12

Rick beat her to it. As she finally reached the top of the stairs, on her way to change into a floppy sweater and a pair of baggy trousers, the study phone rang.

'How did it go?' he said when she managed to pick it up.

'In what way?' She knew what he was asking.

'Come on, spill.'

She relayed what she had learned from Jean and Jonathan.

'It makes it easier with Jonathan having told you about it as well as Jean,' he said.

'Yes, that's exactly what I was thinking. I don't feel I'm betraying a confidence. But was Rose definitely a blackmailer? If she was, she was obviously successful at it. Also, it must have been going on for some time, if her house and the cash that went through her account are anything to go by.' Clarice spoke with frustration. 'But rather than keeping her head down, she'd started ripping people off locally. As far as I can work out, she only took ten thousand pounds from the friendship scam – there were five of them, who put in two thousand pounds each – while by your estimation a great deal more than that has gone through the bank account. Why risk losing the bigger amounts? It doesn't make sense!'

'She's a thief, obviously couldn't resist.'

'Maybe she got a buzz out of it. Winning, as she saw it.'

The light was just beginning to fade. She heard a car engine and saw headlights sweep across the room. Both dogs started to bark.

'Who's that?' she spoke out loud as she walked to the window.

'Sandra and Bob?'

'No, they've been and gone.'

Looking out, she saw a vehicle she didn't recognise.

'It's a beaten-up white van with a green stripe. Looks like the rust's holding it together.' She paused. 'And a really big bloke with a small skinny woman has just got out.'

'Has he got tattoos around his neck?'

'They aren't near enough to see. I'm upstairs in the study, and it's getting dark.'

'It sounds like the Smiths,' Rick said urgently. 'Get downstairs, lock the door and don't let them in.'

Looking out, Clarice saw that the pair had disappeared below her eyeline to reach the door. The dogs' barking increased. 'It might be too late for that.'

'Stall them. I'm on my way.'

Having put the phone down, she moved with alacrity down the stairs, her crutches and measured pace forgotten. Instinctively not putting weight on her damaged ankle, she hopped on her good foot, while grabbing at the banister arm over arm, as a swimmer might, to propel her downward. As she reached the bottom, she could feel her heart racing. The anxiety in Rick's voice still echoed in her head.

Blue, her nose an inch from the door, had doubled in size, the fur standing up over her entire body, bristling down her back in a ridge of spikes. The friendly, affable clown, gift permanently dangling from mouth, was gone; in its place was a black beast, aggression mounting with each extended growl. For every rumble a small yap came from Jazz, leaping in the air as if by reaching a greater height she might become as fierce and as forceful as her companion.

As she got to the door, Clarice heard the shout of a male voice, followed by a bang against the frame. She stood close to the door, allowing the dogs to continue barking. Then gently, soundlessly, she slid the bolt shut at the bottom and slipped the security chain into place.

The fist banging on the door came again, then again. Then silence.

After a while, instead of further shouts, there was the sound of the car engine. She moved to look through the window from behind the curtain to see the beam of the headlights moving upward as the vehicle was driven out.

Ten minutes later, she heard the engine that signalled the arrival of another car, its lights dipping as it moved down the incline. Blue, glancing at her, started to growl, Jazz to witter. Clarice made a short whistling sound to gain their attention, before holding her right hand in the air, palm flat, a signal for silence. The room fell quiet. She tilted her hand downwards and both dogs sat obediently, their eyes going back and forth from her to the door.

'It's me.' Rick's voice came from outside.

Clarice slid the bolt and removed the chain.

'Go see,' she instructed the dogs, who bounded to welcome him, Jazz jumping joyfully around, Blue pushing hard against his legs.

'How long have they been gone?' he questioned, his body taut with anxiety.

'About ten minutes.'

'No problems?'

She shook her head. 'He knocked and shouted hello three times after I'd come downstairs, then left. Think Blue put the wind up him.'

'Clever girl.' Rick, visibly relaxing, rubbed Blue's ears. 'And you, pipsqueak,' he said, bending down to pat Jazz. He looked up at Clarice. 'Are you all right?'

She nodded.

'I wish I could stay.'

'I know,' she said. 'I'm OK, honest.'

'There's been an incident, a man stabbed, I've got to go there.'

She nodded again.

'Why has he come here?' Clarice sounded mystified. 'I don't get it.'

'He's shaking the tree,' Rick said, 'to see what falls. Anyone who even vaguely knew Rose will get a visit.'

Clarice stood quietly, thinking.

'I must go,' Rick said with urgency, turning to leave.

'Yes, take care.'

He gave her a quick kiss on the cheek before departing.

She shuddered involuntarily as she stood watching his headlights climb the slope to depart, then quickly pushed the door closed and locked it. She listened to the sound of the car engine until the evening again became silent. She felt not lonely but ... what? Vulnerable? She experienced a hot flood of anger. Turning back to face the closed door, she made her right hand into a fist to press it hard against it. 'No!' She spoke the word out loud, the dogs, alert again, looking at her. She would not allow that man to make her feel insecure in her own home. That wasn't going to happen.

The phone rang just after 6 a.m.

'It's me,' Rick said.

'I guessed it might be.'

'Thought I'd catch you before you go out to walk the dogs. Everything OK?'

'I'm fine, just having a cuppa. Are you at work?'

'Yep, afraid so.'

There was an awkward silence.

'How did it go last night?' she asked.

'One fatality and one arrest,' he said, then, after another silence, 'I'd better go.'

Five minutes later, Clarice, in her usual dog-walking uniform, left the house. After closing the door, she hovered for a moment before pushing the key into the lock and turning it. Locking the door had never been part of her morning routine; she would be back soon enough and there was nobody about at this time in the morning. She felt again the rise of anger. She moved carefully over the wet, slippery ground, swinging forward with the crutches around the garden. The dogs ran back and forth gleefully, enjoying their freedom after the night's incarceration, Jazz barking, Blue with an old tennis ball, a recently rediscovered treasure, clamped between her teeth. Since the accident, Clarice had replaced the regular three laps of the boundary with one slow hobble, allowing the dogs to have a good run. Bob took them out on a three-lap afternoon walk, for which she was grateful.

The overnight rain began again. Having left the dogs locked in her workshop, she stopped at the willow tree, putting out her hand for a moment to feel the reassuring solid roughness of its bark. Pulling her hat off and tilting her head back, she let the rain dripping through the branches fall onto her upturned face. It was a new day and she was determined to put her fears of last night behind her.

Unlocking the gate and going into the enclosure, she paused again; then, her head and heart fighting over the decision, finally locked it behind her.

Inside, she went through the regular routine of feeding and fussing. It was when she was washing the cat dishes that she heard Blue barking. If the dog was disturbed by a noise, she might bark for a few moments before falling quiet, but now the sound was relentless.

Clarice went out, closing the door to walk to the gate.

That was when she saw him.

He had been peering closely at the lock, one hand resting against the gate. He looked up to see her, less than thirty feet away. The mesh fence and the locked gate lay between them.

He was a big man, with a solid waistline, and threaded red and blue broken veins on the nose and cheeks of his bloated face. His salt-and-pepper hair, thinning and untidy, was plastered against his skull by the rain. Around his neck, what looked like a blue scarf was, Clarice realised, actually a band of tattoos. He wore jeans, a battered black leather jacket and dirty trainers.

'Hello, luv!' he called out to her, his voice heavy with forced civility.

'Can I help you?' Clarice asked.

He smiled, showing dark damaged teeth. 'Came last night,' he said. 'Surprised the dogs didn't let you know.'

She listened now to Blue's frantic barking from the workshop.

'I don't open the door when it gets late,' she said. If she hadn't put the gate lock on and had left the door to the cat barn open, she'd be stuck inside with him now. He had small eyes, bloodshot and peevish, the irritability behind them undisguised by his pretence of politeness.

There was a movement from further back and she saw a scrawny, pale woman wearing an oversized beige raincoat. She had bleached hair, half blonde, with several inches of visible grey roots. She hovered near the willow, watching.

'It's the wife,' he said impassively, the way Clarice imagined he might say 'it's the dog' or 'it's the car'. They were all things he felt he had ownership of. As he looked her up and down, her gut instinct screamed that this was a man who didn't like women, especially if they were intelligent.

'What was it you wanted?' She forced a half-smile.

'It's about the sister-in-law . . . Sharon. You found her.'

She looked at him quizzically.

'At the Hanging Barn?' he said.

'You must mean Rose.' She spoke with as much innocence as she could muster.

'That's what she called herself around here, but her name was Sharon.'

'Yes, I found her, but that's it. You need to speak to the police if you have any questions.' She stared at him.

'Yeah, well, I've been to the police.' His voice had taken on a sharper tone. 'Tried to stitch us up, making out we might be involved.'

'I don't know about that. I expect they're just trying to find out what happened.' She wondered where this was going.

'Can't even get into our own house. We're staying at the pub.'

'Are you from around here?' She put surprise into her words.

'It's called the Old Vicarage, luv, her sister's house.' He nodded back to his wife as he spoke. 'What's hers is mine.'

She had heard the expression before – what's hers is mine and what's mine's my own.

'There was another sister, I gather, so your wife will probably have to do a split with her on that.'

'Yeah,' he sneered knowingly, 'if they can find her – which is doubtful.' He spoke with his head to one side, staring at her, before his glance fell down to the lock and up again. 'Proper little know-all, aren't you?' The rain, which had started to ease, suddenly picked up. 'The wife and I, we're trying to put it all together, what happened.' His tone was wheedling again. 'Speak to anyone who might know something.' He paused, eyeing her speculatively. 'Aren't you going to invite us in? It's bleeding wet and cold.' He rubbed his hands together. 'A nice cup of tea and a chat to put the wife's mind at rest, and she needs a pee … Use your bathroom?'

'I'm sorry, but I've got friends coming over.'

'What, at seven in the morning? That's bollocks.' He lost the amiability. 'A man in the pub told us you were a nosy old cow. He said your ex was filth, the one wasting my time trying to stitch me up, and that with you being so nosy you'd know everything going on around here. He said he'd sent you to that barn to find a cat.' He looked her up and down again, leering. 'One of those sad bitches who prefers cats to men, are you?'

'I don't know what he's told you,' Clarice kept her voice even, 'but I can't tell you more than the police because I don't know any more.' She looked towards the woman by the willow. 'There's an outside loo, that small building over there, it's clean.' She pointed. 'Your wife is welcome to use it.'

He stood silent, staring. Menace radiated from him, his eyes vicious slits. Then, after what seemed an age, he turned away. 'I'll come back another time, then.'

The woman didn't go to use the outside lavatory; instead, they both returned to sit in the van.

Clarice considered going to her workshop to let Blue out, but the distance was further than the van, and she was afraid that on the crutches she might slip and fall, or that he might get out and sprint forward, cutting her off. She returned inside the cat barn to watch from a window, wishing she had thought to carry her mobile phone with her.

They sat in the van for a further twenty minutes, Clarice trapped inside the barn listening to Blue's ceaseless barking. Finally they drove off, their attempt at intimidation at an end – for the moment.

# Chapter 13

Less than an hour later, Daisy Bodey drew up in a dark blue car, which Clarice recognised as being from the carpool of shared police vehicles.

'I did say that they'd gone!' Clarice said, welcoming her into the cottage, to which she'd returned with relief once the van had disappeared.

'Rick was concerned.'

She nodded. 'I understand now why Rick said Smith was trouble,' she said ruefully.

'You said he didn't threaten you directly?' asked Daisy.

'No, he was rude and I felt that he was a threatening man.' Clarice tried to be precise. 'But he made no specific threat to me, not unless you count him saying he would come back another time.'

'You're at a disadvantage with your injury, unfortunately. How long do you think it will be before you get rid of the flat boot and return to normal?' Daisy talked as she munched on a biscuit, wrapping her hands gratefully around the mug of coffee Clarice had placed in front of her.

'If I'm lucky, another six weeks before my X-rays, then around twelve weeks for full recovery. It depends on a lot of factors – people heal at different rates.'

'Age, lifestyle and health?'

'Yes, all of those.'

'That's a bugger.' Daisy rolled her eyes, dipping into the tin. 'Jammy dodgers, my favourites,' she commented. 'Good job you've got the automatic.'

'Yes, thanks to Jim; he's a real life-saver.'

'You're paying for the use of it?'

'Of course,' Clarice said. 'The garage is his business; he couldn't let me use it for twelve weeks for free. But he's given me a good deal.'

A long, thin, black-and-white cat sidled up to Daisy, turning his black face upwards watchfully.

'Hello, Howlin', how are you?'

The cat looked at her, then rubbed his whiskery face against her leg before slipping away.

'Is he the diabetic?'

'No.' Clarice shook her head. 'That's BB, but he's also black and white. Easy to mix them up.'

'Why's this one called Howlin' – apart from the obvious blues connection?'

'You ought to hear him when he's eaten his dinner and all is well with the world.'

'That good?'

'Yep.' Clarice grinned.

'I don't know how you manage a diabetic cat, having to jab it every day!'

'BB doesn't like it, though some cats don't seem to mind. It was easier when Rick held him while I did the injection.' Clarice shrugged. 'Bob and Sandra help.'

'They are brilliant.' Daisy nodded enthusiastically.

Clarice looked pensive. 'I wonder who'll be next on Pete's visiting list.'

'Maybe he'll give up and go home, but somehow I doubt it.'

'Mm, their problem's the same as ours,' Clarice said. 'The most likely suspect as Rose's killer is someone she'd been blackmailing – that's logical – but what did she have on them that was worth paying thousands of pounds for? And that got her murdered in the end. That's what Pete wants to find out. If the money was from blackmail, he wants to know the details so that he can take it over.'

'But look how it turned out for her!' Daisy exclaimed, shooting out biscuit crumbs.

'That was Rose, though,' said Clarice. 'She was *only* a woman, to his way of thinking, and anyway, blackmailers don't see that it might get them killed. The greed blinds them.'

When the phone rang, Clarice guessed it would be Rick.

'I warned you Pete Smith is a complete bastard,' he said grimly as soon as she picked up.

'I suspect you're not wrong', she answered wryly. 'From what he said, he'd been talking to Rex in the pub, buying him pints.'

'Rex'd sell his soul for a pint.' Rick sounded exasperated. 'He must have told him that you walk the dogs early.'

'You know what it's like here. Everyone knows everyone else, and most of their business.'

'A positive and a negative, depending upon the circumstances,' he agreed. 'You will keep the doors locked, just to be on the safe side?'

'I will, and I'll carry my mobile in future.'

'OK,' he said, sounding weary, 'a few more things. The brooch with human hair has gone for analysis.

'Right,' Clarice muttered.

'In the spirit of information-sharing – and you'll hear it on the village tom-toms soon enough – we've brought in Bill Whittle for questioning.'

'About Rose?'

'He did threaten her.'

'What about Frank Pembroke?'

'He has too good an alibi.'

'What is it?'

'Heart attack. He was in Lincoln hospital for over a week during the period Rose would have been killed.'

'Yes, OK. I see where you're going with Bill, but I'm thinking that it's the bigger thing, the thousands that Rose was getting. The friendship group was small change in comparison, though having said that, it's all relative. Two thousand is a lot to Jean and Bill.' She paused, thoughtful. 'What else?'

'We heard back about the aunt, Peggy Little. She died in hospital of pneumonia two years and seven months ago. Not a great deal to say about her. Her house in Norfolk was rented, so there wasn't much of an inheritance involved.'

'Did someone go round to where she lived?'

'Yes,' Rick gave a sigh, 'naturally. According to a neighbour, she was a lovely person, kind, a churchgoer and a volunteer for a charity. The neighbour had only known her for a short time but said she was a decent woman, nothing like the nieces.'

'Which charity?'

'Cancer Research, but the volunteers there have changed, and nobody could remember her.'

'Two of the nieces were nothing like their aunt – Jackie and Rose. We don't know yet about Maggie. Any trace of her?'

'Nothing yet.'

'Was there anything else?'

'Yes, tell Daisy to get her hand out of the biscuit tin and move her bony arse back here. She's needed. But use the polite version.'

'Will do,' Clarice replied, watching Daisy dipping for a custard cream.

'Are you part of the artists' day at Winterby Hall tomorrow?' Daisy asked as she was leaving.

'I said I'll help out.'

'So what does it involve?'

'Twelve contemporary makers are taking part, not all ceramicists – two jewellers and one glass maker, I think – and not all of them from Lincolnshire,' Clarice explained. 'They will be in the Orangery. It's a lovely setting for their work. They set up in the morning between nine and ten thirty. Then up to fifty guests will arrive from eleven onwards to look at the exhibition, and possibly buy or commission pieces. There's a buffet lunch for the guests between twelve and one thirty, and the day will probably go on until about half past three.'

'It all sounds regimented – precise.'

Clarice nodded.

'But you're not displaying your work?'

'No, I'm too well established. It's for people new to the game, graduates possibly, or perhaps some that are older but starting in a new direction.'

'So,' Daisy said as they went outside, 'what does Lady Vita get from it?'

Clarice twisted her face into a mock grin. 'Mainly kudos, but the ladies who lunch pay for the privilege – it's forty quid a ticket to cover the buffet, and the food's minimal. And if an artist makes a sale, Vita gets a small commission.'

'You don't pay for your lunch?'

'No.' Clarice shook her head. 'I'm there to support the cause – *the Arts*.' She threw her head back dramatically, putting the back of her hand against her brow.

Daisy giggled.

'And to be Vita's dogsbody, I imagine, but I don't mind. It's interesting meeting the artists and makers.'

'Was your mother a ceramicist? The boss told me you were called Clarice after a potter.'

'No, Mum went to lots of evening classes and produced things for fun, but never on a professional basis. She was the chief librarian at Castlewick library when she married Dad, which as there were only three people working there sounds grander than it was. After Dad died, she needed the money but wanted to be at home when I got in from school, so she went back to the library part-time. She'd have described herself as a housewife – if you had children, that's what people did back then.'

'Sounds like the Dark Ages,' Daisy laughed.

'We are talking about Castlewick – it's still a throwback to the 1940s, so imagine what it was like when I was a child.'

Daisy hesitated by the door.

'What is it?' Clarice asked.

'I shouldn't stick my nose in, but ... you and Rick, you're getting on so well – I wondered ...'

'It's good that we're still friends.' Clarice felt awkward.

'You always seemed the perfect couple.'

'Just goes to show, there's no such thing as perfect – all relationships have their dips. He might have got himself a girlfriend.'

'Not that I'm aware of – although Sarah Cane, one of the girls working at headquarters, has her eye on him.'

'I know that name,' Clarice said thoughtfully. 'The animal welfare inspector's daughter.'

'That's the one. It's a hoot, canteen gossip – she walks into a room, and he finds excuses to leave.'

'I've met her. Rick took me to a party, someone's leaving do.' Clarice suddenly pictured the small, pretty blonde. 'But he's not interested in her?'

'That's an understatement, but she's not the shy type. It's obvious she fancies him big time – she'll try every trick in the book. If he succumbed to her charms, she'd be angling for an engagement ring within a month. She was engaged to a sergeant six months ago. An inspector would be a step up.'

'Poor Rick.'

'I suppose if you no longer care for him it shouldn't matter.'

'I never said I'd stopped caring for him; it's more that I don't have a right to interfere in his life,' Clarice said, her eyes steely. 'He is a free agent.'

The look on Daisy's face as she departed was oddly smug.


After Daisy had gone, Clarice locked the door of the cottage before, mobile phone in pocket, heading to her workshop, the dogs following. The best way to put Pete Smith out of her mind was to work.

The workshop was warm and the dogs immediately made for the small sofa, Blue climbing onto the blanket that covered it and Jazz settling next to her.

In one corner of the room was a potter's wheel. On every wall shelves of varying heights accommodated vases, dishes and pots at different stages of creation. Bags of clay were neatly placed under the bench that ran the length of one wall; along the windowsill stood different-coloured glass jars, one full of small shells.

She had decided to make a new batch of small tiles for test-firing glazes. The firings would provide a huge amount of information about the visual effect of the glazes, and also show her how they would sit on the clay body. Producing tiles or doing test firings sent her into automatic mode, freeing up her mind for thought.

As she worked, she recalled Vita's reaction on the one occasion she'd taken up Clarice's offer to visit the workshop to see the process that produced her pieces. It had been a short session, Vita's eyes glazing over with boredom within the first twenty minutes. Her desire for knowledge about the production process had clearly been superficial, aimed at allowing her to go through a mental list when talking to makers, to show interest. In reality, she found the nitty-gritty a bore.

An hour later, absorbed by the results of her work, Clarice heard Blue let out a low rumbling growl, and she was back in an instant from the quiet place her work had taken her. Blue stood by the door, her hackles rising.

Picking up her mobile from a shelf, Clarice grabbed her crutches and moved across the room to peer out through the small square window in the top part of the door. Georgie Lowe was walking from her car towards the cottage. With an overwhelming sense of relief, she opened the door and let the dogs run out to greet her friend, Blue grabbing a stick en route by way of a present.

'Hello, babies.' Georgie knelt down with her arms wide open. 'Come to Momma.'

Hobbling some way behind the dogs, Clarice pulled a face. '*Babies . . . Momma,*' she said as she drew nearer. 'You get worse.'

Georgie stood up, holding out her arms to Clarice. 'Give Momma a big hug,' she said, followed by a loud cackle of laughter.

Going into the cottage, Clarice busied herself with coffee while Georgie, as usual, skipped from one subject to another.

'Alan made the breakfast this morning. I say *made* – two rounds of toast and a pot of jam plonked next to it; a first!' She lifted her arms dramatically. 'And Jessica said, "Mummy, is Daddy going to make dinner tonight?" The little minx, I could tell she was having a laugh. Only eleven, but going on twenty-five. She knows how to wind her daddy up. I like the borrowed car, nice colour. I like silver anywhere – bags, shoes, jewellery – *and* I'd love an automatic.' She paused. 'Have you heard that Jean's husband Bill's been arrested. He killed that Rose woman – the one that you landed on in the Hanging Barn – bashed her head in.'

'That's not true, Georgie.' Clarice held her hand up to cut off Georgie's flow, speaking sternly. 'Whoever told you that?'

'Carol, the hairdresser, I saw her in the Co-op.' Georgie looked put out. 'How do you know it's not true? Has Rick told you something?'

'No, he has not, but that sounds like a huge exaggeration without any facts. I know the police have been talking to Bill as well as other people. Did Carol say he'd bashed her head in?'

'They weren't her *exact* words, but something similar.' Georgie looked awkward. 'Who can remember every conversation word for word?'

Clarice leant against the kitchen surface, surveying her friend. She could never decide who was the biggest gossip in Castlewick, but Georgie had to be near the top of the list, with her added tendency to beef it up. 'Please don't say that to anyone else, Georgie. If he's innocent, which he probably is, it would be awful.'

Georgie looked unabashed. 'Did you hear they'd been running a money-laundering scam?'

'Georgie, that's utter rubbish!'

'I'm only repeating what Carol told me. She said Pat Leach is in on it!'

Clarice looked at her steadily, not responding.

'So what's been happening here?' Georgie asked cheerfully when Clarice stayed silent. 'Are you ready for the charity fund-raiser a week on Sunday?'

'Yes, I'll help as much as I can.'

'As long as you're sitting down.' Georgie let out a guffaw. 'Did you see Ginny and Lucy at Winterby Hall when you had your girly lunch with Lady Vita?'

'I saw Ginny, but not Lucy.'

'Any chance either of them might help out at the fund-raiser? You know how desperate I get if someone lets me down.'

'You'll need to ask them,' Clarice said. 'You know Ginny doesn't like doing things Paula's involved in. Lucy might, but the two of them tend to work as a team.'

'I can't say I blame Ginny. Paula is a nightmare. Can you imagine her as your mum-in-law? Ginny and Jack would be married or at least living together if it wasn't for her.'

'We don't know that,' Clarice said.

'So what else has been going on here? Any juicy gossip?'

Clarice decided against telling her about the problems she'd encountered with Pete Smith and his wife; if she did, it would be around the town by tomorrow magnified tenfold into something approaching a potential massacre. Instead, she talked about the arts event at Winterby Hall. Georgie, who yearned to be taken up by Vita, hung on every word. Her eyes, attentive over the top of her coffee cup, showed her to be captivated.

'Could I come and help?' she asked eagerly after Clarice had finished explaining how the day would pan out.

'An assistant to the assistant!' Clarice joked. When Georgie looked confused, she added, 'I'm there to assist Vita. Are you suggesting you come as well to assist me?'

'Well, yes,' Georgie said, 'if I can square it with Alan to keep an eye on the kids. I'd love to have a poke around Winterby – they don't open the hall to the public.'

'You are outrageous!' Clarice roared with laughter. 'You know zero about ceramics or displaying work for exhibition, but you want to come along anyway so that you can have a poke around someone's private home!'

'It's not that funny,' Georgie said with a sheepish grin.

'Georgie.' Clarice found it hard to hide her surprise at the audacity of the suggestion. 'Vita is one very on-the-ball lady. Once she started to ask you questions about your tastes and experience, and it became obvious that you knew nothing about art and were only there for a nosy around and a free lunch, my reputation would be toast!'

Georgie looked down at her empty coffee mug for a moment, then up again. 'If you lend me a book, I could read up on ceramics.'

Clarice began to laugh again, and even Georgie couldn't suppress a grin this time. 'OK, OK,' she admitted. 'I'm not that fast a learner.'

# Chapter 14

Walking into the Orangery at Winterby Hall the following morning, Clarice was greeted by mayhem. Open boxes and bags spilled their contents onto the floor; large shapes in bubble wrap and plinths of varying sizes, heights and construction were scattered around the room. In the centre, like a sergeant major organising her troops, Vita stood within a circle of people of varying ages, all wearing the same expression of rapt attention.

Having exhibited her work on numerous occasions, Clarice understood the landscape. Setting up was a time of jangling nerves, trying to get every detail to the point where the objects on display created a wow factor. The taking-down at the end took a fraction of the time.

The Orangery had high ceilings, ornamented with honeysuckle plasterwork and a frieze of acanthus leaves. Large windows provided natural light and gave a dramatic view of the estate's rolling landscape. To the left was a pathway ending at a corridor of roses that led to the formal gardens. During the summer, the large outdoor terrace held glass tables and chairs and an abundance of leafy greenery. On warm summer evenings, guests attending receptions would sit sipping Champagne and watch the sky turn red as the sun went down.

'Here she is,' exclaimed Vita, spotting Clarice as she joined the circle. All eyes turned to her. 'Many of you will know Clarice Beech by her work or her reputation.' Several people nodded with enthusiasm. 'Clarice has kindly offered to help today, so don't be shy if you need tips for getting the best visual effect in your display; she's your girl.'

Clarice adopted what she hoped was an agreeable expression.

'And,' continued Vita, 'don't ask what happened to her – how she ended up on those crutches. It's a strange and scary tale!'

Great, thought Clarice, trying to hide her annoyance, her smile becoming in an instant a frozen rictus mask as the group directed their quizzical gazes towards her. Vita had whetted their appetite. It was going to be a long day.

Going into the annexe to hang up her coat, she returned to speak to each exhibitor in turn, discussing techniques with the ceramicists and making general suggestions for the displays. Several makers had attended her classes or talks; seeing them again was like meeting up with old friends.

A little later, Paula came into the room with plates of hand-made French lemon biscuits. 'Tea and coffee over here,' she called, leaving the plates next to Thermos flasks filled with coffee and hot water, alongside milk, cups and tea bags. 'Help yourselves.'

She wandered around the room passing the message to each group. When she got to the ceramicist Clarice was with, whose husband was attempting to put together a collapsible plinth, she stopped to watch. Never exactly cheerful, she looked more downcast than normal.

123

'Is everything OK?' Clarice asked.

'What do you think?' Paula spoke in a whisper.

Clarice looked at her with incomprehension.

'Do I look like a tea lady?'

'Well . . . no.' Clarice didn't know how to respond. 'All hands to the pump, I expect.'

'Hardly,' Paula sniffed. 'I am the housekeeper; we have two girls who do this sort of thing. But Lucy's away sick – or, if I'm correct, throwing a sickie to be with her boyfriend – and Ginny, the little madam, has gone on leave with immediate effect.'

'Have she and Jack broken up?' Clarice's voice showed her surprise.

'It's not for me to say.' Paula glanced around the room. 'Her highness told me to sort out the refreshments, and now it's done.'

Clarice watched as she left. That Paula should be snippy about Vita was unheard of. She was her ladyship's shadow, learning and mimicking, a cheerless exercise in imitation. What could have happened? Still puzzling, she dragged her attention back to the couple now wrestling with the white-painted fibre boards that were meant to slot together to form the plinth.

As planned, guests started to arrive at 11 a.m. The flurry and stress of the setting-up now behind them, the makers stood or sat near their own displays, smiling nervously. The room was stunning. The debris had been packed away out of sight, showcases and plinths were arranged around the room in a circle, and eight large bay trees had been brought in to give the room a rich, lush feel. The air had a honeyed smell, sweet but not sickly or artificial. Clarice guessed that it came from the warm drinks being handed out to guests as they arrived.

124

She watched as Vita went from one maker to another, talking at length, asking intelligent, informed questions about the nature of their work, small groups of guests hovering in her wake.

Time for some fresh air, she decided. She went through the annexe to pick up her coat. Outside it was dry but bitingly cold. To the side of the terrace, where Vita had instructed a large plant pot be left filled with earth, a couple of smokers had already lit up. They pulled their cashmere coats and scarves closer to keep out the cold as they puffed on their cigarettes, chatting companionably.

Walking past the terrace, Clarice decided to keep away from the grass, fearful that she might slip, going instead along the pebbled path that led to the formal gardens.

Although she was enjoying the day, she had a sensation that had become familiar over the last six months: being part of something while at the same time feeling outside of it, detached. She did not feel introverted in the company of close friends, but in the wider context, mixing with acquaintances, she was no longer sure where she fitted. Perhaps she was that strange, sad woman as suggested by Pete Smith; or, she rationalised, had she just lost her confidence? Reaching the rose corridor, she paused to remember its beauty when in season; now it was clinically neat and sleeping, awaiting the change of seasons to bring it back to life. She stayed for five minutes, then, feeling the cold, turned and retraced her steps.

As she approached the entrance, she saw the two smokers making their way back. They slowed to hover, listening, as they neared the Orangery. Hidden to the side of the door, out of sight and oblivious to their audience, two men were arguing.

'If I say jump, you say how high – get it?'

There was a short silence.

'It doesn't work like that. You aren't the boss.'

'Not yet, but Pa won't be around for ever and you should remember who your boss will be one day.'

Clarice recognised the supercilious tone of Harry's voice.

'I'm not a beater. Lots of the village boys would be happy to be asked.'

It was Jack, thought Clarice, who Harry was targeting with such bullish aggression.

'It's not one of the village boys I'm asking; it's you, and you should think it an honour.'

'My job is managing the fishery business. You must be aware of the hours I put in.' Jack spoke in a measured manner, not rising to Harry's belligerence.

'Are you complaining?' Harry growled. 'People would bite my hand off for your job. It's well paid, and you get to live in a nice house in the grounds. It's a cushy number.'

'Nobody's going to bite your hand off, Harry, because it's not up to you who's employed here.' The answer was cool.

'Well maybe I need to speak to Pa about it.'

'Yes,' Jack's voice took on a sour sarcasm, 'go ask Daddy, why don't you.'

'Don't talk to me like that.'

'I'll say what I want, and if your father decides to sack me, so be it.'

Clarice moved closer to the smokers, prompting them, after a meaningful glance at one another, to walk forward through the door. She herself paused with her hand against the glass.

'Where do you think you're going?' Harry snapped. 'I haven't finished.'

'*I* have.'

'If I say I need an extra beater, and I say it's going to be you, then you *will* do it.'

'We'll see,' Jack retorted sharply.

'You're pissed off because Ginny's dumped you.' There was a sneer in Harry's voice.

'I have not been dumped. Ginny's using up her annual leave.' There was a silence before Jack continued. 'She's not here to speak for herself. And I find it a bit coincidental that I've never been forced to be involved with one of the shoots before – but hey, you've made a play for Ginny and she kicked you into touch, so you decide to get your own back by abusing your position!'

'Did she kick me into touch? Think she fancied something more upmarket than the servant son of a bastard.'

There was silence before Jack spoke again. 'Leave Ginny out of your game-playing, and if you ever hurt her, you'll pay.' His tone this time was low and threatening.

Clarice stepped forward, pushing open the door to enter the Orangery. She'd heard enough. She had an image of the open-backed trucks carrying men and boys from one field to another near her home. The shoots organised by the local farmers were not on as grand a scale as those on the Winterby estate, but they were organised in the same way. The beaters' remuneration was not monetary, though they did get lunch after the event; rather, being asked to partake was considered a privilege. What Harry wanted, Clarice reflected, was to emasculate Jack by putting him in a position that demoted him from being the man responsible for the management of the fisheries to one of a group of local boys sitting huddled together in the back of a truck, while he himself strutted with the VIPs. This would define their roles at Winterby Hall. Master and servant, that was what Harry wanted.

After lunch, Clarice went back to offer the makers her help to aid their departure. Now she was sitting on the oak parquet floor of the Orangery, wrapping precious items. Seven out of the twelve had made sales, but all had given out their contact details, with postcards showing images of their work. Clarice assured them that, from her own experience, the money made on these days might come weeks or months after the event, and the impressions formed and the contacts they had established were often invaluable.

'Have a coffee with me before you leave.' Vita was looking happy with the day's results as the last of the exhibitors departed. 'Let's go into the drawing room.'

As Clarice moved at a steady pace across the marble-floored hall, Vita caught up to overtake her, pushing at the partly open door.

'It's not on, Pa.' Harry's voice rose into a whine. 'You must back me up – sack the bugger if need be.'

'Don't be such a bloody hothead!' Roland's response was equally angry. 'I don't go around sacking people just because you want to jump their girlfriend. That's ridiculous.'

Both men turned to look at Vita and Clarice, Roland holding his usual glass of whisky, his face redder than normal. Harry, facing his father, clenched his hands into fists by his sides.

'What is going on?' Vita spoke sharply to Harry. 'I've been told you were arguing outside like a common lout, and now I can hear you in the hall.'

'Nothing important.' Roland glanced from Vita to Clarice. 'Staff problems.'

Clarice felt her presence was causing an awkwardness. 'Look, I'd better get going.' She smiled at Vita. 'I need to feed all those animals.'

'Yes . . .' Vita paused. 'Come back for that coffee during the week, and I'd love to see photos of your new work; we ran out of time today.'

'Sounds good to me.' Clarice nodded.

'Thursday OK?'

'Day of the shoot,' Roland butted in.

'Perfect,' Vita said, throwing a cold glare at her husband. 'That's the last thing I want to be involved in. Is ten OK?' She turned to Clarice.

'Yes, ten on Thursday, see you then.' As Clarice walked away, the door was closed firmly behind her.

After collecting her coat, she moved outside slowly, feeling the hit of the cold air biting the back of her throat. The light was beginning to fade, and walking to the car, she was greeted by the shrill sound of a lone pheasant.

'Clarice!'

She heard her name and turned. 'Laura – how are you?'

Tom and Paula's daughter looked like neither of her parents, with her brown-blonde hair, green eyes and round cherubic face. She had complained to Clarice about the weight she had gained since the split with her husband, blaming it on her recent addiction to chocolate. But she was always neat and well turned out: her father's daughter.

'I'm OK, just taking Dad his sandwiches. You're pretty speedy on those.' Laura pointed at Clarice's crutches.

'I'm just getting the hang of them,' Clarice smiled.

'I never did when I had to use crutches; tripped over a paving slab, about four years ago. It could only happen to me.'

Laura, Clarice was reminded, often finished a sentence on a mournful note. She was not just a glass-half-empty sort of person; with her the glass was completely empty and someone had stolen it.

'I haven't seen Tom today,' Clarice said.

'He's working in the office.'

'Now let me guess.' She put a finger against her lips as if in deep concentration while looking at the supermarket carrier bag she knew would contain a plastic box with Tom's snack. 'Cheese and tomato?'

'Warm,' Laura chuckled.

'OK – cheese and pickle, cheese and ham, cheese and onion, cheese and . . .'

'Coleslaw.'

'I nearly got it.' Clarice joined in with Laura's laughter. 'Does he *ever* have anything without cheese?'

'Not for his afternoon snack. He probably missed lunch or just picked at something. The next time he eats properly'll be this evening.'

'How's his arm?'

'Coming on. You know Dad, he's just accident-prone.'

'Yes, I'd forgotten . . . He had a black eye last year.'

'That's Dad.' Laura shrugged. 'Something he was getting down from a high shelf fell on him. A big book about Scotland, I think it was.'

'Poor Tom.' Clarice smiled. 'Are you coming to the book club next week?'

'Yes, I've nearly finished the new one.'

'I'm glad you'll be there. We keep missing one another.'

'Have you heard the latest hue and cry?' Laura's face twisted involuntarily.

'What's happened?'

'Ginny's taken holiday leave without getting Mum's permission.'

'Maybe she asked Vita.'

'No, it was Jack's idea. He said that as he was the manager of the fisheries and Ginny's boss more than fifty per cent of the time, it was acceptable.'

'Your mother obviously doesn't agree.'

'You know Mum, it's all about control. Ginny's gone to visit her parents.'

'They run a bar in Spain, don't they?' Clarice said.

Laura nodded. 'And Mum thinks Lucy's skiving.'

'What do you think?'

She shrugged. 'I really don't know. She's never skived before. It might be Mum being peevish because of Ginny taking the holiday so suddenly.'

'Why do you think Ginny might have gone at such short notice?' Clarice asked.

Laura's cherubic face screwed itself into a scowl. 'Harry's been up to his old tricks. He's such a stirrer. Flirting with Ginny because he knows she's Jack's girlfriend. He just wants to make things difficult between the two of them – which he has. If Ginny took him up, he'd drop her – it's just a joke to him.'

'So she's not interested in him.'

'I don't think so.' Laura lifted her shoulders. 'Harry's like his grandfather – nasty. Everyone says what an old bugger Horace was in lots of ways. They say his personality skipped a generation. Harry's not at all like his dad, our very own bumbling Lord Fayrepoynt.'

'I heard Horace was a difficult man,' Clarice said, 'but I didn't know him, though I've seen his portrait in the drawing room.'

'Yes, you're right not to judge. I didn't know him either,' Laura smiled, 'even though he was my grandpa, albeit from the wrong side of the blanket.'

'When did Ginny go?' Clarice asked.

'Jack took her to the station this morning. She's flying from Luton.' Laura looked down at the carrier bag. 'Better get this sandwich to Dad.'

'Yes, you must – but how are things with you on the husband front?'

'Probably the same as you, Clarice: still separated, getting a divorce, wondering how the wheels dropped off and whether if I'd done something different we'd still be together.'

'We beat ourselves up with all the what-ifs.'

'It's not easy, is it?' Laura put her hand out as she spoke, to rest against Clarice's arm.

'No, it's bloody not.' Clarice smiled, injecting humour into the words while putting her hand on Laura's. 'Let's meet for a drink soon, talk properly. I want to hear all about the floristry course. I know how much you hated working in that accounts office.'

'And the jogging.'

'You – jogging!'

'Yes, every morning, whatever the weather. I'll tell you about it when we meet. What about after the book club? We could go to the new Thai restaurant, have a drink and something to eat.'

'It's a plan,' Clarice said. 'Take care.'

Laura stepped closer and the two exchanged a hug.

'And you,' she said.

After Laura had gone, Clarice eased herself into her car and called Lucy Marriot.

# Chapter 15

'I'm so sorry for intruding.' Clarice sat in an armchair opposite Lucy, who was stretched out on a sofa, engulfed within a large pink duvet. Looking at her pale, drawn, make-up-free face, Clarice did not doubt that she was ill. On the table next to her was a glass of water, a glucose drink and paracetamol tablets.

The smell in the room combined burnt toast and damp. The ceiling had faint brown circles, and although it had been painted with a heavy hand, as had the window frames, the layers of paint were unable to disguise the damage beneath.

'You're someone I'm always pleased to see.' Lucy sounded sincere.

'That's kind, but I doubt you really want visitors when you're poorly.'

'I felt rough this morning, but I'm much better now.' Lucy snuggled down as she spoke. 'It's a twenty-four-hour viral thing and I'll probably be as good as new tomorrow.'

'I do hope that's all it is.'

'I hope so too. You're my second visitor,' Lucy said. 'You've just missed Daniel – he was in and out.'

'Ah, the new boyfriend. He didn't stay long.'

'He's a bloke; I don't think he wanted to hang around the sickbed.'

The rented flat was on the second floor, above a junk shop with pretensions of selling antiques. It was one of a row of shops overlooking the River Bain, which twisted through Castlewick, dividing the old town from the new.

'Welcome to my kingdom,' Lucy had said when she let Clarice in. She was wearing a pair of oversized pyjamas, the black and white fabric giving her the appearance of an urchin wearing a zebra suit. Her light brown hair dropped to touch her slim shoulders. A list of her features might have suggested her to be plain – her mouth was over-wide, her nose sported a slight bump and she had a broad forehead – but when she was speaking, her face became mobile, lighting up with animation: a transformation that touched on beauty.

'I think you've acquired more gear.' Clarice cast her eyes about the stuffy room as she spoke. She had visited the flat on a previous occasion, noting then the mix of Lucy's personal tastes: tall peacock feathers in vases and cushions with red ribbon bows living side by side with worn, heavy furniture the landlord had failed to sell in the shop downstairs. It was now more crammed than on her first visit, with no visible clear surface space. She noticed an acoustic guitar propped against a wall.

'Can you play that?'

'Are you joking?' Lucy glanced at the instrument. 'I can't even hold a tune. It's Daniel's.'

'Is he nice?'

'In what way?'

'Is he fun, good to be with, and does he make you happy?'

'Absolutely.' Lucy's face lit up. 'But if you're asking is he the

135

one, the answer is probably no, though he's *a* one until I meet *the* one, if you understand. And I know this place is a crap hole – Winterby servants' quarters were a palace in comparison. But I still prefer to live here.'

'Much more freedom,' Clarice prompted.

Lucy shrugged. 'It was lonely, everyone was old, and there was nobody of my age to talk to. Not forgetting Paula's list of rules – non-negotiable, the lot of them.' She paused thoughtfully. 'Ginny's twenty now; she's been there since she was eighteen, but she clicked immediately with Jack. There's ten years between them but they work as if they were always meant to be a couple.'

Clarice nodded, recalling the first time she'd met Ginny at Winterby Hall. She'd gone into the kitchen to collect a book left there by Vita, who was hosting a ladies' lunch. A pot containing quail soup had been dropped by the cook, Mrs Ray. Its contents had spread rapidly, and she'd watched as Lucy and another young woman rushed back and forth with mops while Mrs Ray shouted, laying blame on everybody. Clarice had spotted the new girl, deep in concentration, standing at a kitchen unit focusing on the task of wrapping a slab of cheese. Her long dark hair hung in a plait down her back, the sleeves of her white blouse rolled back. Amidst the noise and confusion, she possessed a quality of stillness, a rock untouched by the storm raging around her. Unhurriedly she folded the sides of the waxed paper up across the cheese, rubbing her hand over it to make it flat, then neatly creased the corners. Finally she placed the perfectly wrapped cheese into a small clear bag before sliding her fingers along the seam to seal it. Ginny and Lucy were polar opposites; was that why they got on so well? Ginny's self-contained composure perhaps acting as a foil to Lucy's boisterous exuberance.

'I knew Jack before I met Ginny. He's fit, but I wasn't his type and we're good mates. I was pleased when Ginny came. She's my best friend. She might seem serious, but she doesn't mind my wackiness – we have a laugh.'

Was Lucy hinting at a relationship with Jack before Ginny had begun to work at the hall? Clarice wondered. She had said that she wasn't his type; did that mean that he was hers? She decided not to go there. 'It's good to work with someone you really like,' she said cheerfully.

'They don't go in for fit young men at Winterby,' said Lucy. 'The only other young bloke is Harry, and apart from the fact that he's younger than me and the boss's son, he's also a bit of an idiot!' When Clarice didn't reply, Lucy continued. 'I can guess why you're here.'

'I'm worried about Ginny,' Clarice said. 'I heard what happened. It's out of character for her to take off like that; she's so self-contained, not much rattles her.' She gave Lucy a long stare.

'Paula didn't ask you to come, did she?' Lucy turned waspish.

'For heaven's sake,' Clarice responded with exasperation. 'Do you really believe I'd ever be Paula's lackey?'

'Not Vita either . . . her ladyship?'

'I'm on friendly terms with Vita, but I certainly wouldn't spy on you for her. You really don't know me if you believe that.'

'No, I'm sorry. It was a stupid suggestion. I feel so edgy with all this going on.'

'What's been happening at Winterby? I'm sure Ginny wouldn't mind you telling me – we are friends, after all.'

Silence fell between them, stretching beyond comfortable.

'Yes, I think you're right,' Lucy said, as if finally making up her mind. 'I think she'd prefer friends who genuinely care about her to know. And I know she likes you. She's upset about Harry and Jack being jealous of each other over her.'

'That doesn't make any sense. She's not interested in Harry.'

'We all know that, but for some reason, Harry has decided Jack is his new spider.'

'Spider?'

Lucy gave a smirk, pulling her legs up under the duvet to rest her arms on her knees and her chin on her arms. 'He was the sort of little boy, or so I've been told, who enjoyed pulling the legs off spiders, watching them struggle to escape. And once when he was ten, he pulled the tail off the gardener's daughter's pet mouse. Last time Harry was home from uni, it was a boy called Mathew, who worked with old Reg Lam the gardener.'

'He was the spider?'

'Harry took against him.' Lucy nodded. 'Poor Mathew was a lovely boy, eighteen, I think. Not the brightest, but he loved being outside and enjoyed the work. Harry thought it a huge joke to move things around, knowing everyone would believe that it was Dumbo Mathew who was responsible for losing valuable garden tools and equipment: he made his life a nightmare.'

'Why didn't someone speak up?'

'Speak up?' Lucy's face held an expression of incredulity. 'Dish the dirt on the golden boy? Don't be silly. Anyone who'd done that would be out on their ear.'

'What happened to Mathew?'

'He was let go. They never use the S word; they never sack them. It's always *we had to let him go.*'

'That's terrible. It's the twenty-first century; that type of behaviour can't be tolerated. Employers have responsibilities! Did Tom know?'

'If he did, he didn't say anything.'

'So,' Clarice said, 'Jack has now replaced Mathew as the spider?'

'That's it. Wind up Jack and . . . What would be the best way to do that?'

'Trying it on with Ginny.'

'You've got it.' Lucy looked gloomy. 'Ginny has no interest in Harry, and Jack knows that, but Harry's been behaving like a git. There are no locks on the bedroom doors in Winterby, and that includes staff rooms. Poor Ginny is having to put a chair against the door.'

'Has he touched her?'

'No, no, I don't think he would lay a finger on anyone. He's a bully and a coward; it's all mind games with Harry. But she woke up in the night last week to find him sitting at the bottom of her bed in his dressing gown, watching her sleep.'

'How awful,' said Clarice. 'So intimidating.'

'When she saw him, he got up and walked out, blowing her a kiss on the way.'

'And I suppose if she complained, it would be her word against his?'

'Yes.' Lucy nodded. 'She told Jack, of course.'

'Which is the whole point of the exercise.'

'It's a game – that's just one example of many.'

'I can imagine,' Clarice said. 'It's a bit obvious, but would Ginny not be better either getting another job or saying she wants to move out?'

'She and Jack have discussed it, but why should she have to change anything?' Lucy sat upright, squaring her shoulders, her expression one of annoyance. 'They enjoy working together in the fishery side of the business; they're in one another's company every day.'

'And if she leaves, Harry wins.'

'Yes.' Lucy looked downcast.

Fifteen minutes later, having established the facts and run out of small talk, Clarice prepared to depart. 'Please pass on my love to Ginny when you speak to her.'

Lucy nodded. 'I think everyone just needs to back off and give her some space for a few days.'

Clarice made her way to the car, deep in thought. It was apparent Ginny was thoroughly sick of the problems caused by Harry and wanted them brought out into public view. She felt sympathy for Jack, who was just as much a victim of Harry's manipulative game-playing as Ginny was. But she could not agree with Lucy's view of Harry. If her stories were to be believed, he hadn't just tormented the mouse and spiders as a child, but physically damaged then destroyed them.

As she made her way past the Dog and Pheasant, she felt the presence behind of someone drawing near.

'Hello, luv.'

She turned to find Pete Smith standing less than three feet away. He was dressed as before, but looked more dishevelled, his face florid, his smell reaching her in a way it hadn't been able to in their previous encounter, the stink of tobacco smoke combining with the odour of unwashed clothes and body, and the crude stench of a habitual heavy drinker that seeped from every pore.

'Nice surprise,' he slurred.

'Hello.' Clarice forced the word out, attempting to act normally. She started to turn to walk on to the car.

'Aren't you going to come in?' He indicated the pub. 'Have that drink with me and the wife. I'll buy you a cider or whatever it is you posh birds drink.'

'No, thank you, I need to get home.'

'No rush, is there?' He gave what was meant to be a smile but made Clarice think of a rabid animal baring its dark teeth.

'I said no.' She felt a strong sense of revulsion and suppressed an involuntarily shudder.

'Why's that, luv?' His voice held the pretence of affability, as if the undercurrent of threat did not exist between them. 'Your friends will have sorted the dogs and cats, walked them ... all that malarkey. Then they leave and that's it, you're all alone, all night.' He bared his teeth again. 'Nothing for you to rush home for, girl; you've not got anybody who gives a shit about you, unless you count the cats.'

Clarice met his eyes to stare him out.

He chuckled, turning his back on her. 'Night then, girl, sleep tight.' He stopped at the door of the pub. 'Make sure them bed bugs don't bite.' He wagged his index finger before stepping inside.

She waited a moment, then turned away, fighting the temptation to break into a run.

Back at the cottage, walking away from the car, she caught sight of something and stopped to look.

There was a gouge the full length of both sides of the vehicle, going over the driver and passenger doors. The car had been keyed.

# Chapter 16

It was just after 6 p.m. as Clarice crossed the garden, silently cursing first Pete Smith and then the crutch that made her progress so laboured. She used only one, carrying a torch in the other hand, aware of the black shadow of Ena trailing her and the dogs.

After feeding the cats and securing the barn for the night, she returned to the cottage where, having beaten her back, Ena waited. She fed all the cats and dogs in the house, then went to a kitchen cupboard to take out a bottle of Chilean red. Once she'd put a match to the fire and poured herself a glass of the wine, she rang Sandra and Bob's number.

'The bastard,' Sandra exploded after being told about Clarice's encounter with Pete Smith and the damage to the car.

'I didn't see him doing it; I'm making an assumption.'

'Sod your fairness, darlin', we know who did it, and it's not even your bleedin' car!'

Clarice's mood lightened. If there was one thing she could count on in moments of crisis, it was Sandra's support.

'Unfortunately,' she said, 'that bit of the town is just out of range for CCTV. And I'm wondering how he knows my routines.' She paused. 'As well as your and Bob's comings and goings. Unless he's driving past counting cars.'

'He's trying to wind you up. Have you phoned Rick?'

'No, the poor sod's up to his eyes, drowning in work as usual.'

'You should tell him.'

Sandra's words brought Rick's face to mind, pallid and drained. 'I will tomorrow, when I get home. And I'll tell Jim about the car on Monday – I'm not bothering him at home on a Saturday night.'

'When you get home?'

'That's the main reason why I'm calling,' Clarice said. 'I need to go to Norfolk.'

'Is it something to do with Rose's murder?' Sandra's voice rose with anxiety.

'Yes. I know her Aunt Peggy was a regular churchgoer. There's only one church in Denhelm, where she lived, and the Sunday-morning service starts at nine thirty. I want to see if anyone remembers her. And if I can find out more about Rose and her sisters. Would you mind coming earlier to do the animals? I need to get away by seven thirty at the latest, and if all goes to plan, I'll be back by early afternoon.'

'Is going to Norfolk a good idea?' The alarm in Sandra's voice increased. 'You might be wasting your time, never mind your petrol.'

'If I can pick up a thread, it just might lead somewhere.'

There was a pause that Clarice felt stretched on indefinitely, but she waited patiently, knowing the response to come. 'We'll see to the animals, but please be careful.'

'I will, Sandra. And not a word to Rick if he calls while I'm away. I'll fill him in about Norfolk and the car when I get home.'

\* \* \*

Early the next morning as she prepared to leave, Clarice, following her senses, closed her eyes for a moment and stood still next to the car, listening. What was different? It was completely silent, only the low moan of the wind. Opening her eyes, she looked upwards to the top branches of the trees and the roof of the cottage. Finally she spotted what she was seeking, on the telephone wire: a sparrowhawk. They were not uncommon in Lincolnshire, and this fellow, if it was a male, was looking for his breakfast. His presence had silenced all the small garden birds. As she started the car, he lifted suddenly into the air to glide majestically, wings outstretched, exploring the wide winter garden.

Driving up the sloping incline to join Long Road, she noted its watery surface, a result of the overnight rain. To either side of the tarmac drive were banks of high grasses and reeds. Ahead, on the opposite side of the main road, were open, undulating fields. Out of season they had an irregular pattern of blonde stubble, evidence of the last harvest. Turning left, the road ahead was straight and glistening. The sky, void of anything other than grey clouds, indicated a lot more rain to come. She ruminated on the idea of installing CCTV. She knew of several local farmers, living in isolated places, who used it. But the installation and management would be expensive, which would mean that Pete Smith's intimidation had succeeded. Although, she mused, she could just park all cars in one of the barns rather than outside the cottage. That would cost nothing, and anyone driving along the top of the Long Road wouldn't know if there was somebody at home or not. She'd ask Sandra and Bob, whose car was there on a daily basis, if they'd oblige. She knew they would.

Thinking about Sandra, she reflected on the stages of their relationship. She had first met her when she was ten years old. Sandra and Clarice's mother, Mary, having got to know each other while attending an evening class on 'Historic Buildings of Castlewick', had signed up for a course on wine appreciation. After the first class, concerned that Sandra might not manage a journey on the bus, and unable to work out where she lived, Mary had collected Clarice from a neighbour with her new, well-oiled friend still in the car. Once home, she'd found the telephone number for Robert Todd in the directory and phoned to ask him to collect his wife. 'You're meant to taste the wine then spit it out,' he'd grumbled when he finally arrived.

Clarice, watching from her bedroom window, had seen Bob walking a wobbly Sandra to the car, Michelle and Susan on the back seat in their pyjamas. Her memory was of an attractive woman, her hair pinned up, smart clothes and the red lippy that hadn't changed to pink until she hit sixty. She'd been a smoker then; always had a cigarette on the go. As a ten-year-old, what Clarice had liked most about her was that she'd listened, and treated her as an equal. She had always been a mate.

With the word 'cool' transferring itself mentally, as a trapeze artist might slip effortlessly from one fly bar through mid-air to another, Clarice absent-mindedly pushed in the disc protruding from the player: *Stompin' at the Savoy* by the late jazz saxophonist Zoot Sims.

The roads were quiet without the weekday business traffic, the weather cold and dull. After passing King's Lynn, the satnav took her away from the main roads until eventually she drove into the village of Denhelm and the detached voice announced, *'You have reached your destination.'*

The church was on the high street, next to a Co-op and opposite a war memorial. It was twenty minutes before the morning service was due to start, but people were already wandering in. In the entrance porch, a small group were deep in conversation. Clarice walked past them, stopping at the end of the aisle to look at the original nineteenth-century stained-glass windows above the pulpit. It was colder inside than out, and she was glad that she'd wrapped up well with her muffler, hat and fur-lined boots.

'Good morning.' An elderly woman stood next to her. 'I'm Norma Hollings. We like to welcome new people to the church.'

Clarice turned to find herself towering over the small woman.

'Hello, I'm Clarice Beech.'

'Are you new to the village?'

'No, I'm visiting a friend today in King's Lynn.' She had worked out her story before her arrival. She had an acquaintance in that town so could give an address if needed. 'I believe a friend of my late mother attended this church. She was someone Mum often visited and talked about, and she had fond memories of them attending church services here together when she was staying in the area.'

'A trip down memory lane.' Norma Hollings moved her head back to look upwards as she spoke.

'In a way, although I've never been here before and I believe my mother's friend died a while back.'

'What was her name?'

'Peggy Little.'

'Yes.' Norma's face lit up in recognition. 'You knew Peggy, didn't you, Sue?' she said, turning to another elderly lady, with snow-white hair, who stood nearby listening.

'Yes,' Sue gave Clarice an inquisitive glance. 'Peggy passed about two years ago.'

Clarice, who hated euphemisms that avoided using the words connected with death, suppressed a strong urge to ask in which direction. Instead, she responded with an acquiescent nod.

'Wait until after the service,' Sue said as people drifted towards the rows of pews. 'I'm sure Jane Taylor would love to chat to you – she's over there.' She pointed at a woman, visible only from the back, seated on the front row wearing a red woollen hat. 'Although Peggy's closest friend was really Linda Bates. But she's no longer in the village; she went to a home in King's Lynn.'

'It would be lovely to say hello,' Clarice said, 'and introduce myself.'

'Yes, and I'm sure the vicar would like to meet you.'

'Lovely.' Clarice spoke with as much brightness as she could muster before taking a place halfway back. There were about thirty people attending the morning service, in a church that could easily hold two hundred, and only a small number looked to be younger than sixty.

The vicar had chosen Luke 10:25–37, the parable of the Good Samaritan. Clarice listened, watching him. A small, wiry man, who by his bearing, and fulsome crop of ginger hair, she supposed to be in his early thirties, but as he delivered his sermon, he gave the impression of being someone much older, someone who in his head might always have been old. His voice droned on without enthusiasm, as if out of boredom he had flicked a switch to autopilot. Her mind went to her conversation yesterday with Lucy. Possibly, for the vicar, God was not *the* one, but would do until he discovered his true direction.

At the end of the service, the vicar announced that if anyone would like to join him and his wife for a cup of tea, they would all be most welcome. Half of the congregation wandered to the door marked *Office*, leading Clarice to assume that the invitation was a regular weekly occurrence. She went to join Sue, who was in conversation with Jane Taylor.

'Here she is,' Sue announced. 'It is Clare, isn't it?'

'Clarice.' She held her hand out to Jane, who, viewed from the front and without her hat, revealed herself as another small, elderly, white-haired lady.

'Come and have a cup of tea with us,' Jane said warmly.

'Yes, I'd like that.'

As she spoke, the vicar swooped. 'Mark Peterson,' he said. 'So good to see a new face.'

Walking to the office, Clarice retold her tale, every step reinforcing the feeling she'd had when he was giving his sermon. Once he'd ascertained that she was a visitor and unlikely to boost the numbers in his congregation on a regular basis, he appeared to lose interest in her, his smile cementing itself into a professional fixture.

The room she entered was small, with ample chairs and an efficient heater, much warmer than the church. Clarice took a seat next to Jane Taylor, who immediately announced her age – 'I'm eighty-four, you know' – as a small child might announce themselves to be four and a half. 'You knew Peggy?'

'Unfortunately, no,' Clarice said, glancing around to make sure Sue was out of earshot. 'My mother did, although I don't think she knew Linda Bates, Peggy's friend.'

'Linda.' Jane nodded. 'She's in Sunnydale retirement home.'

'Yes,' agreed Clarice. 'King's Lynn.'

'Poor thing,' Jane said. 'She's years younger than me – only seventy-nine.'

'Do you visit her?' Clarice asked.

'No, never, I'm far too old for that. People visit me now. *You* must visit me; I like visitors, especially if they bring cakes. I like chocolate and cream.'

Clarice smiled. 'Did Peggy's family ever visit you, the nieces?'

'Peggy Little?' Jane thought. 'No, I can't remember them, but I've only lived here for the last twenty-two years, since my husband died. I have a lovely bungalow.'

'That's nice,' nodded Clarice.

'Linda and Peggy went way back. They lived near one another as children, went to the same schools.'

'Amazing.' Clarice's heart lifted with hope.

'Are you getting to know one another, ladies?' Mark Peterson was suddenly next to them. 'Let me top your tea up, Clare.'

'No, thank you.' Clarice stood up, not bothering to correct him regarding her name. 'It was nice to have met you,' she said to Jane, smiling.

'You know where we are should you come this way again.' Jane reflected back the smile.

'I certainly do, and you've made me feel very welcome.' Clarice rested her hand briefly on the old lady's before turning towards the exit.

'You're going?' The vicar stated the obvious as he followed her to the door of the vestry.

'Yes, my friend's expecting me.'

Before she turned to depart, she returned a small wave from Norma Hollings. The vicar accompanied her as far as the church doorway before wishing her a good journey.

On her way out of the village, Clarice pulled up outside the pub. Behind her the main street was quiet, in limbo between the exodus from the church and the arrival of families heading to the pub and the children's menu advertised on a blackboard outside the main entrance. She googled the Sunnydale retirement home website. When, after multiple rings, the phone was answered, she asked to speak to the person in charge.

'What's it about? I'm Mrs Freeman, the manager.' The female voice was pleasant and to the point.

'I understand Linda Bates is one of your residents,' Clarice said.

'Yes.'

'I'd like to visit her if possible. I'm in the area for a few days and I believe she knew a friend of my mother.'

'You can't come today, it's a special birthday for one of our other residents. She's one hundred years old.'

'How lovely,' said Clarice. 'Telegram from the Queen.'

'Quite so, and tomorrow, after all the excitement, Linda will be having her monthly visit from her nephew, though he won't stay long . . . never does. She's quite fragile.'

'Is she well enough for me to visit another day'

'Linda loves visitors. She's as sharp as a knife, despite being so frail. Apart from the nephew, there's no one else comes. What about Tuesday at two? We encourage visitors on weekdays between two and four p.m.?'

'That's great,' Clarice responded, thinking that Mrs Freeman's tone suggested 'encourage' wasn't quite the word. 'I'll look forward to it.'

'Good, and what is your name?'

'She won't recognise it, but it's Clarice Beech.'

'Yes, I understand. I'll tell her that you intend to visit at two o'clock on Tuesday. Having a visitor is something for her to look forward to.'

Driving home, Clarice mentally worked on a script, thinking of the things she could ask Linda Bates, and how to put them to her without giving cause for alarm.

# Chapter 17

Clarice checked her mobile before setting off. There was a text message from Laura saying she'd booked a table at the Thai restaurant for next Thursday. Also four texts from Georgie. It was usual, a week before a charity event, for Georgie to start to panic. Did she have enough volunteers, were there sufficient items for the tombola stall, and would Clarice be organising the floats and cashing up at the end of the event? Clarice told herself she would phone her when she arrived home.

The return journey was slower, with a broken-down lorry outside King's Lynn reducing the road to single file, resulting in a long tailback. Arriving home a little after 2 p.m., Clarice drove down the incline to the cottage. The two cars outside, parked side by side, meant that Sandra and Bob had not yet left and that they had been joined by Rick.

Sandra was at the door, coming outside, before Clarice could reach it. Blue followed, dragging Bob's scarf with her, and Jazz zipped in and out, not wanting to miss being part of the welcome-home committee.

'He turned up an hour ago, so I've fed him,' Sandra muttered.

'I've not told him where you've been.' Having delivered her message, she turned and went back inside.

'Hello, you.' Clarice smiled with genuine warmth at Rick. 'What a lovely surprise.'

'You did say I didn't need to ask to call in.'

He lounged in his chair, legs outstretched, looking at her. On the table in front of him were the remains of lunch: cheese, biscuits and fruit. Not expecting anyone, Clarice had left nothing other than fruit cake and salad for her own evening meal.

'So how were your friends?' he asked as he watched her hang up her jacket.

'Are you on a fishing trip?' she asked drily.

'I've got to start somewhere.' He looked at Sandra and Bob with a sly smirk. 'These two have been tighter than a duck's arse for the last hour.'

'Cheeky bugger,' Sandra sniggered, 'and after we fed you, too!'

'Yes.' Rick smiled at her. 'So you did.'

'Time we were away,' Bob said as he got up.

'What, and leave these two buggers to argue without us listening?' Sandra laughed.

After Clarice watched their car depart, she returned to find that Rick had poured her a coffee and set it in her usual position at the table, having refilled his own.

'No cream today?' he said.

'There's still some in the freezer. I didn't know you were coming.'

'Ah, so there are benefits in phoning first.'

They sat in companionable silence for a few minutes, and Clarice couldn't help wondering why it couldn't be like this always.

'So?' he said questioningly.

'Norfolk,' she said.

He nodded silently. When she told him why she had gone and what she had found, he nodded again.

'There is something else.' She hesitated.

'What?'

'I think Pete Smith keyed the side of my car . . . or to be accurate, Jim's car.'

He jerked upright. She told him about her visit to Lucy and the meeting with Smith.

'That piece of shit.' He spat out the words. 'I warned you what he was like!'

'I hardly went in pursuit of him . . .'

He shook his head. 'I know it's not your fault.' He stood up to pace agitatedly around the kitchen. 'As long as he stays in Castlewick, there's a good chance your paths'll cross again.'

Clarice nodded.

'As you say, there's no proof it was him – he can't be arrested for just being in the town.'

'No, I realise that.'

'Going back to Ginny . . .' Rick came back to sit at the table, 'if Harry hasn't done anything other than flirt with her—'

'It sounds like more than flirting,' Clarice cut in. 'From what Lucy told me, he's trying to intimidate Ginny to get at Jack.'

'But as you rightly said, there's no proof. It's just hearsay, what Lucy told you Ginny said.'

'I know,' said Clarice. 'It's Ginny's word against his.'

'Ginny and Jack should really take it up with their employer, but . . .' Rick let the word hang. 'She's on a hiding to nothing complaining about Harry.'

Clarice nodded.

'There is something I wanted to tell you.' He hesitated. 'We've found where Rose was killed.'

'Where?'

'It's about a quarter of a mile from the vicarage, one of the secluded routes she used to walk into town.'

'How did you find it? You've covered that ground before.'

'A general search, though not in great detail. Doing the inch-by-inch search of all the possible places she might have gone, this one came up trumps.'

'Is it definite?'

'It is, but the weather has been bad and the track has been used by a number of vehicles. We won't get evidence now of tyres or boots, but there are sufficient traces of blood to establish that it's where she bled out. Before her body was moved.'

'Anything else?'

'No bag or keys; long gone by now, I imagine.'

'Whoever broke in to the vicarage must have used a key,' Clarice said thoughtfully. 'If it was one of her blackmail victims looking for what she had on them, we need to think about who might have had access to one.'

He nodded, then changed the subject. 'What did you hope to find in Norfolk?' Resting his elbows on the table, he leaned in. 'Remember, Julie Buckley as FLO is responsible for making contact with family members. She's a good officer, very thorough. Victimology is so often about relationships the subject had with other people, including family members. In a large percentage of murders, the perpetrator is known to the victim.'

'Yes, I'm well aware of that, Rick.' Clarice modulated her voice to sound reasonable, not wanting to tell him he was stating the obvious. 'But did Julie mention Linda Bates? It's the first time I've come across the name. She might throw some light on the relationship between the three sisters. Have you discovered any more about what happened to Maggie?'

'I'll check with Julie, but I don't remember a Linda Bates. Maybe she went into the home before Peggy Little died. And we've hit a dead end on Maggie; it's possible she moved abroad. It would help if we knew the surname of the boyfriend or husband, but that's another blank.'

'I wonder if Jackie might give me something.'

Rick held up his hands in protest, shaking his head vehemently. 'That would blow Pete Smith's tiny mind, and he doesn't need much to become really aggressive. You were right about the booze – there's a lot that relates to alcohol and anger issues in his police record. If he's tanked up, he's dangerous. And I promise you, talking to his wife wouldn't lead anywhere. I doubt that woman knows what year it is, let alone what day.'

'OK,' she said, 'I believe you. But don't you think they're connected to Rose's murder?'

'No, I don't. I reckon they fell out over whatever dodgy business they were engaged in at the time, and parted company over two years ago, as Smith said. It's only since the FLO contacted them after Rose's death that they've had an interest in her. It's all about what her estate is worth, and whoever she was fleecing, be it blackmail or another scam, they want to stick their grubby fingers into that little honey pot.'

'Isn't it a little too coincidental that the aunt died about the same time they appear to have fallen out?'

'It might be relevant, but I think it's more likely that the parting of the ways was related to getting caught selling holidays that didn't exist.'

Clarice thought about what he'd said. 'So Bill Whittle has been completely ruled out?'

'Victimology again. Rose was seen alive by two people on the morning after his visit, and forensics have been all over his house and car, as well as his wife's, his son's and his daughter-in-law's. Nothing, but . . .'

'But?' Clarice waited.

'The reason for our interest was that he has a conviction for GBH.'

'Bill?'

'Yes, it doesn't seem likely, does it? It was over forty years ago – he described himself then as being a young hothead. While Jean was pregnant with their son, he visited a prostitute, who apparently stole his wallet containing his week's wages. When she denied it, he hit her.'

'Did he say anything else about the incident?' Clarice asked.

'He was pissed off.' Rick gave a wry smile. 'What galled him most was that the prostitute kept the money she'd stolen because he had no proof she had taken it. While he had to live with a police record for slapping her.'

'So that avenue, the friendship club, is a dead end, you reckon? It's back to the blackmail?'

'No, not completely. There's still Frank and Lydia Pembroke.' He raised his eyes.

'I thought you said Frank had a watertight alibi, by way of a heart attack. And Lydia would have been too fragile to take Rose on.'

'I agree, and Frank does have an alibi, but his grandson Ollie doesn't.'

'Ah, have you taken him in?'

He grimaced. 'No, we have to find him first. He's nineteen, a little sod, on our books but all minor things. He is very close to his grandparents.'

'Does he blame the run-in with Rose for the heart attack?'

Rick moved his head, clicking his tongue. 'You've got it.'

'Where do you think he might have gone?'

'The grandparents are keeping quiet, but we know he used to hang out with friends in Skegness.'

'Rather him than me. Skegness in November's pretty grim.'

Rick nodded with a half-smile. 'So you'll go back to Norfolk?'

'Yes, I arranged to call on Linda Bates. It can't do any harm.'

'You'll let me know if she tells you anything that seems relevant?'

'Of course, but as you say, the family liaison officer is on the ball. I probably won't find out anything you don't already know.'

'Just need to go with that gut instinct?' He gave his half-smile.

'Something like that.'

After he'd helped her clear the table, he made a move to leave.

'Are you still renting the same house?' she asked as he shrugged on his heavy wool coat.

'Yes.' His response was hesitant and followed by a silence that cut through the openness of the last two hours. He gave her a look she was unable to fathom before bending towards her to kiss her cheek, then striding away briskly into the darkening evening.

Sitting alone with Ella the tabby stretched across her lap, she wondered why he had reacted to her question with such difficulty. How had she misread their meetings and conversations, and was what she now read as sadness in reality discomfort? Since the accident in the barn, he had clearly been concerned for her. She realised now that his solicitude had rekindled some kind of hope in her. But hope for what? That he still cared for her, wanted a reconciliation? Yes, certainly the first; whatever direction their relationship took, she would always care about him and want his friendship. But reconciliation?

She sat for over an hour rerunning every detail of their recent encounters. They had become closer, certainly. 'We used to be a good team, you and me,' he'd said at the hospital. Putting Ella down, she picked up her crutches and, followed by the dogs, left the cottage. Crossing the garden, she entered the workshop and stood looking at the shelf on which the beautiful Clarice Cliff vase was displayed. She stepped forward and put out her hands to gently move her long fingers over its outer surface. It had been mended by an expert and she couldn't feel the cracks, but she knew the fine hairline fractures were visible inside. How far, she wondered, could something be put back together once it had been broken?

# Chapter 18

The following morning in her workshop, Clarice's mind still moved from one extreme to another. Overnight sleep had eluded her. She had tried to work out what was happening between her and Rick, whether the possibility of a future for them really existed, exhausting herself by examining every possible permutation of the way the relationship *might* proceed. It was impossible, she decided: like trying to shackle the wind.

To distract herself, she had begun a thorough clean-up. A blue plastic bag spilled over with torn-up paper, and the sink was filled with soapy water. A call from Jonathan asking for her help in caring for a damaged dog finally put yesterday's encounter out of her mind.

'Do you want me to go this afternoon?'

'If it suits you, my lovely, but you're on your own, I'm afraid; I can't come with you.'

'What do you know about the dog?' As she spoke, she put the cleaning sponge into the sink and pulled the yellow plastic gloves from her hands. As she put on her jacket, the dogs, recognising the telltale signs that signified an imminent departure from the workshop, jumped down from their sofa to run to the door.

'He's a bit of everything, a small boy called Micky, aged between two and three. He was in a terrible state when I brought him in. I operated on his cruciate ligament on Friday, and naturally he's now very slow-moving on his three good legs. I kept him at the surgery for two nights and he went into a kennel yesterday. Unfortunately, Leanne said he needs a lot of TLC, and kennels won't suit him. The poor little chap's terrified.'

'You mean Leanne at the Dog and Puss Purple Mansion?'

'Yes, that's the one.'

'She's been running that kennels and cattery for years and it's one of the best in the region. If she says he won't thrive in kennels, I trust her judgement,' Clarice said. 'Who's the animal welfare officer – is it Chris or Mark?'

'You know my expression about life in general?'

'The one with the double S?'

'That's it, my lovely – life is either shit or sugar. Well, today it's your turn for the shit.'

'So it's Inspector Chris.'

'Spot on.'

Clarice smiled, knowing Jonathan was being polite – he usually referred to Chris Cane as the Fat Inspector. Chris was known to be greedy, always turning up when there was the chance of a freebie – fruit crops at Clarice's or pheasants after a farmer's shoot. Mark Snell, in contrast, in his mid thirties, had moved from London to Lincoln with his wife and young daughters a year earlier and had quickly acclimatised to country living, becoming a popular figure with the locals. It would be Chris who would call or phone on a regular basis to check on Micky's progress – there was no escaping him.

With the mobile squeezed against her ear, Clarice talked while she moved across the garden to the house on her crutches. The edge of cold had gone, with the sun occasionally splitting the sky to create a sheen across the wet grass.

'The couple who owned the two dogs refused to sign them over to the inspector,' Jonathan continued, 'so the police were called in. A constable called Lenny attended. I agreed with Inspector Cane that removal was necessary – wait until you see the state of poor little Micky. The other dog sadly didn't make it; she was a PTS.'

'So heart-rending when they have to be put to sleep. I assume this one is going to prosecution?'

'Yes, it looks like it – you know the score. If the case is lost, he could go back to the owners, the people who did this to him.'

'Not much chance of that, though?'

'No, I think not, and they could still decide to sign him over to the inspector. With photographic evidence of starvation and my evidence of the dogs' condition, I doubt the prosecution could fail.'

'Ligaments can be torn for a variety of reasons,' Clarice said.

'Micky has had damage to that leg for a while. He should have been treated for it, and he and the other dog were badly neglected. I wouldn't ask, Clarice – I know your situation – but there is nobody else. Chris said he's running out of options. Leanne feels quite certain Micky's too nervous to thrive in kennels, so it's pointless just moving him to another. And Chris would be happy for you to take him.'

'Sounds like me and Micky were made for each other – him on three legs and me on crutches.'

'I didn't want to be the one to mention that!'

'So at present he's in no-man's-land until the prosecution. My role is to get him returned to full health.' Clarice spoke from experience. 'He can't be re-homed until after the court case is won, unless the owners agree to sign him over, because he's still legally owned by them.'

'You've got it. Are you OK to take him?'

'Yes, no problem,' Clarice said. 'Team Clarice is ready and waiting. I won't be seeing Sandra and Bob until later, but I know they'll help.'

Ending the conversation with a rueful smile, she went into the small room she used for storage at the end of the kitchen. It would be warm in there and was near enough for her to pop in and out to make a fuss of Micky. As she began to move things around to make space, the dogs' barking alerted her to an arrival.

She looked out to see a blue Volvo that she didn't recognise. She watched from the window until the tall, slim figure of Jack Lyme emerged from the vehicle. A first: he had never called on her before. She hid her surprise as she went outside with the dogs.

'Hi, Jack,' she beamed as he walked towards her.

'Hello, Clarice, I hope you don't mind my dropping by.'

Looking at him striding towards her, she understood why Lucy had described him as fit and Daisy had called him gorgeous. But he also looked haggard and wound up today, the pressure on him showing.

'Lovely to see you, come in. Do you want a coffee?' She spoke as he followed her into the cottage.

'Thank you, I won't. I think you can guess why I'm here.'

'Ginny?'

He nodded. 'I know you paid a visit to Lucy.'

'I did go and see her, yes.'

Clarice had gone to sit at the kitchen table, where Jack followed her to sit opposite.

'What did she tell you?'

'She told me that Ginny's OK and that she just needs some space.'

'It was my idea that she had a break from Winterby. Harry's behaviour had become unbearable.' Jack's face contorted for a second before he continued, 'I don't want anyone to think badly of Ginny. Her nerves were in shreds.'

'How are things at Winterby?' She changed the topic to move him on.

'About the same. I've managed not to smash Harry in the face, but it's taken a lot of restraint.' As he talked, Jack passed his car keys from one hand to the other nervously.

'I can imagine, but punching him's not the best plan,' Clarice agreed.

'I know. Mum and Dad have said I'd be playing into his hands.'

'They're right.'

'The problem is, Dad is the most laid-back man in the county, but Mum's the opposite. She's furious – it might just be her who punches Harry's lights out. The atmosphere at Winterby is shit.'

'Mothers can be overprotective.'

'I suppose so . . .' He paused. 'But you know Mum.'

Clarice considered what he had said, thinking about Paula. Her competitiveness at the charity events, her treatment of staff that bordered on rudeness, and the pushy behaviour with her children. There was no compromise with Paula, no meeting halfway, but it surprised her that Jack should be so open about it. Had he been pushed to the point where he wasn't thinking about being disloyal to his mother?

'Does Paula like Ginny?'

He lifted his hands to give an indication of his impotence. 'She doesn't think anyone's good enough for either Laura or myself, but she knows that if she doesn't get on with Ginny, I'll move out.'

'That sounds diplomatic.' Clarice tried to lift the mood. 'At least if you leave and start again somewhere else, you and your mum won't go into meltdown. And you won't lose the relationship with your Dad and Laura.'

'Yes,' he looked at her, 'that's true.' He twisted his lips into the semblance of a smile, but his eyes did not connect with hers. 'When Laura got married, she left home to live in the town with her husband. Look how that ended. Mum was always on their doorstep. I won't have her picking away at my relationship the way she did with Laura's. I'd rather Ginny and I moved completely away from Castlewick, made a start fresh somewhere else.'

'Whatever you decide, I hope it works out.' Clarice smiled as she spoke. 'Ginny's a lovely girl.'

'Yes.' Unexpectedly, he returned her smile. 'She is.'

'I'm coming over to Winterby Hall on Thursday.'

'When the shoot's on?' he said.

'Yes, but it's nothing to do with that. I said I'd call by for a coffee with Vita.'

There was a silence between them. Clarice felt unsure what to say next.

'I'd better get back,' Jack said.

As she watched his car pulling away from the drive, Clarice

could not help but think how desperate he must be. He was clearly wretched with fear that he might have lost Ginny. Did he believe that Harry had succeeded in destroying their relationship?

Half an hour later, after leaving a note for Sandra and Bob about Micky and telephoning Leanne at the kennels, she set off.

Driving along Long Road, she looked to her left at the dark outline of the Hanging Barn. She would, she thought, never be able to pass this point without remembering Rose and her own part in the discovery of her putrid corpse.

Twenty minutes later, she pulled into the kennels to be greeted by a wall of noise from twenty dogs all barking at once. Poor Micky, it would be a frightening experience for him after all he'd been through.

Leanne came out to meet her, a large woman in her late sixties with a shadow above her top lip that hinted at a moustache. She wore old jeans, a padded jacket and ankle-length purple wellies, with a purple hat pulled down to touch her eyebrows.

'Hi, Leanne,' Clarice called. 'Is Micky ready to go?'

'Yes, I'll just give you his special food first. I do think he'll get on better on a one-to-one basis; he's *really* nervous in kennels.'

After depositing the food in the back of Clarice's car, Leanne led her to a kennel with an outside run. The hatch to the inside was open and they could see the outline of the small, bony dog in the internal enclosed area. The PVC doors leading to each dog kennel were painted a vivid purple, as was the garden fence and the front door to the house. It was rumoured that Leanne as a young woman had been a hippy, a flower child, her penchant for purple a reminder of her youth.

As Clarice ventured into Micky's run, she could see he was a long-haired brown mongrel, not identifiable as belonging to any specific breed. His face was square, his body whippet-like and his ears erect. His condition was as Jonathan had described: he had bald patches and was pitifully thin, his ribcage protruding. He looked back at her with woeful brown eyes, his posture one of resignation, and as she approached him, he lowered his eyes, licking his lips in a gesture of appeasement. His left back leg, completely encased in a blue bandage, stuck out straight behind him.

After ten minutes of petting, talking to him all the while, she gently eased him up to carry him out to the car, settling him in the middle of a nest of old blankets. The sky was black, and as she set forth with a wave to Leanne, the rain swept down, turning to sleet, then back to driving rain. When she reached the Hanging Barn again, barely visible through the waves of water hitting her windscreen, she spotted movement. A figure, hunched forward, was striding in a determined fashion along the edge of the road.

Clarice pulled up while at the same time pressing the button to open the window on the passenger side. 'Hello,' she called, 'are you all right?'

The sodden figure stopped and turned to look at her. It was Jackie Smith.

'Hello – Jackie, isn't it? Are you OK?'

Jackie clutched at the collar of her raincoat, pulling it to her chin. Her hair was flattened against her head. She stared hard into Clarice's face, as if unable to identify her. The rain continued to drive down ceaselessly.

'I knew your sister Rose – sorry, I mean Sharon.'

'I know who you are.' She snapped out the words, her strange stare unblinking.

'Are you lost? You're soaked.' Clarice dithered, not sure what to say.

'You're that funny woman – the nosy one with the cats.'

'Where's your husband?' Clarice asked. She looked around, suddenly panicking. Could this be a trick? Could Pete Smith be hiding, ready to jump out and get into the car? But then how would he know she would be driving past at this time?

'He's meant to be coming back.' Jackie paused as she too looked around. 'He said I had to wait for half an hour, he was seeing someone. He left me here,' she threw a glance towards the barn, 'and didn't come back.'

'It's a long walk to Castlewick,' Clarice said.

Jackie hesitated; then, as if suddenly making up her mind, opened the car door and climbed into the passenger seat. She slammed the door hard behind her.

Micky gave a low rumble.

'What's that?'

'It's a dog, but there's a grid across – he won't hurt you.'

Close to, Jackie's face was an unhealthy, pallid white. Her eye make-up had run in the rain, leaving her with a smudgy panda effect. Her hands resting in her lap were small and child-like, the nails bitten to the quick. Looking at her, Clarice would never have identified her as Rose's sister. Rose, with her fifties garb, had had style.

She pressed the accelerator to move away at speed, thinking that if Pete was hanging about, she'd like to put some distance between them.

'Are you still staying at the pub?'

Jackie gave her another long, silent stare before she responded.

'Don't know where else we could afford to stay.' Her accent was pure Norfolk, her speech slow and ponderous.

'Right, I'll drop you outside,' Clarice said.

Jackie seemed to visibly relax, pulling down the collar of her coat and stroking her hair absent-mindedly. 'He'd been gone a long time.'

'Who had he gone to meet?'

'None of your business,' Jackie snarled, then, after a few moments: 'Anyway, I don't know, he don't tell me things like that.'

Clarice nodded. Rick had it right: the woman was slow and decidedly odd.

'You didn't know Maggie?'

'No,' Clarice said, surprised by the question. 'It was your other sister, Sharon, I knew.'

'Well if you'd said you'd known Maggie, I'd know you were a liar. Pete didn't know her; she went a long time ago.'

'Did she die?'

'Why did you say that?'

'You said *she went*.'

'She *went* to Scotland, but Auntie Peggy didn't tell us much, didn't say nothing about her being dead!'

'That's mean. She should have told you everything – you're her sister.'

'Too bloody right.' The words burst out. 'I'm her sister, but she was always Auntie Peggy's favourite, couldn't do nothing wrong. I couldn't do nothing right.'

'That's not fair.'

Jackie stared at Clarice again. 'Pete said you're trouble.'

'Why?' Clarice spoke with surprise. Keeping her eyes focused forward to concentrate on driving through the downpour, she could feel Jackie's gaze fixed on her face.

'Don't know. I expect it's because you're nosy and bossy. Pete doesn't like people like that, especially not women.'

'I don't know why he would think that.' Clarice struggled to find the right words to respond. 'I've only spoken to him twice.'

'I'm not saying any more,' Jackie said, sounding like a petulant child. 'I've got a man and you've only got a load of stinking cats.'

Clarice considered the strangely competitive reply, the words she imagined copied from Pete. Jackie looked straight ahead and didn't speak again until she was getting out of the car outside the pub.

'You won't tell him?'

'Tell who what?' Clarice queried.

'Pete . . . you won't tell him I spoke to you.'

'You didn't,' Clarice said.

Jackie gave her an odd combination of a sneer and a smirk. 'No, I didn't,' she said, slamming the car door shut, then turning to run towards the pub.


'To describe her as odd doesn't cover it,' Clarice told Bob and Sandra when, an hour later, they were all sitting in the storeroom with Micky.

The dog had come into the house submissively and, after eating every scrap of the small meal he was allowed, had curled into his box, half hidden under the blankets, his large brown eyes going from person to person.

He stank of the kennels and she knew Sandra was itching to bath him, but they would have to tolerate the smell for now.

'It would be too much for him, Sandra. Let him settle tonight,' she said.

Sandra nodded her agreement. 'We can change his bedding when we've bathed him,' she said, gazing at the small curled creature. 'Get rid of that horrible smell.'

'We were starting to get worried about you.' Bob looked at Clarice anxiously. 'With the weather being so bad.'

'I didn't like to leave Jackie there.'

'You're too bloody soft, darlin',' Sandra said.

'I can't help feeling sorry for her. I think she probably has some form of mental disability – she must have found life quite confusing and difficult.' Clarice sounded gloomy.

'She's not your problem.' As she spoke, Sandra kept her eyes fixed on Micky. Then slowly she leaned over to stroke him. 'Auntie Sandra is going to look after you.' Clarice watched as Micky tentatively pushed his face against Sandra's hand.

'We'd best get going.' Bob spoke as he got up. Reluctantly Sandra followed him out of the room to collect their coats.

'Thanks for covering for me again tomorrow,' Clarice said.

'We don't mind as long as you're careful,' Bob told her sternly.

'I will be,' she assured them, 'and I'm not getting away until nearly midday, so I'll see you before I go.' She wondered, as she had in the past, if Sandra and Bob saw themselves as parent substitutes. But she'd never considered them as anything other than good friends – invaluable ones.

# Chapter 19

'Remember to take care, darlin'.' Sandra took her attention away temporarily from washing Micky to call to Clarice. Not wanting to frighten him, or wet his dressings, she had sat him on towels in a dry tub and was gently sponging him down to remove the dog shampoo. Micky's eyes, large, adoring orbs, never moved from her face.

'I will,' Clarice called back as she withdrew from the room. Going to the car, she looked at the deep gouges along the sides. She'd told Jim about it and had suggested that she get it repaired the following week when both of them were less busy.

As she started the engine, her phone rang. Georgie came into her mind, but when she looked at the screen, she didn't recognise the number. She pressed to accept the call.

'Bitch!' She immediately recognised the voice, guttural and aggressive, as Pete Smith's.

'How did you get my number?' She tried to keep her voice calm, as if unaffected by his vitriol.

'You don't interfere with *mine*!'

'If you mean interfering by giving your wife a lift, I thought I was being kind – it was chucking it down.'

'She waits where I tell her to wait. If she'd done that, she wouldn't have got wet.'

'It wasn't very nice for her to have to wait in the barn where her sister's body had been found, and it's hardly dry in there, with half the roof missing.'

'None of your fuckin' business, bitch. If you tell your dogs to sit, you don't want some sod to give a different command to confuse them.'

'OK, well if I see her again, I won't offer her a lift.' She realised he was baiting her. She wouldn't respond to his suggestion that he treated his wife as she might a dog.

'That's not good enough.'

A frigid silence descended: a stand-off. Clarice cut the call without replying.

Minutes later, driving to the main road, she checked her rear-view mirror and quickly turned her head, back and forth, to search around in a circle. She didn't want to admit to herself that she felt rattled. He was not a man who'd respond to reason; he would, she thought, work on plots of retaliation to feed the malice he nurtured. It was obvious from Jackie's comments that he had taken a strong dislike to her. She remembered what Rick had said about Pete's problems with alcohol and anger.

But the journey turned out to be uneventful, and the thought that Pete Smith might be pursuing her dwindled from her mind. The weather, after yesterday's downpour, was dry, and a few hours later Clarice, having entered the postcode for the Sunnydale retirement home into her satnav, found herself driving directly through King's Lynn to a long, low, single-storey building in a quiet street and next to a primary school, both probably built in the late 1970s.

At just after 2 p.m. the car park had already filled up, and she took the last unoccupied place. There were the usual indications that the building was used for the infirm, with a wide ramp to one side of the entrance porch, and as she approached the main door, she could see through the window four wheelchairs in a neat line. She pressed the buzzer, and a few moments later a smartly dressed woman in her mid forties came to use a keypad to open the door.

'Hello,' Clarice smiled, 'I'm Clarice Beech and I've come to visit Linda Bates.'

'We spoke on the phone, I'm Mrs Freeman.'

Clarice juggled with her crutch to take the extended hand.

'Poor you, you've had an accident?' Mrs Freeman was looking at Clarice's crutches.

'A fall.' Clarice did not go into detail. She followed the smell of hairspray emitting from the head of the tightly coiffured manager.

'We get a lot of those in here,' Mrs Freeman said. 'It goes with the territory.'

'I imagine it does.'

'Linda is looking forward to your visit. She's told the other residents you're the niece of an old friend.'

'Has she got confused?'

'She only gets confused when it suits her.' Mrs Freeman spoke over her shoulder, raising her pitch meaningfully. 'As I explained when we spoke on Sunday, her body is fragile but her mind is sharp. She's certainly not befuddled.'

She strode forward purposefully, Clarice gamely trying to match her pace, along a seemingly never-ending beige corridor, a row of green plastic seats down one side of it. Clarice imagined the residents filling their daytime hours sitting on the hard, easy-sponge seats, staring at the beige wall opposite. They passed a long room, its doors propped open, filled with tables and chairs and emitting food smells not dissimilar to those she remembered from her childhood school canteen. In the room next to it, elderly people were slumped in armchairs in a semicircle around a large television. Despite its high volume, many of the residents appeared to be asleep. Others sat in groups of two or three, looking bored, as if, having run dry of conversation, they awaited a time when it would be acceptable, duty done, to leave.

The building's dominant smells of urine, disinfectant and handwash reminded her of her recent visit to A & E. But the hospital had smelt of fear too, at the presence of death, while here there was a feeling of sitting in wait for its not altogether unwelcome arrival.

Two young women, probably by appearance Filipinos, wheeled a trolley around with teacups, biscuits and two large stainless-steel urns. In another smaller sitting room, without a television, a lone, shrunken, elderly lady sat with a blanket over her lap and legs.

'This is Clarice Beech, Linda.' Mrs Freeman raised her voice, the genteel veneer coarsening.

Clarice went forward, offering her hand to Linda, who clasped it between her own.

'Here.' Mrs Freeman pulled another armchair forward. Clarice, detaching her hand to lay her crutches side by side on the floor, sat opposite Linda, their knees almost touching.

'I'll get Aclan to bring you both some tea.' Mrs Freeman gave her brittle professional smile before leaving.

Turning back to Linda, Clarice saw that the old lady hadn't taken her eyes away from her. Her arthritic hands, like claws, now rested in her lap and her small brown eyes were active in her wrinkled, age-weathered face. Then, unexpectedly, she smiled, a hinged jaw swinging awry, her lips moving to show her gums and two lone teeth.

'I don't know you, do I?' The question, in a soft voice with a Norfolk accent, was to the point but not unfriendly.

'No, you don't,' Clarice responded. 'I wanted to pick your brain about the nieces of a friend of yours – Peggy Little.'

'Peggy and I were at school together,' Linda said.

'Yes, I know.' As Clarice spoke, one of the young women she had seen earlier brought in a tray with a small pot of tea for two, milk, sugar and a plate that displayed four digestive biscuits.

'Are we getting special treatment?' she asked when they were on their own again.

'You don't miss much.'

Linda nodded. 'It's because you're not a regular and you speak with a good accent.'

'Do I?'

'Your accent isn't posh, but it's not common.' Linda gave a crafty smile. 'The Queen's English impresses Mrs Freeman. She's a bit of a snob.'

'So next time,' Clarice whispered conspiratorially, 'it might well be the tea urn?'

'It would be nice if there was a next time.' Linda's stare was penetrating. 'Did you know Peggy? Mrs Freeman told me that she was the reason you wanted to visit me.'

'No, I didn't,' Clarice said. She liked Linda; she was

inquisitive and sharp, and she felt instinctively that she would respect honesty. She decided to ditch the story she'd concocted about her mother having known Peggy – the elderly lady would pick it apart in minutes.

'Let me tell you who I am,' she said. She explained what she did professionally before going over what had happened to her, from finding Rose in the barn, to her thoughts about why Rose had died, up to the present moment.

'Well,' exclaimed Linda when she had finished, 'you've been on quite an adventure. I feel envious!'

'I'd give away the memory of finding Rose's body in an instant if I could.'

'Yes,' she nodded, 'you poor girl, I can understand that.' She hesitated as if needing to think about her words before she spoke them. 'People always say that it's unkind to speak ill of the dead, but Sharon – I'm sorry, I can't call her Rose – was an absolute horror both as a child and as an adult. It doesn't surprise me it's ended badly for her.'

'In what way?' Clarice said, watching the animated face.

'It was very much a case of black and white. I knew Peggy and her sister Barbara, Sharon's mother, at school. Peggy and I were in the same class; Barbara was two years older than us. I didn't like her – she was the black to Peggy's white, a thief and a liar. She had the two girls, Sharon and Jackie, with her husband Jerry. One day he upped and left – he'd discovered that she'd been having an affair with Ian, the village butcher. When Barbara found out she was pregnant with young Maggie, Ian left his wife and moved in with her.'

'So,' Clarice said, 'they had a stable life.'

'No, sadly not. After Maggie was born, Barbara started to get up to her old tricks: alcohol and men. Ian dumped her to go back to his wife. Then, when Maggie was five, Barbara died.'

'That is sad.'

'In a car with two drunks, an accident; the men survived but Barbara was killed outright.'

'What happened to the girls?'

'Jerry, the ex-husband, had remarried. His new wife didn't want them. Jerry's mother took them in, but she only wanted her own grandchildren, not Maggie.'

'What a shame to split them up. Did Maggie's father take her?'

'His wife didn't want her, so she went to live with her Aunt Peggy.'

'I didn't realise Maggie had been brought up by Peggy,' Clarice said with surprise.

'Why should you? I always felt Peggy was lucky to get her. It's back to the black and white: Sharon and Jackie were very much like their mother, picking fights, swearing, light-fingered and terrible liars. I asked Peggy not to bring them into my home when they were visiting. Although . . .'

'Yes?' Clarice leaned forward.

'Jackie was never what I would describe as being quite right.' Linda touched the side of her head. 'As a child, she could stand for more than an hour at a time with her mouth open, just staring. I don't know what was wrong with her, but she was odd. They have more understanding of different conditions these days, don't they?'

'I met her.'

'Yes, you did, you've just told me!'

'But,' said Clarice, 'you liked Maggie?'

'Lovely girl, a real sweetheart and so pretty. It destroyed

Peggy when she went away. Peggy was more like a mother to her than an aunt, and she had brought her up to be honest, God-fearing and decent.'

'How old was Maggie when she moved away?'

'When she was sixteen, she was employed at a place about twenty miles from here called Snarebrook Hall. She lived in the servants' quarters and was a dogsbody, doing a bit of everything: helping in the kitchen, cleaning. She'd get the bus home on her break days to visit her aunt.'

'I know that place,' Clarice said. 'It belongs to the Fayrepoynt family; it's their country residence. Their main home is Winterby Hall, not far from me in the Lincolnshire Wolds, and they also have an apartment in Eaton Square in London and a small house in Scotland that Lady Vita calls "the shack". Although I doubt it really is a shack.'

Linda appeared captivated by the information. 'I've never been to Snarebrook Hall, so I've no idea what it's like. Peggy told me that Maggie had fallen in love. It was someone she worked with, but Peggy was worried about her because she was so naïve, far too trusting.'

'So,' said Clarice, 'she married him?'

'Peggy thought that was what had happened.'

'You don't sound sure.'

'I'm not positive that Peggy was one hundred per cent convinced. There hadn't been a church service, Maggie didn't wear a ring and she never saw a marriage certificate.'

'Then why did she think Maggie had married?'

'Because Maggie wasn't like Sharon or Jackie; she had never told lies. But Peggy said she had become secretive, which was strange. Maggie had visited to tell her that she and the boyfriend had taken a holiday together in Scotland, and while they were there, they'd got married.'

'Ah,' said Clarice. 'Gretna Green?'

'She didn't say where, but she was only sixteen,' Linda said. 'Maggie said that when the boy told his family, they weren't happy about the relationship. He said that Maggie had to not tell anyone about him, and lie low until they came around to the idea.'

'So they weren't living as man and wife?'

'No.'

'The husband sounds a bit weak.'

'Peggy was very unhappy about the situation, but Maggie said if she interfered, she'd go away and Peggy wouldn't ever see her again.'

'How very mean!'

'My dear,' Linda leaned forward, putting her gnarled old hand on Clarice's, 'you've been in love?'

Clarice nodded. She had. 'What happened next?'

'Peggy didn't see her for six or seven months, but Maggie always phoned her on a Sunday afternoon. Then she came to visit – it was the last time Peggy saw her. Maggie told her she was meeting her husband's family later on that day. Peggy said she was really excited, in a nervous way.'

'What was his name ... her husband?'

'I didn't know at that point. Maggie said he'd asked her not to say anything until it was all settled, and she'd given her word. When Peggy asked her what they were going to live on, she said that he had his future sorted out and that money wouldn't be a problem.'

'So that could mean he was a student with a career plan, or

that his parents might support him. She didn't give any clues about his parents or siblings?'

'No, nothing. Peggy thought that as they were both so young, perhaps his mother and father would have preferred him to concentrate on his training or studies at college, although she couldn't work out how that would fit with him working at Snarebrook Hall.'

'How strange. Maggie must have had amazing control to keep her promise to tell no one about him, when she was in love and only sixteen.'

'I agree.'

'So that was it?'

'She told Peggy she might not be in touch for some time, told her not to worry because it was all going to work out. And she left a locked case with her, saying it contained private stuff and that she'd be back to collect it.'

'What was in the case?'

'Well,' Linda said thoughtfully, 'I shouldn't say. I've never spoken a word about it before.'

Clarice waited.

'Peggy did have a peek. I don't know if she had to break the lock.'

'And?'

'She was upset when she told me about it because she felt that she'd betrayed Maggie.'

'What was in there?' Clarice's voice was eager.

'Nothing much: a wedding ring wrapped in tissue and a framed print of part of Scotland. Peggy thought it was probably where they went on holiday, a keepsake.'

'Did she never try to trace her?'

'Yes, about three months after she last saw her, she phoned Snarebrook Hall and spoke to the housekeeper, who told her that Maggie had moved to Scotland with her new husband but that they had no contact details. She told her that the man had been a gardener – his name was Brian Curtis – and that Maggie had been pregnant.'

'Did Peggy believe her?'

'She didn't know what to believe. Remember, this was years ago and Peggy wasn't what you'd call a worldly woman. She couldn't understand why Maggie hadn't told her about being pregnant. If she and this man loved one another *and* they were married, what was there to hide? And why not tell her she was going to live in Scotland? But she did contact the police.'

'What did they do?' Clarice asked.

'Very little.' Linda sniffed. 'They told her that they had also contacted the housekeeper, who had told them the same story. And that although the Curtises were moving around looking for work, the housekeeper had managed to get a message to them. The policeman said that they had had telephone contact from Mr and Mrs Curtis to let them know that they were living in Scotland. And that they were sorry that Aunt Peggy was upset, but they had made a joint decision not to contact her.'

'That sounds callous!'

'Peggy was so upset. She couldn't understand why Maggie would behave in that way. She always thought she would change her mind and come to see her. She lived in hope, a kind of limbo.'

'Apart from Maggie's odd behaviour,' Clarice said, 'gardeners aren't well paid. How could he not have to worry about money, especially if they had to keep moving around to find work? The housekeeper would have been Denise Lyme. It does sound like either she or Maggie, or both, were lying.'

'I can't remember her name.' Linda looked puzzled. 'There was a man who dropped Maggie at her aunt's a couple of times. He was older than her, in his twenties. He came and collected her later, but he never came into the house.'

Clarice nodded encouragingly.

'His car was old, nothing special, and he was smart, obviously took pride in himself, but his clothes weren't expensive or fashionable. Peggy did ask if he was the husband, but Maggie said that he was just a friend giving her a lift.'

'What happened to the case?'

'I've no idea. After Peggy died, Sharon came to clear the house, and she sold everything.'

'Not Jackie and Pete?'

'No, apparently they'd had a falling-out. They'd argued a few years before, one of the times Pete was in prison. I do remember,' Linda was reflective, 'Sharon turning up at Peggy's house once when Maggie was there, bold as brass wanting money.'

'Did Peggy give her any?'

'No, she didn't have it to give, and then Sharon asked Maggie, who must only have been young. Of course she didn't have anything either.'

'Was Sharon worried or concerned about her sister when she lost touch?'

Linda's answer was to laugh.

'But she was interested when there might be money involved, clearing her aunt's house,' Clarice spoke thoughtfully. 'Perhaps she was able to use what was in the case to blackmail someone with.'

'It might be a possibility.'

They looked at one another without speaking, then Clarice leant forward to pick up Linda's hand. 'Thank you, Linda, you've helped me so much.'

Linda gave her a smile, brightness lighting up her age-crumpled face. 'I've enjoyed it,' she said. 'I haven't talked so much for ages.'

Clarice had an image of the line of plastic chairs with the beige wall opposite.

'I've got to come back in a few days. Can I call again?' she asked.

'Yes, please,' Linda beamed. 'What are you coming back for?'

'Apart from seeing you,' Clarice said, 'I took photographs of the jewellery at Sharon's house, and I've researched two of the maker's marks in the initialled gold wedding rings. One of them led to a Birmingham maker, a dead end. The other is a Norwich goldsmith. He's moved and is now retired. I'm still trying to get in contact with him to show him the photograph.'

'To see if he can enlighten you further,' Linda finished excitedly.

'That's it.'

'I might have something for you.'

'Really?'

'I've got photographs that you can look at, ones I took of the girls and Peggy. There's one I'm sure I took on Maggie's last visit. I passed on all the good ones to Peggy, of course, but there were a couple a bit out of focus that I still have.'

'I'd love to see them,' Clarice said with enthusiasm. 'I'll leave a message with Mrs Freeman when I've managed to make an appointment with the jeweller.'

'Wonderful,' said Linda. She looked suddenly sheepish. 'I told the other ladies that you're the niece of a close friend. I didn't tell them that we hadn't met before.'

'Did you?' Clarice's smile was indulgent.

'It'll be nice to say you're coming again. Not everyone gets visitors, and even in God's waiting room people are incredibly competitive!'

'You tell them I'm coming again within the next few days,' Clarice said, 'and we'll see if we get put in here or have to make do with the telly room and the tea urns.'

She bent down to kiss the wrinkled cheek before leaving, and was rewarded when Linda's face split again into the near-toothless grin.

# Chapter 20

'I'm pissed off with Jonathan!' Rick said.

Having first phoned to check Clarice would be at home, and turned down her offer of a meal, he'd driven over on Wednesday evening. They sat in front of the living room fire, mugs of tea by their sides.

'I'm amazed how quickly he's settled in,' Clarice said proudly, beaming at Micky. 'Just look at him, it's only his third day but you'd think he'd been here forever.'

Rick observed the scrawny dog coolly as he dozed in the prime position in the centre of the hearthrug, his leg, still encased in the blue bandage, stretched out behind him. Blue and Jazz bunched up on either side, as near to Clarice on the sofa as possible, while studiously ignoring the interloper. There was a notable absence of cats.

'That isn't the point and you know it. Whatever possessed Jonathan – asking you to take him in when you can hardly take care of yourself?'

'I agreed to take Micky, nobody forced me,' Clarice protested.

'The name's right; in your state, that's what Jonathan doing – he's taking the mickey.'

Clarice looked at him silently, her face set. There had been no reference to their last encounter; his awkwardness had gone. It felt almost as if it had never happened, and yet she knew it had.

'I wouldn't have taken him if he had anywhere else to go. Too many animals, not enough people – you know that.'

'I get it, Clarice.' Rick, as usual, having let go of his irritation, appeared to be resigning himself to the situation. 'But you can't save the world, and if you completely knacker yourself, you'll be no use to the animals you've already got.'

'Jonathan mentioned on Monday that you'd released Bill Whittle.'

'Why doesn't that surprise me?'

'Has he got the station bugged?' Clarice said. 'To pick up all the juicy gossip.'

Rick's face implied that her attempt to manoeuvre him away from giving his opinion about her fostering the dog was not working. He remained deadpan.

'Although he hasn't told me yet that you've found where Rose was murdered,' she continued.

'Enough about Jonathan.' His voice was sombre. 'I want to hear about you. Tell me more about the meeting with Jackie. Why the hell did you pick her up?'

'I didn't know who it was until I'd wound down the window. The rain was coming in waves, it's isolated around here, and it's normal to offer help to people stuck in remote places.'

'Not when it's the wife of Pete Smith – and she wasn't stuck.'

'It's done.'

'Yeah – and you got payback with that phone call. What did you expect, flowers or a thank-you card?'

'Rick!' Her voice rasped.

'OK.' He looked at her pensively. 'I wonder who he was meeting and why he'd left Jackie there.'

'I wondered that. Do you know, I think she has some type of medical disorder. From what I can see, all the significant people in her life have been deeply flawed, but I didn't get the impression that she had the intellectual ability to work that out. The only way for her to survive might be to reflect back what she receives, to behave to others as they have to her. Her mother Barbara and sister Sharon both sound like nightmares, and then there's Pete!'

'You're probably right.' He nodded. 'You say that her mother was a nightmare. I'm assuming that Linda Bates told you that. Was there anything else?'

'As a matter of fact,' she said, 'there was.'

'Really?' She had his interest.

Half an hour later, after she had been through every aspect of her discussion with Linda, he said, 'I'm *very* interested in the link with the Fayrepoynt family home. If Maggie worked for them and married one of the gardeners, there might be a possibility, even after all this time, of tracing her, especially knowing the surname.'

'The most interesting fact is that the housekeeper at Snarebrook Hall was Tom's mother, Denise.'

'Really!'

'Yes,' Clarice said, 'although I should say his *late* mother; she died some years ago. Linda Bates didn't seem to know about the connection between Snarebrook and Winterby. And there is a question about whether Maggie actually got married – Linda told me that Aunt Peggy had some doubts.'

'But she said that the housekeeper told Peggy that Maggie had married and been pregnant when she went to Scotland?'

'Yes,' agreed Clarice, 'but was that the truth?'

'One sister worked for the Fayrepoynts thirty years ago in Norfolk, and another is a murder victim, her body found a few miles away from their Lincolnshire home.' Rick spoke as if he was thinking out loud.

'Mm.' Clarice was thoughtful. 'I keep asking myself why, if they had a good relationship, Maggie didn't tell her aunt her plans. It could be that Brian Curtis, the husband, had something to hide, like a criminal record. Maggie would have known how her aunt viewed Jackie's husband Pete, and might have felt that Brian would be viewed in the same way. If that were the case, she might have feared she would be a disappointment to Aunt Peggy.' She sat quietly, reflecting for a moment, before continuing. 'She told her aunt that financially he wasn't badly off. And there seemed to be an implication that he had prospects. The man who dropped her at the aunt's wasn't well off; his clothes weren't up to much and he was driving an old banger. The problem I'm trying to get my head around is that it's odd she didn't introduce him. Why, if he was just a friend, would that be a problem?'

'That backs up your first idea,' Rick said, 'that she was ashamed of him.'

Clarice nodded. 'My other thought is that she was only sixteen when she started work at the hall, seventeen when she went away; at that age, imagination can take over.'

'In what way?'

'Her husband couldn't just be ordinary or average; he had to be amazing, and he had to fight for her, slay the dragon.'

'Which was his family?'

Clarice nodded. 'It sounds like a fantasy from a book or film, with Maggie casting herself to play the romantic female lead.'

Rick nodded. 'The retired jeweller sounds a bit of a long shot. You're talking about a single customer from thirty years ago. Is it worth the journey? Why not try to catch him by phone? It would save you doing the round trip.'

'Well, it probably won't lead anywhere, but I've already told Linda I'm going to call on her again, and it meant so much to her.'

'Clarice,' Rick put on his serious face, 'what have we just said about you not being able to save the world? Linda Bates isn't your mother, sister or aunt. She has a nephew, for goodness' sake; she isn't your problem.'

'A nephew who hardly visits and then probably only out of duty,' Clarice said stubbornly. 'I've said I'll call in, so I will.'

Rick gave his half-smile, a sign that Clarice knew meant he had lost the battle. 'But you believe that the framed map of Scotland holds a clue?'

'It *could*,' she corrected him. 'The map covers Dumfries and Galloway, which is where you find ...'

'Gretna Green,' he finished for her.

'Will you get someone to look at it tomorrow; open the frame to see if there's something behind the print?'

'No,' he said, getting up. 'Bugger that, I'll go now. Are you too tired, or do you want to come?'

'I'm with you,' she said. 'Just give me a minute to put Micky in his room.'

They went in Rick's car, arriving after 8 p.m. to walk along the pathway to the porch. The weather forecast had suggested there would be below-freezing temperatures overnight, and it was already cold. The sky was clear, with the moon giving some light to their passage. Rick carried his torch from the car, which spread a powerful beam.

Going into the house, Clarice reflected upon Rose coming and going from there and had an unsettling feeling. This was what she had died for. The ownership of a *thing* that she had thought of as being proof of her self-worth. The knowledge gained about Rose's past life and aspirations cast a new sense of wretchedness on the property.

Rick clicked the hall light switch, but it remained dark. The living room curtains were pulled together, but a long, narrow ladder of moonlight had penetrated through a gap, dividing the darkened room. Clarice, remembering Rose's doll collection, imagined the hundreds of dead, fixed eyes surveying them. She followed Rick upstairs.

The torch picked out the blank spaces on the bedroom wall where the framed prints had been. The curtains were open, and the moonlight filling the room gave it a grey other-worldliness, with the light from Rick's torch acting as an advancing sprite. She heard the crunch of glass underfoot as he moved ahead of her.

'Someone's beaten us to it.' He spoke as he swept the torch beam across the debris of wood, paper and glass on the floor. All the prints had been removed, and the frames were in pieces on the floor. He bent to shine the torch on the map of Scotland.

'If there was something there, it's gone.'

Clarice nodded. After the rise of optimism from her conversation with Linda, she now felt deflated. She turned to look at the antique bureau; Rick, as if following the same line of thought, turned too. The drawers that had contained the jewellery were scattered across the floor, their contents gone.

'Don't touch anything,' Rick said, moving towards the door. 'Let's go down.'

191

The kitchen door was half open. The lock hung away from the main frame, indicating that the intruder had used brute force to gain entry.

Rick wandered away to use his mobile phone. Clarice followed as far as the hall, listening to the low buzz of his voice and watching the movement of the torchlight, giving away his agitated state as he paced to and fro in the living room.

'What's in the black bin liners?' she asked when he returned, pointing to the three bags under a hall table.

'It's the dolls we took to the station. The constable who checked them, Meghan, returned them this morning. The place hadn't been broken into then, so that gives us a ten-hour slot when it must have happened.'

'Nothing in them?'

'Nope,' he said, glancing at the bags. 'I've called in the break-in; the team will be coming out.' She sensed his awkwardness. 'It might be easier if you're not here.'

'I'll wait in the car.'

Half an hour later, Clarice saw the headlights of an arriving vehicle cutting across the end of the lane to continue and park at the rear of the building, probably on Rick's instructions. She wondered what the police constables would think of the boss checking out this house late in the evening with his ex. And would they call her his ex, or still refer to her as his wife? She realised that any awkwardness Rick might feel would be due to the gossip factor. If she was seen with him in the house, the canteen would be buzzing tomorrow. The gossip within the force was as ardent as that in any other place of work. The feeling she had had in the garden at Winterby Hall returned to swamp her. The boundaries of her world had changed so much that she no longer had any certainty about where she fitted.

Rick drove her home.

'It was Rob and Meghan,' he told her. 'I've left them there.'

'How is Rob?'

'Between girlfriends again.'

'Now why doesn't that surprise me?' Then, after a moment: 'What happens next, with the investigation?'

'I need to talk to Tom and look at the staff records, if they still have them going back that far.'

'I'm going over to Winterby tomorrow,' she said, 'for a coffee with Vita.'

'Our paths might cross then,' he said. 'I'll phone Tom to arrange a time.'

'There's a shoot going on tomorrow.'

'Great!' Rick grimaced. 'A chance to jostle with the checked jacket and Barbour brigade.'

Looking at his poker-faced expression, Clarice began to snigger. Rick turned to look at her and cracked a smile. And for that moment, she felt that she belonged.

# Chapter 21

Arriving at Winterby Hall the following morning just before eleven, Clarice realised she would have a problem parking. Row upon row of four-by-fours of various makes and types filled the gravel outside the hall.

Seeing the men wandering away from their vehicles to the hall, clad uniformly in their finest tweed jackets or Barbours and green wellies, Rick's words from the previous evening flashed into her mind, and a brief smile lit her face. Near the end of the driveway, young men, teenagers to mid twenties, had gathered ready to climb aboard the open-backed trucks. They would go ahead, ready on the given command to walk in rows through the long grass, hitting out in front with sticks, driving the birds into the path of the shooters.

Clarice thought of Jack, wondering if he had heard from Ginny yet. She gave the group a brief glance and, not seeing him amongst them, took hope that he had won that battle.

Managing to find a spot at the edge of the car park, further away than she had anticipated, with the pebbled ground not ideal for crutches, she walked slowly to the house. As she approached the door, it opened and Tom stepped out. For a fraction of a second, his eyes focusing on her were unguarded and cold before they flicked to professional cordiality.

'Clarice.' His voice held its usual warmth. 'You missed your husband – he was here early on.'

'Really?' Clarice sensed his agitation.

'Yes, he wanted to know about the staff at Snarebrook Hall when my mother was housekeeper there.' He appeared to expect a response.

'Ah, I imagine you'd be the first person he'd think about for that sort of information. The current staff wouldn't have a clue.'

'I dare say you're right, but as my mother never told me anything about the comings and goings there, I wouldn't have a clue either. There was a huge turnover back then, when jobs were more plentiful.'

'But you *were* living there at the time?'

'No, Clarice,' he said firmly. 'I visited my mother, but I would have been married and living with Paula.'

Clarice noted the steeliness in his words, a tone she'd never heard before. The only face she had ever seen Tom wearing was that of the calm, polished professional estate manager. She thought it wise to change the subject. 'No sling today?' she said, looking at his right arm. 'Are you fully mended?'

He lifted his index finger to his lips, implying a secret. 'It's not supposed to come off, but it's more comfortable not to wear it, just for a few hours, while I'm so busy. Don't tell.'

'I won't,' she smiled, moving to the door.

'Allow me.' He stepped forward to push it open with his left arm.

'Thank you.' As she moved past him, her eyes were drawn to his hand. His shirtsleeve had ridden up, revealing several long red welts in the exposed flesh. She wondered how much further they might reach up his arm. Were they scratches that had been made by human nails? Or just an accident sustained as part of his day's work – some animal he'd had to cope with? He was a keen gardener, but they looked too deep for thorns. They were blood red, so fairly recently inflicted. They could not have had anything to do with Rose's death.

From the Orangery came the loud noise of conjoined men's voices battling to be heard, the occasional booming of a dominant male followed by guffaws and hoots of merriment. And all this, she thought, before the shooting, the lunch and the drinking.

'Clarice.' She turned to find Lucy, wearing a black dress and white apron, holding an empty tray by her side. 'Hi, I've been doing the coffees for the men – before they start killing things.' She voiced the last words in a stage whisper, moving her eyes towards the Orangery. She looked pink and flustered.

'Any news on Ginny?' Clarice asked.

'Yes, she's arriving back from Spain this morning; she said four days apart from Jack was enough. She's getting a taxi from Lincoln station. You may well bump into her, unless she goes straight to the fisheries to find Jack.'

'That's great,' Clarice beamed. 'Does Jack know she's on her way?'

Lucy smiled. 'No, and if you see him, don't say anything – it's a surprise.'

Clarice, as Tom had done earlier, put her finger to her lips. 'And it'll be a lovely one.'

'You're to go into the drawing room.' Lucy ushered her forward. 'Lady Vita will be along in a moment.'

Closing the heavy door behind her brought instant silence. Clarice stood for a moment to admire the beautiful room. Everything in it was polished and cleaned until it glowed. The wood and the silver shone; the fire was laid neatly and ready to be lit. Fresh flowers – white Michaelmas daisies and long-stemmed spotted spider orchids – were displayed on a table behind the sofa; maybe one of Laura's arrangements.

She hovered for a moment, awaiting Vita's arrival, before walking across to look at the portrait of Horace Fayrepoynt. In evening dress, he looked to have been in his mid forties when he sat for the artist. His hair, as was fashionable in the 1950s, was short and brushed back from his face. He held his head high, looking down with impenetrable piercing blue eyes. His aquiline nose, something both sons had managed to escape, reinforced the image of haughty arrogance. The artist, she suspected, might have tried to improve on his lack of chin, but doubtless too much adjustment would have made the portrait unrealistic. She made a square with her fingers and thumbs, looked through it to take in just the face. Could it ever have belonged to someone ordinary – a plumber, perhaps, or a teacher? No – she brought her hands down – the conceit and arrogance of the man had been captured.

Clarice thought of Mary, her mother, who had for a couple of years attended watercolour painting classes. There were two of her efforts framed and hanging side by side in her bedroom at home, both of wild flowers: bright red poppies, harebells, cornflowers and larkspur.

She was distracted by movement outside, and going to the window alcove, she slipped inside to sit and watch as the men, refreshed by their coffee, started to drift outside. The beaters were now sitting, obedient as schoolboys, on the benches of the trucks, the drivers awaiting the signal to move away. She imagined the feeling of being pressed on either side by bodies, the friction as the trucks bounced along, knees touching in the centre. Claustrophobia swamped her momentarily, making her feel clammy. She had always, when possible, avoided using lifts. She assumed the men in the trucks did not have a problem with confined spaces.

She heard the door open and turned to look through the hanging drapes, expecting to see Vita. Instead, Harry came into the room, calling over his shoulder, 'There in a mo, Pa, just picking something up.' He was dressed in brown corduroy trousers with green wellies, a Barbour coat zipped up to his brown scarf and a green hat. As joint host of the shoot, he was important, second only to his father.

Clarice, having hesitated, felt that it might be awkward now to suddenly reveal herself. Instead, balancing her crutch carefully, she watched him go to an antique chair next to the fireplace. He leaned behind it and in a second retrieved what he had come to collect: a handsome-looking double-barrelled shotgun. Having participated in clay pigeon shoots with Rick, she knew that the value of the more upmarket guns could be staggering. It should have been kept locked away until it was needed, she thought ruefully. The law required guns to be locked in a cabinet when not being attended to or in use, but it seemed typical of Harry's lazy ways to hide it there.

After he'd left the room, she went back again to stand before the portrait.

'Apparently he hated that,' Vita said, coming into the room. She looked sleek, her hair shiny and glossy and swinging against her face. Her blood-red lipstick matched her linen top, paired with dark blue slim-fit chinos.

'Horace?' Clarice asked.

'Yes,' Vita said. 'He insisted that it didn't do him justice.'

'Was he tall?'

'Yes, he was. Tom inherited his height, but not poor Rolly. It skipped a generation, though; Harry is as tall as his grandfather.'

'What does Roland think of the portrait?' Clarice said, smiling. 'Does he think it's a good likeness of his father?'

Vita pursed her lips while she considered. 'He's never really expressed an opinion either way, but he did say that his father was a difficult man – hard to please. I imagine it might have been a challenge finding an artist of sufficient eminence to take on the commission.'

'He was a strong character?'

'Very much so; not someone to get on the wrong side of. But I do believe that he adored Rolly.' She chose her words carefully. 'He was a tad eccentric, and he *loved* his pigs.'

'Really?' said Clarice. 'I never realised you kept pigs.'

'We don't now, but Horace did, as did his father before him. Naturally he didn't look after them himself, but he was often caught feeding them the odd apple. Apparently, they were Gloucestershire Old Spots, but Horace continued to call them by their original description, which was orchard pigs. Rolly said that he's never eaten bacon like it since the estate closed down the piggery.'

'Why did they stop keeping pigs?'

'It was after Horace died. Roland was living in Devon at the time; Ben, one of Horace's cousins, was teaching him the basics of fishery management. Horace always said that it was important for him to understand every aspect of what an employee should be doing, and how an estate should be managed.'

'Very wise,' Clarice agreed.

'From what Rolly told me, Tom didn't want the management of the piggery; he said that he'd be happy to manage the estate in general, but not that.' Vita sighed. 'Rolly must have allowed Tom to browbeat him. After all, Tom should just have done as he was instructed!' She sniffed. 'I sometimes forget that Rolly was *so* young – he was the same age as Harry is now.'

'And with all that responsibility,' Clarice said.

'Yes, absolutely.' Vita turned towards the door. 'Let's go upstairs to my private sitting room. Mrs Ray is leaving the coffee in there for us. Did you bring the photographs of your new work?'

'Of course,' Clarice said as she followed her.

'I'd like to get away from the shooting mob. What my husband and son get so excited about is beyond my comprehension.'

Upstairs, the door to the sitting room was open. As Clarice approached, she was hit by the smell of lemons, and she recalled the word Vita had used to describe her late father-in-law – eccentric. Knowing how hard Vita worked on her image, enjoying being photographed and interviewed for upmarket magazines, Clarice wondered fleetingly how much of *her* eccentricity was contrived.

Mrs Ray was leaving as they arrived. 'I've put everything as you like it, your ladyship,' she said. 'I've left both warm and cold milk.'

'Thank you, Mrs Ray, you are a gem.' Vita was at her most charming. 'And you have so much on today with the shoot lunch; don't let us keep you.' With a nod, she swept past the cook, Clarice following.

'It's so good to see *real* photographs,' Vita said as she looked closely at each of the images in the portfolio that Clarice had brought with her, asking questions about their glazes and production.

'They're only ones I've printed off using my home printer,' Clarice said self-deprecatingly.

'I appreciate that,' Vita sounded sniffy, 'but you'd be amazed how many aspiring artists show photographs on their mobile phones. So unprofessional. And people stand *too* close, invading my personal space, then witter at great length about each and every aspect of their work.' She gave a mock shudder, followed by an amused chortle.

Their coffee-drinking, image-perusing and random chatter was accompanied by the background noise of the multiple popping sounds made by the guns. Suddenly, hearing the slamming of a car door, then a few minutes later a male voice in the corridor outside the room, Clarice realised the shooting had ceased.

'Have they finished already?' she said, looking at her watch.

'Hardly,' Vita replied, getting up to walk to the window and look out. 'They've only been at it an hour. It's going to be a late lunch – it'll be gone two before they eat.'

The words had barely left her mouth when the door opened and Roland rushed in, followed closely by Tom.

'Are you sure about all this?' Tom was asking. Clarice noticed he was now wearing his sling.

'That's a bloody stupid question!' Roland shouted the words at Tom, who continued to follow him across the room to where Vita was standing. Roland's face and neck were reddened by exertion, beads of perspiration standing out on his forehead, and Clarice noticed that his hands were shaking.

'What the hell is going on?' Vita addressed her husband, her face taut.

'It's at the edge of the woods,' he said. 'It's a woman.'

'Who?' Tom asked, going to Roland to take hold of his arm. 'Who is she?'

'You aren't making sense!' Vita snapped. 'Speak slowly.' She glowered at Tom before looking back at her husband.

'The beaters found her. It's a woman ... her body. They phoned the police straight away.' He looked at Tom. 'I don't know who she is. Half her face has been blasted away.'

'An accident?' Vita's hands rose to cover her mouth.

Into the long silence that followed came the approaching sound of a police siren.

# Chapter 22

They stood frozen until the police car and its siren had stopped. Then all at once, as if mannequins that had been given life, they moved towards the door.

'Has anyone seen Ginny?' Clarice asked.

They became still again, exchanging puzzled looks.

'Ginny?' Vita said sharply. 'She's still on holiday.'

'I understood from what Lucy told me that she's coming back this morning,' Clarice said.

'I'll phone Jack.' Tom spoke as he fished his phone from his pocket.

'We must go down to speak to the police.' Vita moved forward, and as flotsam on a wave, the three men moved ahead of her, Clarice at the rear swinging speedily forward on her crutches in a plucky attempt to keep up. They went out of the room to descend the stairs as Tom spoke to his son.

'Is Ginny there?'

Reaching the bottom, the group stood together, awaiting the answer.

'Clarice has said that that Ginny was planning to come back this morning.' Tom's eyes moved to DS Daisy Bodey and DC

203

Rob Stanley as they advanced towards them. 'OK, she's obviously not arrived yet. Can you come to the hall, please, Jack?' There was a pause while he listened. 'I know about the police car; please come here now!' He clicked off.

The sound of sirens alerted them to the arrival of more emergency services vehicles.

'Can you tell me where the victim of the shooting is, sir?' Daisy's voice carried authority. As she spoke, the men returning from the shoot started to drift in and hover in the hallway, the constant opening of the door ushering in blasts of cold air. Those with shotguns carried them over the crook of their arms, breached to reveal empty barrels.

'I can get one of these fellows to show you where she is.' As Roland spoke, a man stepped forward.

'Is it within easy walking distance?'

'Quicker if you drive.'

'Right,' Daisy said, 'I'll go over to the scene of the incident.' She turned to her colleague. 'Rob, get everybody to wait in there.' She pointed to the Orangery. 'Nobody is to leave the premises.'

'Right, Sarge.' Rob nodded.

'Meghan, you can come with me.' Daisy addressed a newly arrived female officer. 'And Lenny,' she said, speaking to the male colleague accompanying her, 'make sure nobody leaves. Go out to the parking area to stop anyone getting into their car and send them in here.'

The man Roland had volunteered to lead Daisy to the crime scene came towards her. Clarice noticed Roland edging towards the drawing room and, she guessed, the whisky decanter.

'And you, please, sir.' Daisy spoke before he could reach the door.

'Me!' Roland sounded horrified.

'Yes, this is your home and it was your shoot.'

'Well, yes, but . . .' he blustered.

'Would you like me to go?' Tom asked.

'Did you take part in the shoot, sir?'

'No.'

'Then I don't want you.'

Roland turned with resignation to be shepherded out.

'The boss is on his way,' Daisy told Rob, before heading off. Rob started to direct the men coming into the house to the Orangery.

'She is rather abrupt.' Vita's voice held an aggressive bite that carried across the hallway. Daisy, at the door, ignored her, following the others outside. 'Don't *you* think she was abrupt?' Vita said, turning to Clarice. 'Anyone would think Roland was at fault in some way.'

'Given the circumstances, I think she's just trying to get on with doing her job.' Clarice spoke evenly, uncomfortable at being put on the spot. Vita's body language, as she pulled herself upright, told her that her response had not been what her ladyship desired.

'What's going down in here, Ma?'

Vita turned to her son as he strode across the hallway. 'Harry, thank goodness you're safe. You've heard about the accident?'

'Of course. It was Paul who found her. He took me to see her and I told him to call the police. There's an ambulance outside. A bit of a wasted journey.'

'You are sure she's dead, not just injured?'

'As a dodo.'

'Harry!' she rebuked him.

'What?' He opened his arms wide, waving his gun as he did so. 'I'm just telling it like it is.'

'Excuse me, sir.' DC Rob Stanley, sturdy, with fair short-cropped hair, came over. 'Is that gun loaded?'

'Wouldn't be much good at a shoot if it wasn't!' Harry spoke in a voice heavy with derision.

'I'll take that, sir, for the time being.' Rob stretched out his arm to firmly clamp his large fist around the barrel of the gun, pulling it from Harry's grasp. Pointing it downwards, he expertly flicked the lever to open the gun and remove the cartridges.

'Cheeky bugger!' Harry was outraged. 'I had the safety on, and that's a Purdy – have some respect, it's worth more than you'd earn in a year!' His voice boomed around the hall.

'Harry!' Vita interjected stopping him from saying more; several of the men heading for the Orangery had stopped to listen.

'What are you gawping at?' Harry called over to them.

'Would you be good enough to join the other men from the shoot, please, sir?' Rob faced Harry with an unyielding expression, then stepped aside to indicate that he should pass him.

Harry opened his mouth to reply.

'Yes, he will,' Vita said firmly. 'My son is the joint host today, so in his father's absence, he will take charge of the men in the Orangery.'

'Yes,' Harry agreed, catching his mother's eye. 'I'll take charge.'

If Vita realised that Harry's behaviour towards one police officer was not dissimilar to her own, moments earlier, to another, she did not reveal it. And what exactly, Clarice thought, watching Harry walk to the Orangery, was he meant to be taking charge of?

'Is it all right if we wait in here?' Tom asked Rob, pointing to the drawing room.

Rob's eyes flicked from Tom to Vita and then Clarice.

'We were all here, in the house, while the shoot was on,' Tom added.

That, thought Clarice, was not provable at that moment. Though she and Vita had been together, it still had to be established if there was someone who might provide an alibi for Tom. Also, where was Tom going when he passed her as she came in, and where had Vita been before she'd joined her in the sitting room?

'Yes,' Rob agreed. 'Wait in there, but don't leave until instructed.'

Vita made a faint snorting noise but said nothing as she led the group to the door.

'Dad!' Jack suddenly appeared, to run and catch up with his father.

'And who are you, sir?' Rob asked.

'He's my son, Jack Lyme,' Tom butted in before Jack could speak. 'We asked him to come over here from his office at the fisheries.'

Rob looked quizzical.

'It's where the lodges are situated, for people staying here,' Tom said. 'Jack manages that aspect of business for the estate.'

'Are there guests staying in the lodges at present?' Rob asked.

'Yes.' Jack took over. 'We're open eleven months of the year. People don't just come for the fishing – the lodges are often booked for holidays.'

'And they're all within walking distance of the woods and fields where today's shoot was taking place?'

'Yes,' Jack said.

'OK.' Rob took out his police phone. 'You may go in with your father, but please don't leave until instructed.'

As they entered the drawing room, Clarice could hear the mumbled sound of Rob's voice as he updated HQ with the new information. She realised that the guests from the lodges, as well as the shooting party, would all be required to give an account of their movements. The police would now have a huge task taking statements from so many people.

Vita walked over to sit in her favourite carved mahogany armchair.

'Tell me what's going on.' Once the door was closed, Jack spoke to his father, an edge of panic in his voice.

'We don't know much, just that there's been an accident during the shoot.'

'Someone's been shot!'

'Yes.'

'Who . . . Do we know them?'

'We don't know any more than that, Jack.' Tom's voice was soothing.

Jack looked confused. 'Why did you ask about Ginny? She's not due back for three days.'

There was an awkward silence while Tom appeared to be thinking of a way to reply.

'The person who's been killed is female.' Vita's voice, as if finding every nook and cranny, filled the room.

'You all think it might be Ginny?'

'No . . . not necessarily.' Tom was flustered. 'But Lucy told Clarice that Ginny had changed her plans and was arriving back this morning.'

'How many of the shooters were female?' Jack asked. 'They're always men, aren't they?'

'None were female.' Vita's tone was cold.

'Then it's obviously *not* an accident involving someone who was part of the shooting party!'

'We don't know who it is,' Clarice said, 'and the police can't let us know until they know themselves.'

'But it could be Ginny,' Jack said. 'Where is Harry?'

'What's that got to do with anything?' Vita responded, her head having instantly swivelled around, her eyes on Jack.

'I told him that if he hurt her there would be trouble. I didn't expect this.'

'What!' Vita started to rise from her seat.

'Jack,' Tom snapped, 'be quiet! We don't know who the woman is. Sit down and shut up. I can't see Harry doing something like this.'

Jack and his father eyeballed one another. Then Jack turned away and walked to the alcove where Clarice had been earlier, sitting down to look out of the window at the movements of the police officers.

Going over to join him, Clarice could see one of the groups of young beaters being herded into the house. Both trucks were standing empty, side by side in the centre of the car park. She assumed that the first group were already inside. The two groups were often split, beaters going ahead to get into their new positions with shooters following on, working their way around the fields of the estate.

Jack glanced up at Clarice, then back outside again, where Rick was getting out of a car and walking towards the house. Passing the window, he glanced in, but if he saw Clarice, he did not acknowledge her presence.

The room fell into silence. Tom had taken a seat away from both Jack and Vita, whilst Clarice had moved from the window to sit on a sofa. The tension was palpable. Glancing at her watch, Clarice checked as ten minutes passed, then another ten, and then another. Jack got up to pace around the room before returning to sit down.

The smell of almond furniture polish seemed suddenly oppressive. For several minutes at a time, the room was brought to life by a flood of sunshine, only to return again to dullness as the clouds hid the sun. It felt as if they had been fixed in a time warp, each minute passing like an hour.

Fifty-five minutes after she'd seen him arriving, Rick walked into the room, followed by DC Rob Stanley. Jack sprang to his feet whilst Tom stood up in a more sedate manner. Vita, who had maintained a frosty silence, remained seated but turned with Clarice to look at Rick.

'Your ladyship.' Rick acknowledged Vita before nodding his head to Clarice and scanning the room. 'I understand from what DC Stanley has told me that you were all here in the house when the incident took place. Apart from you, sir.' He indicated Jack. 'You were at your office at the fisheries.'

'What about the woman?' Jack asked. 'Ginny, my girlfriend, was apparently coming back today, but I haven't seen her. Who is the woman, the one who's been shot?'

'The team is out there at present, but they've only been there for a short time.' Rick spoke directly to Jack. 'We don't yet have identification of the victim.'

'It's been over an hour. Don't you know any more?'

'They will take as long as they need. We must allow them to do their jobs thoroughly.'

'Was it an accident?' Vita said. 'At the shoot?'

'I can't answer that question either,' Rick replied before his eyes swept over Tom, Jack and Clarice. 'DC Stanley will be taking you to another room, one at a time, so that you can give your statements. We need to know where everybody has been this morning.' He turned again to Vita. 'We will need to use several rooms for interviewing. There's not only the shooting party to consider, but also guests and visitors at the lodges, as well as the staff.'

Vita nodded. 'I imagine this will not be over by the end of today.'

'No,' Rick said. 'The first thing we will need to establish is whether or not this was an accident. Whatever the outcome – accident or otherwise – we will be here until we're satisfied that the case has been fully resolved.'

'When you say "otherwise", you mean murder?' Vita said.

'Yes, I do.' Rick looked directly at her.

Clarice noticed a trembling in Vita's hand before she placed it over the other in her lap.

'And where is my husband?' Her voice was querulous. 'Lord Fayrepoynt went out with that woman officer and he hasn't returned!'

'He has returned. He's been with DS Bodey and the housekeeper, Mrs Lyme, helping to allocate the rooms that can be used by my officers to interview and take statements. And he's now in one of those rooms giving his own statement about his whereabouts earlier this morning.' Rick's voice was modulated, controlled; it was clear he would tolerate no arguments. He held Vita's gaze until her eyes dropped downward, her mouth an angry red slash.

He looked around the room, then nodded at Jack. 'You, sir, please come with me. You too, Clarice.'

Once outside, Rob directed Jack to follow him, while Rick led Clarice to a small storage room off the kitchen, in which a small table had been set up with two chairs.

'Who is it?' The words came out immediately. 'Is it Ginny?'

'I can't say, Clarice,' he said. 'She was shot in the face.'

'Will you tell me when you know?'

He nodded silently.

'Well?' she said as they sat facing one another across the table.

'I have to ask.' Rick leaned back in his chair.

She nodded. 'How much I know about what's been going on?'

'Yes.'

She recounted to him what had happened since her arrival. 'So . . . not a lot,' she concluded.

'I disagree. The scratches on Tom's arm are a cause for concern. I didn't see them when I spoke to him earlier.'

They sat for a moment deep in their own thoughts before Clarice asked, 'Have you any more information on the break-in at the vicarage?'

'No. The house has been secured. Pete and Jackie Smith checked out of the pub early yesterday morning.'

'Are you thinking that it might have been Pete who broke in?'

'I wouldn't put anything past him, although in reality he's stealing his own stuff – or rather Jackie and Maggie's stuff, since they're the next of kin to Rose.'

'What do you want me to do now?'

'Nothing. Just go home.'

'Don't you want a statement?'

'Yes, but we've got a lot of people to get through, and I know you can account for your movements. We can take your statement later.'

'Can I go and speak to Lucy? She'll be worried about Ginny.'

'No, I'm sorry, you can't. She's about to be interviewed, and I'd rather anything that she might have to say is said to one of my officers.'

Clarice nodded.

'I'll walk you to your car, let Lenny know you've been cleared to go, then I want to brief Daisy. She has a good interview technique; she can have a talk with Tom.'

As she drove away, Clarice glanced in her rear-view mirror to see Rick standing watching her departure before turning to walk back to the hall.

# Chapter 23

Arriving home, Clarice felt drained. There was a note on the table from Sandra telling her that as well as tending to the cats in the barn and Micky, they had walked the dogs. Feeling restless, she called the dogs to her before going outside. It was dull and cloudy, and as she walked slowly around the boundary of the garden, the weather reflected back her heavy gloom, mooring her spirit to the earth with its invisible ropes. The thought that Ginny might be dead depressed her deeply. But then, she rationalised, it might not be Ginny and there should be sadness for whoever had died. Blue and Jazz ran back and forth whilst Micky kept to her pace, but their antics and boisterous fun could not shift her pessimism.

It was nearly 4 p.m. when, back in the house, she remembered she had missed lunch. As she poked aimlessly through the contents of the fridge, finding nothing that appealed to her, she realised that what she was feeling was not hunger, but nausea.

A random thought came into her mind and, following it, she brought out bread-making flour and dried yeast, putting them on the kitchen table. But after fetching a large mixing bowl, she stood back to look at the assembled items and realised that she couldn't muster the enthusiasm to make bread today. Instead she went into the sitting room to use the downstairs phone to call Sandra. It rang as she crossed the room.

'Clarice?'

She recognised Laura's voice; remembered guiltily that they had arranged to meet at the book club and then go on for a meal.

'Laura, where are you?' Clarice asked.

'I've just come from the college to the book club. Clare Robbins has told me that it's been on the local radio news that there's been an accident at Winterby Hall and somebody's been shot.' She spoke rapidly, breathless, as if trying to get the words out as quickly as possible. 'I've tried phoning home and I've tried Dad on his mobile, but no one's picking up, and when I phoned the hall, I was told by a policewoman that nobody's being allowed in!'

'Laura, I'm so sorry – our arrangement for tonight went completely out of my mind.' Clarice thought of Daisy interviewing Tom, an image of the scratches on his arm penetrating her mind.

'You've been there today. Jack said you were meeting Lady Vita for a coffee.'

'Yes, I haven't been home long.'

'Are Dad and Mum OK, and Jack?' There was fear in Laura's voice.

'Yes, I didn't see Paula but I know Rick did. And I saw your dad and Jack. They're all fine.'

'Thank goodness, I was so worried.' She stopped talking, but Clarice could still hear her breathing. 'Can I come over to you? I'm just outside the library but I don't really want to go back into the book club, and I expect you've gone off the idea of a meal. I know I have.'

'I have. Come over, Laura. I'll give the restaurant a ring and cancel our booking.'

'OK,' Laura said. 'I'll see you soon.'

Half an hour later, after Clarice had cancelled the restaurant and brought Micky into the sitting room with the other dogs, Laura arrived. She was, as always, immaculate in a navy-blue suit with a floral blouse. Clarice wondered if the other students in her group were as smartly attired.

'Were you going to make some bread?' Laura stood in the centre of the kitchen, looking at the assorted items on the table.

'No,' Clarice sighed, 'I can't muster any enthusiasm for it.' She moved the flour, yeast and bowl back into the cupboard.

'Mum makes good bread,' Laura said, watching her clearing the table. 'We never have shop-bought.'

'Paula's such a brilliant baker; her cakes always sell out at the charity events. Does she use the airing cupboard to prove the bread?'

'No, she puts it into a plastic supermarket bag, near the Aga. It rises beautifully.'

'A spray of water?' asked Clarice.

'No, a sprinkling of seeds; she does the spray later.'

'Sounds like she's perfected the art.'

'Except poor old Dad gets annoyed with the recycled bags.' Laura smiled.

'In what way?'

'Well,' Laura said, 'I shouldn't say, but everyone knows Mum's mean, she never parts with anything unless she has to. The bags Dad gets his plastic box in with his afternoon sandwich are the bags Mum's already used once, for her bread to prove in. Dad says they're always full of flour dust and seeds. Being so pernickety and smart, he moans if it all comes out onto his trousers, or worse still, his office desk.'

'He moans to your mum?'

'No, you are joking! He moans to me and Jack.' Laura talked as she wandered into the living room. 'Is he one you're fostering?' she asked, seeing Micky on the rug.

Clarice told her Micky's tale.

'Poor boy,' Laura said, having taken a seat on the floor next to him.

'You'll get a hairy bum sitting there,' Clarice said, looking at the navy wool skirt of Laura's suit. 'Don't forget I've got long- and short-haired cats as well as the dogs.'

She waited for the usual response: 'That could only happen to me.' But instead, Laura waved her arm as if pushing something away from her. 'I'm not bothered about a few cat hairs. You wouldn't believe how worried I was after I heard about the shooting.'

'That's only natural,' Clarice said.

'Mum phoned and left a message while I was driving over here, I've just left one back for her. Can you tell me what happened while you were there?'

Watching Laura stroke Micky, Clarice told her what she knew about the shooting.

'So you don't know who the woman is?' Laura asked. 'And Ginny's not turned up or phoned?'

Clarice shook her head.

'Poor Jack,' Laura said.

'Poor Jack and Ginny, and poor woman, whoever she is,' Clarice added.

'You don't think it is Ginny?'

Clarice lifted her shoulders. 'I don't know. Let me make us some tea or coffee. If we feel hungry later, I'll rustle up an omelette or something.' She got up. 'Tell me about the floristry course.'

'Loving it,' Laura said with enthusiasm. 'People think it's just arranging a few flowers, but there is so much more to it. The jogging is about trying to lose weight. New career, new slim body. I want to leave the past behind.'

'Brilliant. You were at Jacob Printing a long time?'

'Don't remind me,' Laura said. 'I left school at sixteen. I wanted to go to art college, but Mum pushed me into an office job. Her plan was for me to take my A levels at evening class while I was earning, then go to college to train as an accountant.'

'It never happened?'

'It was never what I wanted. I was in that job for eighteen years, during which time I married and then separated from a man my mother disapproved of.'

'I did office work for a while,' Clarice said. 'I needed the money but I always felt I was treading water.'

'That's how I felt too. You were lucky; you escaped and went to art college. I guess I might have left sooner if I hadn't met Geoff and got married. The end of the marriage acted as a trigger to change my life.'

Later, mug of coffee in hand, Laura, still sitting on the floor with Micky, asked, 'Do you see much of Rick? Do you still get on, as friends, I mean?'

'I hadn't really seen much of him for about six months, just in passing. Castlewick's a small place. I've seen a lot more of him since I found Rose's body at the Hanging Barn.'

'That must have been awful,' said Laura.

'It was,' Clarice agreed, not wanting to think about it. 'What about you and your ex? Are you still friends?'

'Not really.' Laura twisted her lips, her eyes cold. 'I thought we could be; I think we both did.'

'Whatever you liked about each other in the beginning, before you married,' Clarice said, 'it's still there, you're both still the same people. Although of course you never know what goes on in other people's marriages, and couples often put up a good front.'

'Yes,' Laura said, looking down. She seemed awkward, and Clarice wondered if she had been putting on a pretence that her marriage was still working long after it had fallen apart. She remembered Jack telling her that he wouldn't allow Paula to pick away at his relationship with Ginny as she had done with Laura's marriage.

'I think it would have worked, just being friends,' Laura continued. 'Until the new girlfriend arrived on the scene.'

'Ah,' said Clarice.

'Who wants to begin a fresh relationship with the ex-wife still hanging around? And I realised that if I met someone else, I wouldn't want him to be best mates with his ex-wife or girlfriend either. If he had kids by her then I'd want him to be civil and friendly for their sake, but that would be it.'

'So he's in a new relationship?'

'Mm.'

'That must be hard.'

'Not hard. I don't blame him for wanting to move on. It just feels overwhelmingly sad.'

Clarice nodded.

'What part of suddenly being alone did you hate the most?' Laura asked.

'I've thought about that,' Clarice said. 'There were two things. One was the sense of loss – it felt like someone had died, though of course it wasn't the death of a person, it was the death of the relationship. And the second thing was the loss of the other friendships.'

'You mean people having to choose to be your friend or his?'

'Yes, there is that, but I had – or rather *have* – a sense of not belonging. I'd been with Rick for years, and now it's just me. I feel all the uncertainties of being sixteen again, trying to discover who I am and where I'm going, but without the thrill of looking to the future. With friendships, it's like trying to walk on quicksand. I believe that I'm on firm territory but then realise I'm not. Do men find it easier? Probably not. If you spoke to a bloke, I expect there'd be another side to the argument.'

'I'm not sure that I understand.'

'Well,' Clarice said, 'I'm trying to think of examples . . . I'm quite a tactile person, and would think nothing of giving a mate a peck on the cheek or a hug, but now it's awkward.'

'Yes,' Laura said. 'I think I get that.'

'I'm OK with female friends but not with male ones, especially if I'm alone with them. When it's time to do the peck on the cheek hello or goodbye, I ever so slightly freeze.'

'Yes, I know what you mean. It's uncomfortable, there's suddenly a barrier where there wasn't one before,' Laura laughed, 'and you think, OMG, will he think I fancy him?'

'Exactly, and his wife might be a really good friend, but then that's awkward because if she thinks you fancy her husband, she perceives you as a threat!'

Laura leant forward, going into fits of giggles.

'What?' asked Clarice.

'It's always the egotists and the bores.'

'Yes,' Clarice hooted, 'the ones Sandra calls "the small pricks".' She wiggled her little finger in the air.

'Does she call them that?' asked Laura, convulsing with laughter again. Micky looked at her quizzically.

'Yes,' said Clarice, 'because it's never the decent ones. The nice ones realise you must feel awkward; it's the ones who think that they are *so* hot!'

'You're right.' Laura wiped a tear away, then turned to follow the sound of the ringtone from her phone. She got up, suddenly serious as she went to retrieve it from her jacket.

Clarice listened, realising that Laura was speaking to her mother. She left the room, going into the kitchen to check that she had enough eggs for two omelettes, only to find that there were an extra six, Sandra having topped them up.

'That's great, Mum, so you'll phone and let me know?' Laura followed a few minutes later, finishing the call.

'Mum thinks I'll be able to go home in about an hour. They're finishing the last of the interviews.'

'Thank goodness. There were a lot of people to get through.' Clarice glanced at her watch. 'It's gone six, shall we have that omelette? Will cheese and tomato be OK?'

'Yes, please,' Laura said. 'I'm suddenly starving.' She went to sit at the table as Clarice brought a pan out.

'So what's new?' Clarice asked.

'Mum said there's still going to be a police presence; they won't be packing up and going home just yet. I think there'll be someone posted where they found the body.'

Clarice listened as she chopped tomatoes before tossing them into the sizzling butter in the omelette pan.

'They haven't said who the woman is, so they haven't said that it's *not* Ginny. And Mum says Jack's going mental!'

'Poor Jack,' Clarice murmured.

'Apparently he's been accusing Harry of all sorts. Mum's insisting he stays in the house with her. And Dad's had a hard time from the sergeant who interviewed him.' Laura drummed her fingers distractedly on the tabletop.

Clarice glanced up as she chopped and felt a fleeting sense of guilt. Laura, who had seemed to be more relaxed after the news that she could go home soon, was now clearly less so.

'Mum said Walter had been a bit of a sod this morning. Because the shoot was on, Dad picked him up to lock him inside the barn that's used for storage.'

Clarice pulled a quizzical face.

'Walter scratched him,' Laura touched one hand against the back of the other, 'on his hand.' Her eyes dropped. 'DS Bodey asked where Dad had got the scratches from . . .' Her voice trailed away.

Clarice sensed that Laura was not being completely honest with her, as if she was lying or omitting something, just as earlier she had sensed she was holding something back about her marriage breakdown.

She turned her attention back to the pan. 'It all sounds a bit of a mess,' she said, before looking up again to see Laura brushing her hand across her eyes, tears spilling downwards.

'Laura,' she said, moving the pan away from the heat before going to put her arm lightly around the other woman's shoulder. 'Are you all right?'

'I'm OK.' Laura spoke as she rose, as if trying to take back control.

Clarice moved away.

'It's been an upsetting day,' Laura spoke firmly, forcing a feeble smile, 'but I'm OK.' She tore a piece of kitchen towel from the roll on the table to noisily blow her nose. Then, as Clarice turned back to the stove, she muttered, 'Families, who'd have them.'

Clarice felt confused by the comment. Laura's mood was swinging from upbeat to tears and back, the stress of today's events making its mark. She decided that asking what she had meant might reduce her to tears again. Instead, she said, 'Let's eat.'

Later, after Laura had gone, Clarice couldn't help but wonder exactly what her friend was withholding. Was she trying to cover up something about her father that might be important? Something Rick might need to know . . .

# Chapter 24

Clarice's night was full of twisting and turning. She awoke several times to find herself hot and sticky, wrapped as tightly as an Egyptian mummy in the white cotton sheet, the duvet on the floor. As it became light, she felt jaded, the sense of foreboding carried over from the previous day.

After coffee, she took Blue, Jazz and Micky out into the garden. It was 6 a.m., icy cold, with a white sky and the crunch of hard frost underfoot. The silence and clinical whiteness of her surroundings contrasted with the mayhem that had been going on inside her head. And despite thinking she was resistant to the possibility of being upbeat, she felt the bitingly cold air infiltrate her melancholy as she watched the innocent joy of the dogs playing chase. Her own leisurely pace matched Micky's slow three-legged movements as they moved around the garden watchfully, stalked by the black shadow that was Ena.

As she returned to the cottage, she recognised the sound of Rick's car driving slowly down the incline. She waited for him to get out and walk to her, Blue and Jazz wild with excitement, Micky uncertain, pressing close to her legs. Rick knelt down, throwing his arms out in welcome to the dogs, rubbing and ear-scratching, before they all followed Clarice inside.

'You're an early bird,' Clarice said.

'So are you. I thought I'd catch you in your dressing gown.'

Ena had beaten them in and sat on the kitchen table, normally a no-go area for cats, gazing majestically at Rick.

'She's still the queen of the castle,' Rick said.

'She certainly is,' Clarice responded distractedly. 'What time did you get away last night?' He looked, she thought, more dishevelled than normal. His clothes appeared to have been slept in, his eyes were baggy, and although he had obviously had a shave, he'd used an old-fashioned razor and she noticed two small nicks where he had cut himself.

'After eleven,' he said, yawning.

Clarice nodded as she opened a cupboard to take out dishes of food she had prepared before going out for the walk. She placed the first one on the floor in front of Ena, who immediately jumped down, then larger ones in front of Blue and Jazz. After that, she put the dishes out for the rest of the cats, as far away from one another as possible, in a circle around the kitchen. The kitchen took on a blended smell of the animal food, last night's log fire and the coffee, now cold, that she had made earlier.

'Last one,' she said, walking towards the storeroom, Micky hobbling unbidden but with enthusiasm behind her. 'I'm feeding him separately because one of the others will nick it if I don't. I'll be with you in a second.'

When she came back into the kitchen, Rick had taken off his jacket and was putting a fresh filter into the coffee machine before spooning in some ground coffee.

'Want something to eat?' Clarice asked. 'I could do you some eggs.'

'I've not got much of an appetite,' Rick said flippantly. He thought for a moment. 'Toast?'

'Toast it is,' she said, going to the bread bin.

She told him about Laura's visit the previous day and how she had felt concerned, with Laura's mood seemingly swinging from laughter to despair. She held off asking him questions until they were seated at the kitchen table, with Rick cutting the butter in slabs for his toast before piling spoonfuls of her last year's strawberry jam on the top, Blue and Jazz on the floor between them.

'Have you made contact with the Norfolk jeweller?' he asked.

'I've spoken to his wife, Helen – he's called Mike, and he's in France with their son. They're in the process of renovating an old farmhouse over there.'

'All right for some!'

'Yes, but they're due back on Monday, about six in the evening. Helen told him about me and I'm going to go over at seven, in case he's running late. I've promised not to keep him for long. I'm seeing Linda Bates in the afternoon.'

'Another long day for you,' Rick said pointedly. 'With all that's going on here, it does seem a bit of a distraction.'

'I'm OK with it,' she replied, sounding non-committal. 'Guess you're on your way over to Winterby?'

He nodded. 'I'll meet the team there. Lady Vita has graciously said we can set up in the Orangery.' He raised his eyebrows mockingly.

'You have to set up somewhere!'

'It's better than one of our mobile units, and I think her

logic is that if we use that area, she gets her house back. The Orangery is linked to the hallway, with toilets, and beyond that, the kitchen. Luxury!'

'That's good,' said Clarice. 'It's warm in there too. I don't blame Vita for not wanting half of the Lincolnshire police force stomping mud back and forth through the house.'

Rick looked at her over the top of his mug as he sipped his coffee. 'The woman who was shot – it's not Ginny.'

Clarice brought her hand to momentarily cover her mouth, surprised at the strength of the feeling of relief that had engulfed her. She felt the prick of unshed tears behind her eyes. 'Thank goodness for that.' Her voice was croaky.

'There was a long delay boarding in Spain, then when she finally got back to the UK, her mobile phone had run out of juice. As her return was meant to be a surprise for Jack, she hadn't worried about contacting him.'

'That's brilliant,' Clarice beamed. 'Jack must have been so relieved.'

'He was. She arrived by taxi, the police at the main gates contacted Jack, and he went up to meet her straight away and brought her back.'

'To Tom and Paula's house, or to Winterby Hall?'

'I don't know about that. I just know that she's safe.'

'And the victim – are you any nearer to identifying her?'

Rick held her gaze. 'It's for your ears only at present, not to be repeated.'

'Yes?'

'It's Jackie Smith.'

'No!' Clarice gasped, both hands forming involuntarily into fists. She recalled Rose's decomposing body, and then thought about Jackie and the strange, disjointed conversation they'd had.

'There was too much going on last night for me to phone you, and I didn't want to turn up on your doorstep at nearly midnight.' Rick watched her closely as he spoke. 'It does make me wonder all the more about where Pete went to on Monday night when he left Jackie near the Hanging Barn.'

'I've thought about that,' Clarice said. 'Knowing Jackie seemed incapable of keeping anything to herself, I still think he might have left her there because he was meeting someone, in case she inadvertently blabbed who it was.'

'He could have left her at the pub,' Rick said.

'Yes, he could, but if she'd got talking to people there, he wouldn't have liked it,' Clarice said. 'Jackie was easily led – she had a very odd conversation with me in the car, asking me not to tell him she'd spoken to me. I think he kept tight control of her.'

Rick nodded slowly while contemplating what she'd said.

'Have you contacted Pete?' Clarice asked.

'We're still trying to trace him.'

'Jackie was shot?'

'Yes, blasted at short range; she didn't stand a chance. It'll be going out in the news today as a murder, not an accident.'

'Was she shot during the shoot?' Clarice asked.

'No, the pathologist says she was killed yesterday, about twenty-four hours before the shoot.'

'So,' Clarice asked, 'was her body moved, like Rose's?'

'No, she was killed where she was found. It's away from the hall, and the noise made by the shotgun could easily have sounded like a bird scarer. Her body was hidden by the long grass; one of the beaters practically tripped over her.'

'I wonder if Pete had arranged to meet whoever he was with on Monday,' Clarice said. 'But this time, because they'd checked out of the pub, he might have planned to leave straight away, with the money he expected to be handed over, in which case he'd have taken Jackie with him.'

'That's one line of thought.'

'Is there another?' Clarice said.

'It might have been an accident that's not been owned up to, or Pete might have killed her, or someone might have killed them both and we have yet to find his body.'

'None of those seem viable.' Clarice was perplexed. 'Why did the murderer not move the body when they moved Rose's?'

'And why was a shotgun used when Rose was battered and then asphyxiated?' Rick said.

'Two killers?'

'Possibly.'

'But they must be connected.'

Rick shrugged. 'I need to consider it from all angles. The press will descend on us when they find out it's a murder, and it's inevitable that, with Rose's body being found so recently, and so near to that of her sister, we're going to get the national press involved. There'll be headlines about a serial killer on the loose, I imagine. But we aren't revealing Jackie's name yet; I'm keeping that quiet for as long as I can. I want more time to dig deeper.'

'What about Tom?' Clarice asked.

'He told Daisy what Laura told you yesterday. That he had picked Walter up to move him inside because of the shoot, and Walter had scratched him.'

'Do you believe him?'

'The jury's still out on that one, but the scratches weren't from Jackie.'

'No,' Clarice agreed, remembering Jackie's small, child-like hands with their nails bitten to the quick. She suppressed a shudder. 'Jackie didn't have nails.'

Rick looked at his watch. 'I'd better make a move. Thanks for the coffee and toast.'

'Any time,' Clarice smiled. 'Hope the day goes well; you've got a lot on.'

'Ha!' he snorted as he got up to collect his jacket. 'It's going to be long and tedious, an inch-by-inch search of the grounds, including the woodland and the fields. I've got maximum reinforcements – they've all been told to turn up at eight. I want to be there well before they start arriving.'

'Plus you'll get a second breakfast.'

'You know me too well,' he said with a chuckle.

'I've got to call over to Winterby Hall at some point,' Clarice said.

'Today?'

'Today or tomorrow. I realised that with everything going down yesterday, I've left the portfolio I took to show Vita. It's upstairs in her sitting room.'

'When you go over, you could call into the Orangery to make that statement. I'll tell them to expect you.'

'Won't they be too busy?'

'They're always going to be too busy. There will have to be a couple of people in there at all times, so I'm sure they can find a space for you. And good luck with seeing Lady Vita. She seemed quite crabby yesterday.'

'She was certainly crabby with me,' Clarice said. 'I wouldn't take her side when Daisy asked Roland to go with her to show her where the body was.'

'Daisy told me,' said Rick. 'She ignored it and you should do the same. Vita can't expect you to join in her hissy fit when an officer's just trying to get on with doing her job.'

Clarice smiled. 'I've seen off tougher customers than Vita in my time, don't worry.'

# Chapter 25

After Rick had left, and with the knowledge that Pete Smith's whereabouts were unknown, Clarice felt edgy. When Sandra and Bob arrived, she told them what had happened but omitted the identity of the victim and the time of the murder.

'We didn't have the radio or the telly on yesterday,' Sandra said, as if disappointed she had missed out on a local event. 'You should have phoned us, darlin',' she said to Clarice.

'I nearly did, just before Laura phoned me.'

'Do you think someone from Winterby might be involved?' Bob asked.

'Impossible to say.' Clarice shrugged her shoulders. 'According to Rick, everybody had someone to vouch for where they were before the shoot.'

'I'm so relieved it's not Ginny,' Sandra sighed. 'I don't really know her, only from when she's been here walking the dogs, but she seems a nice girl.'

'Whoever the dead woman is, she's someone's daughter or mother!' Bob spoke sharply to Sandra before turning to Clarice. 'Did Rick not give a hint who it might be?'

'Stop being so bleedin' nosy.' Sandra shot the words at him. 'If Clarice says she doesn't know, then she doesn't, and if she does and is keeping quiet, it's because Rick's asked her to.'

'I'm going to ring Winterby Hall,' Clarice said, heading for the stairs and thinking how difficult it was to tell only half a tale, 'to see if I can call over for that folder of photographs and get my statement out of the way.'

Paula answered the Winterby Hall phone.

'Oh, *hello*, Clarice.' She sounded at her most supercilious, and Clarice wondered if she had an audience.

'How's Ginny?'

'She's fine,' Paula said without elaborating.

Clarice told her about the portfolio she had left behind the previous day, before asking to speak to Vita.

'Lady Vita's tied up today, but she did mention you might want to call over for the photographs.'

Clarice had an image of Vita standing nearby doing a sideways cutting motion with her hand. She had witnessed it on a couple of occasions when Vita had decided that her relationship with someone was at an end.

'Not to worry,' she said. 'I'll collect them later. I'm sure I can catch up with Vita another time.'

'Of course,' Paula said. 'I was wondering about your Sunday fundraiser. With everything that's been going on, perhaps I should give it a miss.'

'Entirely up to you, though everybody will miss you and your delicious cakes. If you decide to do that, please tell Georgie. Unless you'd like me to tell her on your behalf?'

'Well . . .' Paula paused.

'The other way to look at it,' Clarice said, 'is that with so much going on, it might be a chance to get away from Winterby for a few hours.'

'There is that.'

'But yet *another* thought is that half of Castlewick will turn up, and with everything that's been happening this week, there's bound to be a lot of gossip. You might prefer to avoid that.'

Clarice considered that if it were possible for a thought to manifest itself into an electric current, the suggestion that there might be gossip about events at Winterby Hall without Paula there to listen or put across her point of view was the signal to switch it on.

'Yes, that's true, Clarice,' she said quickly, 'but I mustn't let you down.' She spoke with newly found conviction. 'And you were so good to Laura yesterday – thank you for that. I will come as planned on Sunday. I won't allow the gossips to put *me* off.'

'That is so good of you, Paula.'

'Your photographs are in Tom's office. You can catch me before two, or Tom after that.'

Hanging up, Clarice decided she'd go after two. She would like the opportunity to have a look at Tom's office, and if Paula was there, she wouldn't get the chance.

For the rest of the morning, she stayed in the office catching up on paperwork. When she'd finished, she headed to the kitchen to join Sandra and Bob for lunch before they went home.

'Nice cup of tea, darlin'?' Clarice realised that Sandra was asking not her but Bob.

'Yes please, sweetheart,' Bob responded.

Clarice smiled, but made no comment. The niggling had obviously finished and they were back to being the best of friends.

\*

Driving up to the gates at Winterby Hall, Clarice saw a number of cars and vans parked on the sides of the road leading to the gate, a small crowd of people clustered around the entrance. Approaching slowly, she realised that three or four people were either photographing or filming her. The press, as Rick had predicted. She could not help but wonder how it would be possible to honour bookings for the fisheries and lodges with all this going on.

She pulled up as two officers she recognised from yesterday approached the car. She opened her window. 'Hello,' she said, 'I'm Clarice—' She was cut off by Meghan.

'You're expected; please go through.'

Nodding in acknowledgement, Clarice drove into the grounds. The parking area outside the hall was half full. Going into the Orangery by the terrace door, she saw Rob.

'Hi, Clarice, have you come to give your statement?' he asked.

'Yes,' she said. 'There are a lot of cars outside. Are they still out combing the land?'

He nodded. 'They've been at it since about eight a.m.'

'Nothing new?'

Rob gave her a look that was a cross between knowing and cautious. She realised he was assessing how much the boss might have told her. 'Did you see the press pack? It's just been on the news that the shooting wasn't an accident, it was murder.'

'Ah, I didn't see the news.'

'There you are then.' He gave her the same look. 'Something new.'

He took her to the small room near the kitchen to take her statement. 'You don't mind this being recorded?' he asked before they started.

Half an hour later, as they finished the interview, she was surprised to see Lucy hovering near the door.

'I saw you going in,' Lucy said. 'Thought I'd catch you as you came out. Paula said you might not arrive until after she'd gone.' Although she was talking to Clarice, Lucy's eyes were on Rob.

'Have I missed Paula?' Clarice asked innocently.

'Yes, and Lady Vita's not here. She went out just after nine this morning.'

Clarice silently apologised to Vita, realising that she could not have been in the room, or even the house, during her conversation with Paula. She wondered if she was becoming oversensitive. 'Are you taking me up to Tom's office, then?'

'Yes.' Lucy was still looking from under her eyelashes at Rob. Clearly it was the handsome constable she had wanted to see, not Clarice. 'Have you got everything you need, Rob? Did you want any more of those orange chocolate biscuits?'

'That's really sweet of you, Lucy,' he said. 'I did especially like the lemon ones.'

'I can find you some,' Lucy cooed. 'Clarice, you know how to find your way to Tom's office, don't you? You're such a regular visitor.'

'That's fine, Lucy, I'll pop up there now.' Lucy would be in deep trouble if Vita found out she was giving hand-made lemon biscuits away to a mere police constable, Clarice thought with a smile.

'Tom's only just come in, and he looks a bit grumpy.' Lucy turned her lips down as she spoke before returning her full attention to Rob and leading him to the kitchen.

Going through to the hallway, Clarice climbed the magnificent ornate staircase to the first floor, where Tom's office was spread over two rooms. She wasn't surprised he was grumpy – having someone murdered in your grounds was hardly conducive to good humour, unless you were as enamoured of the police presence as Lucy was. The door to the office was ajar, and she pushed it open curiously – although she had previously glanced in, she had never had a reason to enter.

The room was painted in an off-white emulsion, on the walls prints of scenes of hunting and gun dogs. Much more Roland or Harry's taste than Tom's, but, thought Clarice, Tom might not have had a say in the decor. There was a desk with pens and pads, and a second desk further away with a computer. Books filled the shelves on one of the walls, everything neat and in perfect order. The fireplace had an ornate fender, no doubt what Tom had damaged his arm on. On the nearer desk was a supermarket carrier bag. Inside, Clarice knew, would be a box holding Tom's afternoon cheese sandwich.

As she took a step further into the room, she saw that the connecting door to the next room was half open, and immediately recognised the voices of Tom and Roland.

'You've got a bloody cheek,' Roland blustered. 'I certainly didn't instruct you to cancel the next shoot. I've never cancelled one before. We always have three, just like my father did. We can't finish on two, it won't do!'

'The shoot is the least of your worries. It will only bring more people and more attention while all this is going on with the police.'

'Don't try to tell me what to do! Between you and Vita, I'm thoroughly sick of it.'

'You need to call Vita off,' Tom's voice was icy, 'and keep Harry in check.'

'It's your bloody son threatening mine that started all this.'

'No, Harry's twisted games started it, and now it's spiralling out of control, with Vita adding her bit of venom on top of Harry's.'

'How dare you talk about my wife like that!'

'If you don't call them off, I won't be responsible for Paula. How do you think this is all going to end, Roland?'

'What can I do? You know Vita, she's got Jack in her sights now, and Paula's your problem.' Roland sounded exasperated.

'Don't be so stupid. You know they're asking questions about Maggie. Whose problem is that? The Fayrepoynt family's dirty little secrets are all going to come spilling out if you don't do something.'

'It's not my fault, none of it, and you're changing the subject. I want the third shoot to go ahead as originally planned.'

'Roland, forget about the shoot. You have to intervene, put your foot down with Vita.'

'I can't! And I had no control over events that happened thirty years ago. I wasn't even here . . . I was, as you bloody well know, in Devon.'

Clarice turned quietly and hobbled back to the top of the stairs. Going down two steps, she stopped to listen. If they were still arguing, she couldn't hear them.

'Hello,' she called out brightly. 'Hello, Tom, are you up here?'

A few seconds later, Tom emerged from his office.

'Clarice!'

'Hi,' she said. 'Just the man I was looking for.'

'You've found him?' Lucy appeared suddenly behind Clarice, coming up the stairs.

'You want your photographs,' he said. 'Let me get them for

you.' He went back into the office, returning a moment later with the portfolio.

'Thank you, Tom,' Clarice said.

Following Lucy back down the stairs, she tried to make sense of the conversation she had just overheard.

# Chapter 26

'I wanted to thank you myself,' Ginny said.

She sat in what Clarice thought of as Rick's armchair, in the living room. A long plait hung down to one side of her shoulder, and she wore an oversized white sweater and fashionably ripped jeans. Her face, without a scrap of make-up, was unsullied, milky white and serene. On her lap, bunched in a heap, with his bandaged leg sticking out, was Micky. Blue and Jazz lay on the floor nearby.

'That's a first!' Clarice joined in Jack's laughter as they looked at the small dog wagging his tail joyfully at conquering the climb onto Ginny's lap unbidden. 'And there really is nothing to thank me for. I didn't do anything.'

'You cared, Clarice,' Ginny said. 'Lucy and Jack told me how worried you were.' As she talked, she gently stroked Micky's head with her long, slender fingers. He looked up at her with adoring eyes. 'I can't wait until he's well enough to go for walks. Can I come over with Lucy to take him out?'

'Of course, it would be lovely to see you both.' Clarice looked at Jack, whose expression as he gazed at Ginny resembled that of the small dog. 'And *you* seem a lot happier.'

'I am,' he beamed.

Ginny turned her gentle smile from Micky to Jack, putting out her hand for a moment to touch his shoulder with her fingertips.

It was late on Saturday morning and Ginny had phoned to ask if they might call in. Clarice had welcomed them with coffee and croissants.

'Are things getting any better – easier – at Winterby Hall?' she asked.

The couple exchanged an expressive glance, drawing out the gap in the conversation.

'It's better than it was,' Jack said eventually. 'Ginny going away brought things to a head. Harry's keeping his distance – from both of us – but . . .'

Ginny picked up where Jack had left it hanging. 'It's like watching a pan of milk you know is just about to boil over.'

Jack nodded his agreement.

'The atmosphere's terrible,' she continued. 'Lady Vita hasn't spoken to me at all since I returned. I was waiting to be told that they were going to have to let me go.'

'Yes, Lucy once told me that they never use the word "sack",' Clarice said.

'It's Dad who's been protecting Ginny from the wrath of Lady Vita,' Jack said.

'*And*,' Ginny butted in, looking gratefully at Jack, 'it was your dad who gave me the chance to move out of the servants' rooms; he invited me to live at your house.'

'But we can't go on like this for much longer,' Jack said decisively. 'We've decided we're going to find new jobs and move away from here completely.'

'Is that what you both really want?' Clarice asked.

They looked at one another again before Jack replied. 'Mum and Dad have been brilliant, but it's not fair to them to have all this awful strain. It's very much them and us – Roland, Vita and Harry on one side and our family on the other. And Dad still has to work with Roland.'

'Do Roland and Vita know what a sod Harry's been?'

'Yes,' Jack said, 'it's all out in the open.'

'Vita's taking Harry's side, no matter what, I imagine,' Clarice asked.

'Yes, but she's just being a mum,' Jack said, 'and I could say the same about my own mother. She's getting more agitated by the day. It's hard enough running the business with the police everywhere and reporters sneaking around. We haven't told them our plans yet, but I've started to drop hints about us moving away, and Mum has become *really* stressed. Her attitude is that if we leave to start again somewhere else, Harry's won.'

'I am sorry to hear that,' Clarice said.

'I'm afraid she's going to lose it with either Lady Vita or Harry, say something they'll find unforgivable, and then it'll be Dad and Mum who will be "let go"!'

'Hello!'

Clarice recognised Sandra's voice as she and Bob let themselves in, Jazz and Blue both jumping up to greet them.

'You've caught us out. None of us heard you arriving,' Clarice said.

'Well hello, darlin'!' Sandra beamed delightedly at Ginny.

'Hi, Sandra,' Ginny said. 'Look, I've been adopted.' She gazed down at Micky.

'You have!' Sandra said. 'Are you being unfaithful to your

Auntie Sandra, Micky?' The little dog wiggled his body in delighted response.

'There's someone else just coming, Clarice,' Bob said as he followed Sandra in. 'Do you want me to go out and see who it is?'

'No,' Clarice said. 'Come in, Bob, and say hello. I'll go and see who it is. I am popular today!' She picked up her jacket and crutches and left the two couples to chat.

Ernie Jones, a local farmer, was climbing from his Range Rover by the time she reached the doorway. She knew immediately why he'd called.

'Now then, duck!' he said as he approached, giving the regular Lincolnshire greeting. 'You look busy, with all these cars.'

'I am. And I can guess why *you're* here,' she added.

Ernie, in his late fifties, was short and stout, with a craggy face and very little hair.

'I bet you can, ducky.'

'The shoot?' she questioned.

'Well guessed, young lady.' He walked towards her, his breathing laboured.

'Which day is it going to be?' she asked, appreciating his kindness in informing her. Ernie was a dog lover and aware that all the loud bangs on his land next to Clarice's large garden might upset some of her animals. She would make arrangements to have someone in the barn to fuss and distract the cats while the shoot was on. She was glad Sandra had not realised who the visitor was. Birds were often winged rather than killed outright, with stragglers sometimes finding their way into the garden, and Sandra would give Ernie a hard time about it, and the morality of shooting itself.

'It's going to be next Friday, Clarice,' he said. 'Nothing like Lord Fayrepoynt's, though!'

'I'm sure your guests will all enjoy the day.' Clarice spoke diplomatically.

'As long as we don't find any dead bodies,' he said.

'I doubt you'll do that.' She waited for what she knew would come next.

'You found that first one, didn't you?' he said. 'At the Hanging Barn.'

'I did, Ernie, though I would prefer not to have had that particular experience.'

'So that's why you're on those sticks?' He pointed to her crutches.

'Yes, I didn't land too well.'

'You landed on top of the dead body, or that's what I was told.'

'That's right.'

'Cor . . .' He wafted his hand across his face as if driving away a bad smell. 'That would be a bit stinky.'

Clarice reacted with a nod of agreement.

'They tried to pin it on poor old Bill Whittle,' he said.

'Who tried to pin it on Bill?'

'Well, not your husband – or ex, I should maybe say – but the police took him in.'

'They took several people in, Ernie, but I don't believe anyone tried to *pin it* on Bill. He was questioned but never charged.'

'That's right. But I feel sorry for Jean. It was upsetting for her, and Bill's a good bloke, decent. I use him if I get stuck for a driver during harvest time. He's always been straight, always does what he's supposed to, a good old boy.'

'I'm sure you're right.'

'At least you didn't find the second one.'

'One was enough.' She nodded.

'They don't know who did it yet, then?'

'No, Ernie, if they had, it would have been on the news.'

'Ah, I expect you're right.' He scratched his chin thoughtfully. 'I was just thinking that with your ex-husband being in the police and you being known as a bit of a local sleuth . . .' He let the words hang between them.

'Sorry to disappoint you, but I don't know anything.'

Ernie nodded, his eyes shrewd, as if not quite believing her.

'How's business?' asked Clarice, changing the subject. 'Are you busy?' Rick maintained that while they always pleaded poverty, there was no such thing as a poor farmer. Ernie had cut the middle man out, his crops going straight to be sorted and bagged, sold on directly to the wholesale market.

'It's a quiet time of year for us,' he said, turning back towards his car.

'I hope you can enjoy your time off while it's peaceful,' Clarice said, as she waved him goodbye.


Later in the afternoon, after Jack and Ginny had left, Bob and Sandra helped to load Clarice's car with bric-a-brac, books and items for the tombola stall at the charity event the following day.

'Are we all done?' Sandra asked as they prepared to leave.

'I think so,' Clarice said. 'I've already had a couple of calls from Georgie, but I expect she'll remember something else before tomorrow.'

Going inside to start to prepare her dinner, she couldn't help thinking back to her conversations with Ginny and Jack. She puzzled over the directions the discussion had taken. There was something that had been said that connected to something else. But what? She could not make the link.

# Chapter 27

The doors of Castlewick town hall were propped open. The cars parked directly outside all had their boots open, and people went to and fro taking boxes and bags into the hall. The stalls would include donated toys and clothes, books, plants, cakes and the tombola. Refreshments would be available from the kitchen area, tables and chairs having already been placed near the open hatch.

Clarice, feeling guilty amid all the bustle that she could not help with the physical side of setting up, had gone to sit in the kitchen. In front of her was a pile of plastic bowls and bags of cash in small denominations. She put an equal amount of the small change into each bowl, one for each table, to act as a float.

In the background, the clashing of tables and chairs being detached from the stacks combined with the chatter and laughter of the volunteers spilling through the hatch. Many of the volunteers only came together for the fundraisers, and it was an opportunity to catch up on gossip. Tucked away out of sight, Clarice had already heard the buzz of gossip about recent events at Winterby Hall. Georgie had told her that rather than putting people off, the number of volunteers making themselves available for the day had increased.

Glancing from her partially hidden place, Clarice watched disparate individuals connecting with one another. These events were like intersections at a crossroads, where people linked up, bonds were strengthened, old ties renewed. Mark Hurst, an old friend and animal lover, was chatting in a corner with Liam Nash, the new manager of the town's homeless shelter. In the centre of the hall, Jean Whittle was holding one end of a trestle table whilst Clare Robbins went to grab the other. The two women were obviously now back on speaking terms. They put the table down to stand and talk, and were joined by Lydia Pembroke. Clarice reminded herself to enquire how Lydia's husband Frank was after his spell in the hospital; had Rick tracked down their grandson Ollie in Skegness? she wondered.

Near the door, Georgie was talking to Rosalind Harper and Chrissy Pine, two women in their early fifties. Looking at the pair always made Clarice think of girls from her school days. Rosalind, on the surface sugar-sweet, the pretty one, smart and savvy, who never appeared to fail; and plain Chrissy, the imitator, Rosalind's little echo. Rosalind coveted Georgie's role as chairperson of the fundraising group, while Chrissy wanted to be Rosalind. The two women organised an upmarket ladies' event for the charity during the summer at a hotel on the edge of the town. Although they were aware that it took weeks to build up sufficient donated articles to produce a good tombola, both women habitually skimmed off any decent items if Sandra ever left her stall unmanned. But Sandra was on to their mean-spirited behaviour. Although she had yet to catch them in the act, she'd noticed items missing and reappearing on Rosalind and Chrissy's stall, and had become more vigilant.

Looking again at Jean, Clare and Lydia, Clarice thought they were at least as competitive as Paula. They all saw themselves reflected through the eyes of others. The damage to the relationships caused by Rose had only been possible because of the greed of those involved. Had they, she wondered, ever considered those at the bottom of the scheme, who would have lost money if it had continued? In the end it was they who had been the losers.

Clarice saw Paula arrive, with Laura's help bringing in her boxes containing cakes and bread. Sandra and Bob, near the main entrance, had left their boxes of bric-a-brac to help others set up in the main hall.

Her phone rang, and she recognised Rick's number. She put down a bowl of change before pressing to accept the call.

'Hi, Clarice, where are you?' he asked.

'I'm at the town hall; can't you hear the noise?'

'So they're setting up,' he said. 'I hope you're not trying to help with the tables!'

'No, I'm sitting in the kitchen sorting out the floats. What's happening with you?' She was curious, knowing he would have phoned for a reason.

'I wanted to tell you that Jackie Smith's name is being given out to the media mid morning, as the victim of the shooting.'

'You couldn't keep it back any longer?'

'No, it's almost forty-eight hours, and a number of newspapers had already established who the victim was, though at our request they held back giving out the details.'

'That was decent of them – normally they all want to grab the headlines. What about Pete, have you found him?'

'No, but his photograph will be going out with the media coverage.'

'Well, thanks for letting me know.'

'Is Paula there?'

'Yes, she's just setting up with Laura.'

'I'm walking over from the hall to the Lymes' house. Roland and Vita were informed by Daisy over two hours ago about the news coverage. I asked them to make sure all members of the household and staff were informed. Daisy said the Lyme family were not contactable when she spoke to Roland and Vita. I want to check that Tom and Paula know. I'm thinking that if the press knows Paula's the housekeeper at Winterby and they find out she's helping at your fundraiser, they might turn up at the town hall asking questions.'

'Did you want me to say something to her?'

'Yes, just ask if the message has been passed on.'

'Will do,' Clarice said. 'But Jack and Ginny called by to see me yesterday and I gather the two families are hardly on speaking terms. According to Jack, it's all pretty fraught.'

'This is police business.' Rick sounded fractious. 'I'm not interested in family squabbles. It's important the Lyme family know what's going on. The press will jump on anyone with a connection to Winterby. And I don't understand why people don't keep their mobiles switched on.'

Clarice could not help but remember the number of times she'd needed to reach Rick and his phone had been switched off. 'I'll make sure Paula knows,' she said.

She ended the call and stood up. Spotting Laura nearby, she called her name and hurriedly repeated what Rick had told her.

'Oh my God,' said Laura. 'Mum doesn't know that – nobody told her.'

A few minutes later, she returned with her mother.

'Laura's just told me they're going to let everyone know this woman's name. Do you know anything else? Is she connected to that Rose woman?' Paula asked.

Clarice explained that the person they knew as Rose had been Jackie's sister, and that Jackie's husband Pete was being sought by the police.

'Do they think he killed them?' Laura asked.

'I don't know,' Clarice said. 'But he's Jackie's next of kin and they can't find him.'

'This is just *too* much.' Paula sounded irritated. 'Why the hell didn't either Roland or Vita tell us? It's going to be embarrassing if it's on the radio and people here – or worse, the press – want to talk to me about it. I've got nothing worth saying, but that won't stop them.'

'But Mum, we've been out since early on,' Laura said. 'Vita might have tried to ring us, but I forgot to recharge my phone and you've not had yours with you . . . and Dad's been out with Jack and Ginny.'

'We're entitled to our days off,' Paula said stubbornly.

'Yes,' Laura said calmly, 'but we normally stagger it, not all taking the same time off together, and we usually make sure that we're contactable.'

'That was before Vita became so irrational and stroppy. She has to learn!'

Learn what? Clarice wondered. Was Paula giving tit for tat, her relationship with Vita locked into a toxic downward spiral?

'Now, girls.' Georgie bounded into the kitchen like an Afghan hound with two tails, her excitement overflowing. 'Is everything OK? Are you all set up, Paula?'

Paula, silent and motionless, looked at her with aloof detachment. Laura lifted her shoulders in incomprehension.

'Unfortunately, we're not able to stay,' Paula said coolly. 'I don't want to be asked questions about something that has nothing to do with me.'

'Right, Mum,' Laura said. 'I'll start packing up.'

'Unless,' Paula turned her back on Georgie to look at Clarice, 'you'd like us to leave the baking. Someone else can man the stall. There isn't room in the freezer, and it's a shame to let it go to waste.'

'Do you have to go?' Georgie pleaded. Clarice recognised that her desperation came from wanting to know what was going on.

'Yes, they do,' she said. 'I'm sure we can find someone to sell your goodies, Paula, thank you. I'll return the tins and bags to you.'

'Well,' Georgie said after the two women had gone, 'are you going to tell me what's going on?'

Clarice explained as briefly as possible why Paula and Laura had to leave. She left out the information about Roland and Vita not having passed on the message.

'So who will take care of the cake stall?' Georgie asked.

'I'm meant to be the floater for the day, so I'll do it,' said Clarice. 'I can still count up the takings later.'

'But you're meant to be taking it easy.'

'How hard can it be?' she said.

The event opened to the public at 1 p.m., and Clarice found there was a ready market for Paula's baking, her first customer arriving with the initial flow when the door opened. Seemingly on a mission, she walked directly to Clarice. She was in her mid thirties, pretty and slim, and Clarice recognised her immediately.

'Hello, Clarice,' she said unsmiling, her eyes flinty.

'Hello.' Clarice smiled at her. 'You're my first customer, so lots of choice.'

'How are you?' she asked, ignoring the baking.

'I'm getting by,' Clarice hedged.

'Do you know who I am?'

'I do,' Clarice said. 'You're Sarah Cane, Inspector Chris Cane's daughter.'

'That's right.' Still she did not smile.

'I've just got another dog from him. Micky,' Clarice said.

'So I've heard.' Sarah gave her a long, silent look, her face unreadable. 'I'll be seeing you,' she said, before walking away without buying anything.

What an odd woman, thought Clarice. Like a Persian cat, lovely to look at but high maintenance and with sharp claws. She was glad that Daisy had told her about Sarah's infatuation with Rick.

Later, as people waited to be served, she was joined by Jean Whittle.

'Georgie said that you might need a hand,' Jean said.

'Thanks, Jean,' Clarice said. 'I hadn't realised quite how busy Paula's stall would be.'

As the number of people decreased, Clarice talked to Jean about the book club's book of the month.

'Laura came to the meeting,' Jean said, 'but she didn't stay.'

'No, she phoned me from the library to say it had started,' said Clarice.

'Thursday,' Jean said. 'The day of the murder at Winterby Hall.'

'What was that?' Lydia Pembroke, in her sixties, with short bleached hair and wearing her usual large gold earrings, came to stand next to them.

253

'We were talking about the book club,' said Clarice.

'The murder was on that Thursday,' added Jean.

'Yes,' Lydia said. 'They've named the woman on today's lunchtime news; it was the sister of the other woman who was murdered, the one you found, Clarice.'

Jean seemed unsurprised and made no comment. Clarice realised that there must already have been discussion, and Jean must know about the connection between the two women.

'I hope they don't try to pin this one on your Bill,' Lydia said to Jean.

Both women gave Clarice furtive glances. She realised that they were awaiting her reaction, perhaps assuming she'd take the side of the police.

'I wasn't aware that your husband had been charged with Rose's murder,' she said coldly.

'No, he wasn't.' Jean's colour heightened. 'But people thought he had something to do with it because he was questioned by the police.'

'Ah,' Clarice said, 'they were drawing the wrong conclusions.'

Both women looked awkward.

'They wanted to speak to my grandson Ollie.' Lydia sounded indignant. 'He's only a youngster, an innocent. We don't even know where he is at the moment.'

'And my Bill wouldn't tell a lie,' Jean said. 'He's as straight as could be.'

'So are you, Jean,' Lydia chipped in.

'Of course.' Jean nodded.

Smiling, Clarice turned from them without responding to serve another customer with the last of Paula's baking. She mentally returned to thoughts she had had earlier about the ways in which people wanted to be perceived. She knew Bill had a police record for violence; that Jean and Bill had discussed their lies when she was in their home. And that Ollie, who had already been in trouble with the police, was not the little innocent that Lydia wanted people to believe him to be.

# Chapter 28

The following afternoon, after a late lunch with Sandra and Bob, Clarice set off to Norfolk. She'd asked Mrs Freeman to let Linda Bates know that she would be arriving at Sunnydale nursing home just after 3 p.m. That would give her an hour with Linda and three hours to fill before meeting Mike, the jeweller. She realised the late afternoon would drag.

The rain that had been forecast had held off. As she drove through the grey country lanes to reach the main road, she felt herself relax. She was looking forward to talking to Linda again.

The fundraising event yesterday had been a success. The money raised would be gratefully received by Castlewick Animal Welfare to be used for pet food and veterinary costs. It had raised ten per cent above the previous event, and although there had been a lot of gossiping about the local murders, there had been no awkward incidents with the press.

Later that evening, Clarice had called Laura to tell her how much her mother's products had raised. 'You will pass on the message to Paula?' she said.

'Normally Mum would have been interested,' Laura said heavily, 'but it's not at the top of her list of priorities at present.'

'Are things still difficult?'

'It gets worse by the day. I asked her not to say anything to Vita and Roland about not getting the police message. I thought the situation might calm down. Mum wasn't having it, and she went straight over to Winterby Hall as soon we arrived home from the town hall. Vita sent Lucy to tell Mum that she was *far* too busy to talk to her and they could discuss any issues tomorrow.' Laura sounded downcast.

'I bet that didn't go down well.'

'No, I'm keeping my head down. Mum has got steam coming out of her ears.'

'Not good.'

'No, when she's agitated, she gets crabby with everyone, especially Dad. And it's harder having a stranger in the house, although I guess it's an honest introduction to the family for Ginny. At least she knows what she's getting into.'

'Ginny's hardly a stranger; she's been going out with Jack for two years. And she works with your mum so she knows what she's like.'

'I get what you're saying, but when Ginny took her leave without Mum's permission, it upped the stress not just for Jack but for all of us.'

'Is Paula blaming her?' Clarice asked.

'Not blaming exactly, but there's been a ripple effect. Ginny's part of the problem, because Harry's appalling behaviour is now out in the open, and Vita won't tolerate any criticism of him. The meltdown between Mum and Vita has made the tension levels at home go completely off the scale.'

'I do hope it all blows over by tomorrow. If not, it won't be pleasant for your mother and Vita trying to work together.'

'You and me both, Clarice. Mum has to work with Vita on a daily basis and pass on instructions to staff. There's a wedding reception coming up in the Orangery, and the bride wants unusual extras but with no extra cost, Mum needs to clear the details with Vita today, but I'm not holding my breath. They're too similar, both of them too stubborn. Mum won't back down and Vita is determined to show who's boss all the time.'

Bringing her mind back to the present, to concentrate on driving down the murky lanes, Clarice re-ran the conversation in her head. By this time, the meeting between Paula and Vita must be over. They would either have made their peace, or the Lymes would have been told that they were going to be let go, their family relationship notwithstanding. Stuck behind a slow-moving flatbed truck, she went back to the conversation she'd had with Jack and Ginny. The road was narrow and the truck long. There was no opportunity to overtake, and she watched the bags in the back bounce as the truck hit potholes on the road, fine dust spraying from the flap at the back. It had started to drizzle, and as the rain stopped and the sun briefly shone, she looked about for a rainbow but failed to see one.

Eventually the road widened and she was able to pass. But the image of the scratches to Tom's hand stayed in her mind, and she thought again about the conversation she'd had with Laura about the supermarket bags Paula used to prove the bread, and Tom not liking the dust and seeds getting onto his desk or clothes. She mentally rewound to an earlier conversation with Rick. Rose had been asphyxiated, and had inhaled grain dust while she was dying. Tom had said that he had fallen in his office, possibly on the day of Rose's murder. With the image of the fine spray of dust from the lorry in her mind, a thought burrowed deep into her consciousness and stuck.

The drive to Norfolk was a blur, with the logic of the reliable facts about the two murders and the possible murderers battling for prominence with supposition and guesswork. She felt a sense of surprise when, just after 3 p.m., she turned into the car park at Sunnydale. As anticipated, Mrs Freeman came to the door to let her in, but instead of taking her in the direction they had followed the last time, she led the way to what Clarice assumed was her office.

'Please sit down.' Mrs Freeman indicated a chair on the opposite side of her desk. Clarice did as she had been instructed as Mrs Freeman walked around to sit opposite her. 'I'm sorry you've had a wasted journey, but I understand you have another port of call and are also visiting someone else today.'

Clarice nodded.

'Mrs Bates died this morning. It was in one way unexpected, but then with her being so fragile, it wasn't.' Mrs Freeman spoke wearily, wearing what Clarice thought would be her professional face for the delivery of bad news. Her voice was quieter than her normal brisk tone, and she rested her hands on the desktop, leaning forward, careful to look directly at Clarice. 'I am sorry,' she said.

Clarice was just thinking that Mrs Freeman had an effective professional sympathetic manner when she added, 'But then you hardly knew her.'

'No, I met her only once, but I'm sorry not to have had an opportunity to enjoy her company this afternoon,' Clarice said stiffly. 'How did she die? You said that she was fragile.'

'Yes. But she was looking forward to seeing you.' Mrs Freeman looked at Clarice suspiciously. 'She'd told everybody here that you were coming back to see her as if you were a long-lost friend.'

'We got on immediately,' Clarice said.

'She wasn't well yesterday,' Mrs Freeman continued. 'She went to bed early, but she had breakfast this morning. One of the girls found her in a chair; she thought she'd fallen asleep, but . . .'

'She was dead.' Clarice finished the sentence.

'She'd had two operations for heart problems.'

'You think she had a heart attack?'

'Yes, I do, but it has to be confirmed,' Mrs Freeman said. 'If it's any comfort, she died peacefully. She looked as if she'd just dozed off and had failed to wake up.'

'Yes, it is a comfort. She was a lovely lady,' Clarice said.

Mrs Freeman gave her a look of incomprehension. Clarice wondered if the woman sitting opposite her had ever attempted to have a meaningful conversation with Linda.

'Thank you for telling me. I expect her nephew will be coming over?' Clarice got up as she spoke.

'No, he's busy today; he loves his golf. He said he would make the arrangements tomorrow and call in for any bits and pieces later in the week.' Mrs Freeman sniffed as if disgruntled.

By arrangements, Clarice assumed Mrs Freeman meant for the funeral, and perhaps bits and pieces referred to personal items such as jewellery. She wanted to get away; the room suddenly felt too small. 'Well, thank you again,' she said.

'There is this.' Mrs Freeman pulled open a drawer and took out a manila envelope, which she passed across the desk. Clarice saw her own name on the front in spidery handwriting.

'It was on her bed,' Mrs Freeman said, 'ready, I suppose, for when the two of you got together.'

Clarice felt an overwhelming sense of sadness.

'It wasn't sealed. I did look inside, just in case.' Mrs Freeman sniffed again. 'It's only a letter and two old photographs. I can tell the nephew that it had no value.'

'Yes,' said Clarice, taking the envelope and turning to the door.

'What I can't understand,' Mrs Freeman's voice caused her to halt, 'is why she wrote you a letter if she was going to see you today. It has yesterday's date on it. It's odd, as if she knew . . .'

Clarice looked at her.

'. . . that she was going to die today,' Mrs Freeman finished.

Slipping the envelope into her bag, Clarice left.

'I forgot to offer you a cup of tea.' Mrs Freeman's words trailed her along the corridor.

An hour later, having driven from King's Lynn to Norwich, Clarice sat in a café with a cup of coffee. Taking the manila envelope from her bag, she brought out the single sheet of paper and looked at the almost illegible words, imagining Linda struggling to write with her twisted, arthritic hands.

> My dear Clarice,
>
> I cannot tell you how much pleasure our meeting last week gave me. It brought back the long-buried memories of my younger self at school with Peggy. We did have such a lovely friendship, both as children and as adults, sharing one another's good times and bad. And I remember young Maggie so well, such a darling child. Her aunt thought of her as a gift, the daughter she never had.

I do hope that we will see each other tomorrow. Although we only met briefly, you would not believe how much I have looked forward to seeing you again. I am putting this letter together with the photographs of Maggie that I promised you – just in case. I feel sure that you will make the journey and that I will be here to receive you, but the things we look forward to the most are often not meant to be. Call it the intuition of a foolish old lady.

Your friend,

Linda

What Mrs Freeman had said was true: Clarice had hardly known the old lady. Rick's words back came to her: *Linda Bates isn't your mother, sister or aunt. She has a nephew, for goodness' sake; she isn't your problem.* But that did not stop her feeling sad for a woman she had thought of as being desperately alone, trapped by her body in a place that was a business, nothing more than one of the items of that business. Mrs Freeman was probably a good manager, keeping the home clean and orderly, but everything that came from her was measured as a commodity, be it the number of minutes of a visit or the biscuits on a plate. Clarice mourned the death of the feisty old lady, saddened that simple kindness could not have been more freely given to her.

She put the letter back into the envelope, bringing out the two photographs to place them side by side on the table next to her coffee cup. Despite them being thirty years old and slightly out of focus, she got an immediate sense of Maggie, who was not as she had imagined. She would not have described her as being pretty; she was truly beautiful. Her cheekbones were chiselled, her curly white-blonde hair tumbling down over the shoulders of her Laura Ashley sleeveless summer frock. The wide smile as she stared straight into the camera was natural. Clarice could not make out the colour of her eyes, but she imagined them to be blue or green. Next to her, with her arm around her shoulders, was a plump, smiling woman in her fifties, obviously Aunt Peggy. She looked not at the photographer, but adoringly at her niece. The second photograph was lighter, perhaps taken at a different time of year. Maggie, in jeans and a sweater, was side by side with her aunt, their shoulders touching but their faces more sombre. Standing slightly apart from the pair was Rose – Sharon as she was known then – wearing a short white dress, her bare brown legs set wide apart, one hand on her hip, striking a pose, her long, straight hair dyed red. She had style, thought Clarice, even back then. It must have been the day Linda had said Sharon had turned up asking for money. Behind the group, some distance away, standing next to an old blue Ford Cortina, his hand resting casually upon the bonnet of the car, was a young Tom Lyme.

# Chapter 29

Clarice wandered the streets of Norwich, visiting galleries and book shops familiar to her. It was something she'd often done with Rick on his precious leave days, combining the delivery of her ceramic pieces to a gallery that sold her work with lunch at their favourite Italian restaurant. After leaving the work at the gallery, they'd wander arm in arm to the restaurant, where she enjoyed practising her rusty Italian on the proprietor, Alberto. Today, as she drew near to Alberto's, she turned sharply to cross the busy street, involuntarily lifting her hand to the side of her face, as if in need of protection against the building that housed ghosts of her past.

She went on to the castle museum to see if there was a current exhibition that might divert her thoughts from the news of Linda's death. She was in luck: the exhibition, with only four more days to run, was the work of Henri Matisse. While not quite the pleasure it might have been otherwise, his vivid, expressive colours did provide a distraction. When the gallery closed at 5 p.m., she wandered around for another half an hour before going into a small restaurant and ordering herself a sandwich and a coffee. As she had anticipated, the time dragged, more so because she carried the jarring feeling of disorientation and confusion death always brought: nothing felt normal.

At 6.40, she walked back to her car. Feeling shattered, she thought how glad she would be to return home, though she was not looking forward to the drive. As she reached the car, her mobile rang – Helen, to let her know that Mike's flight had been delayed.

'I'm sorry, Clarice, but he's still at the airport, just about to board his flight. He thinks it will be nearer ten o'clock before he arrives home. Would you like to leave it and speak to him on the phone tomorrow?'

Clarice thought about it. After waiting most of the afternoon to call on Mike, she was loath to end up with a phone call, and she now also wanted to show him the photograph Linda had left for her.

'Is it going to put you out if I come over later?' she asked. 'I don't suppose he'll feel like talking to me when he's had a long day waiting around at an airport.'

'No,' Helen said, 'quite the contrary: he's intrigued and wants to meet you. He knows you've been waiting around yourself after visiting your friend, so please do come over to talk to him if you still want to.'

'That's really kind,' Clarice said. 'I'll ring you later before I set off.'

Sitting in the car, Clarice called Sandra to tell her what had happened.

'Come home, darlin',' Sandra said. 'You're just going to knacker yourself.'

'I would rather hang on,' Clarice said. 'Having waited this long, I'd rather not have it dragging on for another day.'

'Shall we take the dogs home with us?' Sandra asked. 'Like we did when you were in the hospital?'

'That would be brilliant. I might stay over if I feel too tired. Will you be able to manage Micky too?'

'Course,' Sandra said. 'We can't leave the little 'un behind. Just as well that he gets on with your two!'

Clarice found a small hotel, one of a national chain, clinically white, personality-free, but inexpensive. She was advised by the receptionist that there was no shortage of rooms. She bought herself an orange juice in the bar area and went to sit at one of the small tables, which, with the open-plan layout, gave a view of the bar itself, the restaurant and the reception area. She decided to wait to see how she was feeling later before committing herself to booking a room.

For the first hour, she people-watched. Couples of varying ages emerged from the lift, to make their way to the restaurant or leave the building for a night out. A crowd of noisy young men, from their loud banter part of a stag group, were egging one another on to drink faster – spirits, beer and shots – all the time making jokes about the sexual prowess of the groom and the horseplay he was to endure before the evening ended. A young couple emerged from the lift, still half locked in an embrace, to take a table in the corner of the bar, each with a glass of wine. Their eyes connected, their heads almost touching. An older couple, perhaps in their sixties, ate a three-course meal in the restaurant without the need for discussion, masticating while looking blankly around the restaurant rather than at one another. After finishing their meal, both glanced at their watches as they stood up to put on jackets hung around their chairs and exit left through the main doors. Ten minutes later, the stag party followed, staggering out into the street, those who were genuinely drunk and the ones who weren't but wanted to be part of the gang. Their noise carried into the distance until it disappeared. The young couple left to go back into the lift.

As Clarice watched new people drift in and out, she ordered herself another orange juice and brought out the photographs, laying them face up like playing cards on the table in front of her.

She thought again about the volunteers at the Sunday charity event, the people they were now and would become, how they might have turned into someone they hadn't ever wanted to be, living their lives in black and white.

She mentally rewound to consider the three sisters. The bar was quiet now. In her mind, she went back to the putrefied body in the Hanging Barn. Rose, the acquisitive one who wanted so badly to escape from her social and economic position. Working as a servant in the home of a wealthy employer, she saw things she wanted to own and the kind of person she wanted to become. Although intelligent, her route would not be through education. Instead, she'd lived on her wits to become a magpie: a thief, blackmailer and swindler. Rich people had big houses; they collected things: books, paintings, artefacts. Moving to Castlewick and transforming herself into Rose, the wealthy widow living in the big house and collecting dolls, she believed she had fulfilled her dream. But Sharon's dubious ways were not easily abandoned. While Rose wanted to play the grand lady, Sharon needed the buzz only a con could deliver.

Jackie was the saddest sister. She'd had the bad fortune to be born without the aptitude to develop basic social skills. It followed that her family circumstances, her role models, also contributed to her disenfranchisement from everything that might be considered normal.

Clarice looked again at the photographic image of beautiful Maggie. Being brought up by her aunt, she had escaped her background. She should have been the lucky one, turning into the person she wanted to be. But Maggie was dead too.

Motionless, deep in thought, Clarice moved back and forward as if sifting and searching through sand to rediscover a lost gem, going over every conversation she had had since finding Rose's body.

At 10.10, having entered the postcode into her satnav and driven the short distance to their home, she at last met with Mike and Helen Shore. Although they both looked younger, they were in their late sixties, smart in casual slacks and loafers.

'I guess you found me by the maker mark?' Mike asked.

'Yes, I traced it through the assay office.' She briefly filled them in on what she wanted to know.

'You sound like a modern-day Miss Marple.' Helen laughed, clearly intrigued.

'Let me show you what Helen dug out for us while I was in France,' Mike said, bringing in a large battered book. 'I've kept everything, going back to the first customers.'

'He worked for someone else until his early thirties,' Helen said, 'then he went into business on his own.'

'Strangely, I do remember the couple,' Mike spoke as he carefully turned the pages, 'because they were so young and *so* in love.'

'And,' Helen teased, 'you did mention that the girl was one of the prettiest you'd ever seen.'

'Only second to you, my dear,' he replied.

Listening to their banter, looking from one to the other, Clarice realised that they were best of friends as well as husband and wife. The conversation flowed easily between the three of them, until, looking at her watch, Clarice realised that it had just gone 11.30.

She left after again thanking them, suddenly overcome by an irresistible urge to get home. Abandoning any thoughts of staying overnight in Norwich, she hit the road, her mind as she drove returning once more to her journey to the retirement home earlier. The thought she had had then had now become rooted. She knew who had killed Rose.

# Chapter 30

Arriving home, she sensed the strangeness of the house, its emptiness without the dogs rushing to greet her. She considered whether to phone Rick, but it was well after midnight and she didn't want to wake him. Still, the information was too important to hang onto. She picked up her mobile and sent a text. He would see it in the morning.

Getting into bed, her body felt taut, as if all her muscles were locked. She considered getting up again to run a warm bath before dismissing the idea. All she wanted was to escape into sleep.

She woke to an unfamiliar sound and for a moment was disorientated. The noise came again, a creak of the floorboards. It was too heavy to be one of the cats. Suddenly she was wide awake, her first thought that the dogs were not here.

She did not move, not even breathe. Someone was creeping about, but were they downstairs or up? Her mobile was downstairs in the kitchen; the nearest phone was in the study. Throwing aside the duvet, she rolled to the left, putting her feet quietly onto the pine wooden floorboards facing the open bedroom door. Her hand went automatically to grab her crutches from the side of the bed; then, fearing that they would slow her down, she made the split-second decision to leave them. She raised herself up slowly, all her weight on her right foot. In the moments it had taken her to roll and stand, the house had grown silent. She glanced at the clock: 6.02 a.m. The morning light was creeping faintly through the slats of the blinds. She put her hand against the wall to fleetingly move her weight onto her left heel before propelling herself forward, returning the weight again to her right and taking a step nearer the door. During the last few days, she had been moving around the small space of the office in this manner, but always while wearing the flat-bottomed boot. The penalty for doing it barefoot was an immediate sharp pain in her ankle and lower leg.

The silence persisted, but she knew she had heard the sounds, and this time it would not be Rick. Walking stealthily, heedless of the soreness from her left foot, she moved from the bedroom onto the landing at the top of the stairs. Keeping herself against the wall to avoid the open central area, she made her way noiselessly towards the study doorway. The half-light turned the familiar items of furniture into strange and silent creatures waiting to come alive. There was a wealth of places for whoever was in the house to hide. Upstairs, in addition to her own bedroom and the study, was another bedroom and the bathroom.

She stayed motionless for what felt like forever, hoping the intruder might make a movement that would give away their position. Then a scuttling sound to one side made her turn. Howlin' darted to a halt in front of her, his eyes huge and fear-filled, and then ran hard in the opposite direction, disappearing into the bathroom.

She waited for a few moments to regain her composure

before sliding along the wall and slipping into the study. Two steps in and she reached forward to lift the telephone receiver from its cradle, bringing it to her ear. It was dead.

Sensing a presence, she turned to see a figure emerge from behind the partially open door. Even in the semi-darkness, she recognised the broad, thickset bulk of Pete Smith. The smell of stale alcohol and cigarette smoke assailed her senses.

'You might need this, luv,' he said. She looked at what in the half-light could be a piece of rope dangling from his hand, then realised that it was the telephone lead, unplugged from the socket.

His breathing was heavy, and as he moved forward, she realised that his head was covered. He was wearing a type of balaclava, black or dark navy, with holes for his eyes, which were alight with febrile hate.

'Why are you wearing that, Pete?' She asked the question mockingly. 'Don't you think I'll recognise you dressed like a big girl?'

He made a low growling noise and raised his hand to pull the balaclava up over his head. In that split second, she took her chance, diving around him through the space in the doorway he had previously occupied.

A howl of rage followed her as he swung around, too late to stop her slipping past but giving her insufficient time to get across the landing to go downstairs. Instead, she dived back into her bedroom, slamming the pine door shut and pressing her body against it.

Her mind went to her mobile, and she pictured it where she had left it yesterday evening, on the table in the kitchen.

She felt a push against the door and knew that in a contest of strength – his bulk against her own slim frame – she would be the loser. She looked at the window. If she could get there without being stopped, she would need to open it, climb up and jump; and then what? If she could get out before he caught her, which was doubtful, it was a long drop. If she landed badly and couldn't run, he would soon catch her. She looked around the room for a weapon, but there was nothing.

A second howl of rage was followed by the door moving, thrusting her forward as he threw his full weight against it. Throwing herself forward, she grabbed one of her aluminium crutches and retreated to the other side of the room, putting the width of the bed between them.

He stood in the doorway, looking at her impassively.

Her mouth was dry, and her foot throbbed from the sudden burst of exertion. Her whole body was a trembling, pounding heartbeat. She was trapped.

'Now, luv.' He was still breathing heavily, but he spoke slowly, making sure she was aware that he was in control. 'You got something that belongs to me.'

'What?' She was surprised by the strength of her own voice.

'Don't piss me off, girl.'

'I can't give you something if I don't know what it is.'

'You've been down to Norfolk at least three times in the last week.'

'How would you know where I've been?'

He curled his lips away from his rotten teeth in the grimace that for him constituted a smile.

'What do you want from me?' Clarice said. 'You took what was behind the map of Scotland – that should have been enough for a payout!'

It was her habit to sleep in an oversized T-shirt, one of Rick's old ones, which reached to the top of her thighs. She realised that Pete was staring, his eyes flicking up and down over her body in the loose garment as dawn began to seep through the window.

'Ain't got much on, have you, girl?' he mocked, baring his teeth and licking his lips in a suggestive manner.

'I wasn't expecting company.' She stared back. With her fingers wrapped around the crutch, she dug her nails into her palms, forcing herself to keep control, desperate not to allow her terror to become obvious. Pete's smell wafted in waves towards her, her body felt clammy with perspiration and she thought she might retch or scream helplessly.

Suddenly he pulled open his jacket and put his hand inside, pulling out a white envelope that he dropped on the bed between them. 'Know what that is?'

She lowered her eyes to look. 'It's what you found inside the frame,' she said. 'The marriage certificate. Left in the locked case at Aunt Peggy's and found by your sister-in-law Sharon, or Rose as I knew her.'

He applauded slowly, a muffled sound. 'Said you were a proper little know-all first time I met you.'

She looked at his hands. Protruding from between the fingers was a long, thin blade. She mentally fought the fear rising up in her.

'Now, girl,' he said, 'I've shown you mine; time for me to show you yours.'

She stood silently, her head lowered as if in thought. 'But,' she said eventually, 'you've not given me anything I didn't already know. If you want to trade, I need something in return.'

'Like what?'

'We both know who Sharon was blackmailing, and why.'

He shrugged.

'You know who killed Jackie.'

'Yes, and once I've got what I want,' he rubbed his thumb and finger together to indicate money before moving the knife across the bed with his other hand, slicing the fabric of the duvet, 'I'll tie that piece of shit down and skin him.' He was silent for a few moments. 'She weren't worth nothing; she was less than nothing, but she were mine.'

'Well,' Clarice spoke calmly, 'I know who killed Sharon. But who killed Jackie? You were there.'

With his head tilted downwards, he looked up, an imitation of a coquette. 'You already know, a clever girl like you.'

'Yes,' she nodded, 'I think I do, but . . . you tell me.'

The room became still and he continued to stare, as if weighing something up. Was he planning to move suddenly forward over the bed, or around it? She had to be ready.

'It was the bastard.' He spoke slowly, drawing out his words.

She nodded again.

'There . . . told you you'd know.' He used the point of the knife to touch the envelope. 'I've got that and the ring,' he patted his pocket, 'and now I want whatever it was that old cow Linda Bates gave you.'

'The only thing she gave me was photographs of Maggie.'

'Just Maggie?'

'No, someone else was with her.'

'Who?'

It was her turn to tease. 'You might know.'

'Where are they?' He spoke impatiently.

'Downstairs. I'll show you.'

'Gonna try to make me chase you around the house?' he smirked. He bent forward to pick up the envelope, then sprang as fast as his large body allowed, throwing himself across the bed, his arms outstretched to grab at Clarice. She was ready, and dipping to one side she moved around the bed, through the open door and onto the landing. Two strides out of the doorway she felt the power of the blow from his fist pounding into her lower back and she sprawled forward face down, rolling over onto her back with effort. She screamed in pain as he grabbed her right ankle, pulling hard to drag her back before moving to position himself between her and the stairs.

Tucking her right foot under her while bending her knee to twist the left leg away from him in a subconscious effort to protect the damaged ankle, she sat in an awkward position, one buttock pressed to the floor, the other raised by her foot. The new morning light, creeping in, caught on the steel of the knife lying between them. She looked up to find his eyes fixed on her.

'Go on, girl,' he sneered. 'Give you a chance.' When she didn't move, he said, 'Take it before I show you my methods – what your ex-husband would call my MO . . . what I'm going to do to the bastard when I'm ready. And then, with all that money, I'll fly away – just disappear!'

Still she sat motionless, her mind racing. She couldn't retreat back into the bedroom, and she knew that he was playing a game with her. If she lunged forward, he would probably move to put his foot on the blade of the knife. She suddenly felt cold and shivery, light-headed; she had no control over the situation. She could feel the hard wood of the pine floor pressed against the bare cheek of her buttocks; time had slowed down as she remembered the words she had spoken out loud in the Hanging

Barn: *Walter, do you really want me to get splinters in my arse?* Part of her felt detached, looking on at her impending fate: so that was to be her final thought – about a three-legged cat and her concern regarding splinters. Then Rick's words came back to her: *We used to be a good team, you and me.*

'Go on, girl.' Pete spoke again, encouragingly, as if chivvying an old friend. 'You've nothing to lose now, you know you're dead meat.' He started to bend forward gradually. 'Look, I'm going slow, take your chance.' He moved lower to the ground, looking into her face as his fingers closed over the handle of the knife. She could see the rotten teeth and the beads of sweat on his face, and smell his vile breath.

That was when she heard the noise: the familiar rattlesnake sound of the tongue clicking against the roof of the mouth. A dark shadow danced forward, and Ena swiped. Pete Smith screamed, trying to cover his face and pull himself up, but Ena was fast and unstoppable, swiping with the long steel-like claws a second time, then a third. Clarice drew her hand across her face to wipe what felt in her confused state like sweat, and realised it was raining blood.

'My eyes, my eyes!' Pete shrieked the words over and over, holding his hands to his face, stumbling towards Clarice and then, as Ena slashed out at the back of his calf, jumping like an ungainly dancer away from the centre of the landing and stepping backwards – into nothing. Clarice saw him fall, disappearing from her view down the metal stairs, and heard the crash of his body as it hit each metal rung, until the scream halted abruptly.

After the banging had ceased, she stayed in the same position until her back hurt, then flopped down sideways to the floor.

Later, she could not decide how long she had remained there – five minutes, ten, twenty. What she remembered was the whole of her body shaking, before she brought up her knees into a foetal position. Then the letting-go of the tension that had held her, kept her going. The thought came that he could climb back up the stairs, and she forced herself to get up, to go to look down.

She knew immediately that he was dead. He was laid out on the floor at the bottom of the staircase, his arms above his head, a still-life puppet. One foot rested on the bottom step, his head almost at a right angle to his body, his neck broken. And around him, as if inspecting the corpse, was a semicircle of five cats, still and silent as stone. On the top step, looking down, majestically surveying the scene, sat Ena.

## Chapter 31

Clarice went back to the study to reconnect the phone before calling first the police, then Sandra and Bob. Going into her bedroom, she dressed quickly, while waiting for her mind and body to feel reconnected. She picked up a small bottle of water from her bedside table and took it into the study to lean against the desk and drink half the contents. The plastic rim hitting her teeth made her aware of how violently she was shivering. Going back into the bedroom, she found a large woollen blanket and wrapped it around herself before sitting on the floor with her head forward. She counted as she breathed, holding the air in her lungs for as long as possible before letting it out. The shivering was replaced by spasms coming in waves that rippled through her body. Eventually, over the minutes that stretched dream-like without end, she felt that she was taking back control. She heard the first distant sound of a siren.

As she walked down the staircase, she focused her eyes past the prone body of Pete Smith. Part of the fear was that he might at any moment suddenly rear up to attack her again. The spasms that had been under control started again, and she pulled the blanket tighter around her body as she went to the door to let in DC Rob Stanley and Constable Meghan Ryan.

'All right, Clarice?' Rob spoke with kindly concern, clearly aware that she wasn't.

Meghan came immediately to her, putting her hands on either side of Clarice to guide her.

'In there.' Rob, knowing the house from his visits to Rick, directed Meghan to the living room while he stared at the body at the bottom of the stairs. Clarice went where she was led. She listened to Rob's voice fading behind her, communicating information to HQ.

'Are you hurt?' Meghan asked the question quietly.

Unable to speak, Clarice shook her head to indicate that she wasn't. She realised that she was still feeling the after-waves of shock, going through the motions of trying to behave in a way that might be considered normal. It was as if part of her was still detached, looking on at what was happening: first the body at the bottom of the stairs and now the living room, which was exactly as she had left it last night. Was it the tension that had kept her upright and able to walk? How would her body feel when the shock had gone?

A man and woman came in wearing some kind of uniform. Clarice looked at Meghan in incomprehension.

'It's the ambulance paramedics, Clarice,' Meghan said.

Clarice shook her head, pulling back.

'Hello, Clarice.' A tall woman in her late twenties came to sit next to her. 'Is it all right if we check you over? You've been in the wars.' She smiled kindly as she spoke.

Meghan left the room.

Later, all Clarice could recall was that the female paramedic had a Birmingham accent and curly hair. And her own repeated insistence that she did not need to be taken to hospital for treatment.

Sandra and Bob were allowed to join her when the paramedics left. Clarice noticed that in all the years she had known Sandra, this was the first time she'd arrived without her lippy. She looked like a small, frightened old lady. She came to sit next to Clarice, wrapping her arms around her over the blanket, whilst Bob laid a fire from the sticks and logs at hand. Outside the living room, the police team began to inspect and photograph the areas where they knew Pete Smith had been. Bob passed on the information from Rob that the door to the small conservatory at the back of the house had been forced to gain access.

Once Bob had got the fire going, he disappeared into the kitchen, returning with the kettle, tea bags, milk and mugs, and proceeded to make cups of tea for them all.

'I'll have to have my hand back,' Clarice said to Sandra, 'to hold my mug.'

Sandra had said very little, just clinging to her, her protectiveness magnifying Clarice's sense of her own vulnerability.

'We could have lost you,' she whispered.

'But we didn't, Sandra,' Bob said sternly. 'Leave her be.'

'That evil, twisted shit!' Sandra's voice was a wail.

Clarice put her arms around her friend. In comforting her, she felt the still-raw fear of last night mingle with relief and an inexplicable wave of elation: he had done his worst, but she had survived.

Over the next hour as she listened to the movement of people and vehicles that spoke of police activity, Clarice felt herself uncoiling, the tension in her body going, to be replaced by aches in her back, legs and foot. Rob had come in to listen and take notes. He wanted to know exactly what had happened, telling her that it was always easier to talk when something was still fresh. She had said that Sandra and Bob could stay, but seeing Sandra's face contort with distress, she wondered if it might have been kinder to have gone into another room. The cats were all calm now, lying around on the floor and chairs, Ena on the windowsill, watching disdainfully. Clarice stroked BB, who had draped himself across her lap, finding the motion soothing. She missed the energy of the dogs. Bob said that once the police had left, he'd go home to fetch them.

Later, when Rob came back into the room to tell her that the body of Pete Smith was being removed, she asked, 'Does Rick know about this?' She felt embarrassed asking, as if she were being needy. 'I didn't phone him. I dialled 999, but . . .'

Sandra gave Bob a knowing look, and Clarice wondered if they, like her, found it odd that Rick had not phoned.

Rob came to sit next to her. She had known him mainly from social situations with Rick, generally celebrations, the pub or restaurants. He had a boisterous personality, full of dry humour, but he also knew when to be quiet. This situation felt surreal, as if she were dreaming.

'I was waiting for everything to be resolved here, as far as possible, and to give you some space before I talked to you.' He looked at her as if assessing her mental state. 'Rick asked me to tell you that he will phone, but there's been an incident at Winterby Hall.'

'Serious?' Clarice asked.

'Yes, it's Paula Lyme . . . She's dead.'

'How?'

'I can't really talk about it, Clarice, sorry,' he said, 'but you can imagine how stretched we are. With the Jackie Smith murder last week and Mrs Lyme last night, and now this . . .'

His phone rang. 'I've got to answer this,' he said, walking towards the door. Clarice nodded, but a moment later, he returned. 'It's the boss,' he said. 'He wants to talk to you.' He passed the phone over.

'How are you?' She could hear the concern in Rick's voice.

'I'm OK, don't worry about me.'

'You're not hurt?'

'I'm fine. How is it for you at Winterby Hall?'

'Complete hell.'

'Paula is *dead*?' Clarice questioned.

'Oh, most definitely, the speed she was hit by the car. Her body was pinned to the wall; she didn't stand a chance.'

'So . . . that cat is definitely out of the bag.'

'What!' There was an explosion down the phone.

'I'm coming over.'

'Don't do that; you're in no fit state, and you'll just be in the way.'

'You got the text I left for you last night?'

'Yes, and acted on it.'

'I know who killed Jackie and Paula, and I know why.' She heard Rick's intake of breath, followed by a long silence.

'I'll ask Rob to come over with you. I don't want you to be on your own.'

'He's here, standing next to me.'

Clarice passed the phone to Rob, who said *yes* three times before passing it back to her.

'He wants to talk to you again.'

'Is there anything I need to know before you get here?' Rick asked.

'Yes, don't let either Tom or Jack Lyme out of your sight.'

'OK – is that all you're going to say?'

'I'll be there in half an hour. I'll fill you in then,' she said, adding as an afterthought, 'Just one more thing . . .'

Rob drove to Winterby Hall in silence, his usual bubbly persona gone. Meghan sat next to him, Clarice in the back. They had left the forensic staff at the house, taking samples from all the surfaces.

Rick was waiting in the car park. He looked haggard, but his eyes in his tense, gaunt face were sharp. As he watched her moving toward him on the crutches, they initially appeared to rake her, as if checking that all her limbs were moving as they should, before locking onto her face.

'Go and talk to Sue,' he instructed Rob and Meghan, nodding towards an officer near the entrance to the hall. 'She'll bring you up to speed.'

As they walked away, he turned to Clarice. 'OK – spill.'

# Chapter 32

The family and staff were gathered in the drawing room. The fire had been banked up, the silence in the room broken only by the sound of flames and spitting logs.

Sergeant Daisy Bodey, who had been standing in the open doorway, moved away to let Rick and Rob enter, followed by Clarice. A uniformed constable, whom Clarice did not recognise, had positioned herself in front of the closed French windows. She realised that officers from other areas of Lincolnshire might have been brought in as an emergency measure.

Roland was sitting in his bergère armchair, cradling a half-empty glass of whisky, Vita leaning against the fireplace with a cup in her hand. A nearby trolley held more cups and two large Thermos jugs. Harry lounged on the sofa, near his father, with an air of boredom. It seemed to Clarice, her eyes moving from the family to the staff, that there was an invisible line, held taut with tension, with the family on one side, the staff on the other. Sitting near the door were Jack and Ginny. A little further away were Lucy and Mrs Ray, then Tom in a low armchair, with Laura on a high-backed chair placed to the side of him. He looked ashen, as if overnight he had become a creature devoid of blood. He did not look up as they came in, but continued to stare down at his hands, twisting his long white fingers together in a rolling movement, as if performing a bizarre ritualistic handshake with himself.

'About bloody time,' Roland thundered. It was apparent he had been drinking for some time; his voice, loud with indignation as well as whisky, was slurred. 'We've been herded in here like cattle for hours.'

'Forty minutes, Rolly, don't exaggerate.' Vita spoke sharply, walking briskly to the trolley to top up her coffee.

'Bloody ridiculous!' Harry suddenly became alive. 'Stuffed in here with bastards, cleaners and cooks.' He glowered around the room, taking in Tom and the other members of staff.

'Harry!' Roland's voice was hard. 'Shut up.'

'Pa, it's not right!' Harry was shrill.

'Just shut up, boy.'

The use of the word 'boy' hit Harry like an electric current. It was delivered in the same tone of voice that Roland used on his dogs. Clarice had never heard him speak like that to his son. Harry's body jolted, his mouth gaped. An icy silence followed.

'Don't worry,' Rick spoke with authority, 'we don't want to be stuck here any longer than you. Come in, Clarice.' He half turned to usher her from behind him.

'What the hell has your ex-wife got to do with this?' Roland stared at her.

'You'll find out if you do as your son has done and shut up,' Rick snapped.

'You can't talk to me like that,' Roland blustered. 'Chief Constable will chop off your balls, I'll make sure of it.'

'That's a chance I'll take.' Rick looked towards Clarice. 'Do you want to sit down?'

'Yes,' she said, 'it might be easier.'

Jack immediately got up and brought his chair over.

'Thank you, Jack.' She sat down and laid her crutches beside her on the floor. Jack walked across the silent room to stand behind Tom and Laura.

'I've just had a conversation with Clarice,' Rick said. 'I've suggested that she now repeats to you what she told me.' He looked around the room; nobody reacted.

'This all started for me,' Clarice said, 'when looking for Walter I fell and landed on the body of Rose Miller, who as we all now know had changed her name from Sharon Cocker.' She paused to look around the room; all eyes were fixed on hers. 'But the issues that led to that death started for this family over thirty years ago.'

The eyes swivelled to look at Roland, who was staring down at his empty whisky glass.

'When Roland was nineteen years old, he divided his time between here and Snarebrook Hall, where he met sixteen-year-old Maggie Cocker. He was smitten. I've seen photographs of her – she was a beauty: curly blonde hair, a lovely figure and huge eyes. I would think she could have had her pick of men.'

Roland made a rumbling sound but didn't look up.

'After the death of their mother, her sisters Sharon and Jackie had gone to live with their fraternal grandmother, while Maggie was brought up by her Aunt Peggy in her council house between Huntingdon and King's Lynn.'

'Near Snarebrook Hall,' Laura said.

Clarice nodded. 'She found a live-in position at the hall. She was a cleaner, helped in the kitchen, a bit of everything wherever she was needed.'

'A cleaner!' Harry looked in disgust at his father, his face contorting.

'I've been told that Aunt Peggy was a lovely person. She didn't know who Maggie had fallen in love with. Maggie told her she couldn't talk about it until his family had resolved their problems and accepted her. Roland told his father that he was in love with Maggie, and Horace's response was to send him to stay with his cousin in Devon to get him out of the way. He sacked Maggie and also sent her on her way.'

The room was completely silent, everyone hanging on Clarice's words.

'What Horace hadn't been told was that Maggie and Roland had already been to Scotland. When they returned, they were married. After she'd been sacked, Roland made her promise not to say anything about their marriage to anyone until he had told his father. That never happened – he was too frightened to do so.'

'Stop there!' Vita spat the words, incandescent with anger. 'How utterly ridiculous!' She spoke directly to Clarice. 'You've lost it big time, Clarice. I want you out of my house.' She swung around to her husband. 'Tell her, Roland . . . tell her!'

The silence dragged while Roland looked down into his empty glass. Finally he spoke, his voice now steady and low. 'I knew that one day . . . one day I would have to face this.'

There was a cry of anguish from Vita, who clutched at her throat in an exaggerated gesture, staggering to press herself against the wall. Never before had Clarice seen her out of control.

'Ma.' Harry went to her and stood next to her helpless, not knowing what to do. She moved away from him to sit down opposite her husband, unable to speak, her gaze piercing him.

Roland was silent, looking down contemplatively.

Clarice paused for a moment. 'It didn't click at first, about the wedding ring; the initials were wrong. Roland's are RF, Roland Fayrepoynt; Maggie's MC, Margaret Cocker. But we're talking about two very immature young people. The initials in the ring were the names they called one another in their secret world: RP, Rolly-Polly, and MM, Maggie-May.'

She looked towards Vita. 'I got the Rolly-Polly from you, Vita; you've always called him Rolly, and it's only a step further to extend it to Rolly-Polly. And the jeweller who made the ring had Maggie's full name in his records: Margaret May Cocker.'

Vita remained motionless, her facial muscles locked.

'The jeweller still lives and works in Norwich. The maker's mark inside the ring led me to him, and his records show that the ring was ordered and paid for by Roland.'

'What happened to Maggie?' Laura stared at Clarice.

'Roland did as his father had instructed and chose to play the role of the dutiful son; he didn't come through for Maggie.'

'Nobody stood up to my father, it wasn't possible.' Roland kept his eyes downcast as he spoke.

'But you always tell me to stand up for myself!' Harry said.

'If you'd stood up to my father,' Roland looked up, his voice sharp, 'you would be dead, or in a hell on earth.'

'In the case of Maggie, it was dead.' The room seemed to grow smaller with Clarice's words. 'Maggie was an innocent – she didn't know who to turn to. When she realised she was pregnant, she went to someone she had met through the family, someone she thought of as a friend, who had always had to do as he was told and be grateful for the scraps he was given. His mother was the housekeeper at Snarebrook Hall. Maggie met Tom when he visited her.'

'She wasn't pregnant,' Roland said suddenly. 'No, that's wrong, I would have known.' As he stared around the room, everyone looked at him for a few moments and then returned their gaze to Clarice, who was looking at Tom.

'Tom was married to Paula.' Clarice turned towards Laura. 'They had a daughter and had broken away from working as part of the Fayrepoynt family.'

'Dad?' Laura spoke to Tom, who ignored her.

'I believe Tom took Maggie in out of the goodness of his heart. He is a kind, decent man, something I realised when all the evidence pointed to him killing Rose. He could never have killed anyone, let alone looked into the face of someone while murdering them. I imagine it would have been Paula who saw the potential of the situation when she agreed to Maggie staying with them and having her baby. Paula worked on long-term gains. She could never have guessed the outcome, but I imagine she would have thought the knowledge would give her power over Lord Horace and Roland.' Clarice looked at Laura. 'I'm sorry, Laura.'

'Dad?' Laura said.

Slowly, as if returning from a different world, Tom lifted his head to gaze at his daughter. 'It's true, Laura, we both know it.'

Laura, covering her face with her hands, started to cry.

Mrs Ray rose and walked across the room to put her arm about her. 'I'm sorry, ducky,' she spoke quietly, 'but she was very controlling. I don't like speaking ill of the dead, especially someone so recently departed, but ... she was cunning and vindictive.'

'She made my life a misery for years,' Tom said. 'All the jokes about me being accident prone ... *poor sod's so clumsy he'd fall over tying his own shoelaces.*'

'I told you to stick up for yourself,' Laura sobbed.

'If I'd hit her back just once . . . but I couldn't do it,' Tom said. The room became silent.

'Go on,' Rick urged Clarice.

'I believe Maggie wrote to Roland to tell him about the birth of their son. But Roland was still in Devon, supposedly to learn about fishery management, and he knew nothing about the letter. Horace had opened it. He asked Tom to bring Maggie and the baby to see him.' She looked again at Tom. 'You took her there, didn't you?'

The fire was beginning to fade, the room in a state of lockdown, the tension draining away any normality. Glancing around, Clarice saw how haggard Roland looked, as if he had suddenly aged by ten years. Vita was still immobile, and Jack had moved back to be closer to Ginny, taking her hand.

'I'd told Maggie that Roland had been sent to the estate in Devon, and she wrote to him there,' Tom said. 'But Horace's cousin intercepted the letter and sent it unopened to Horace, as he'd been instructed to do if there was any correspondence. Roland never saw it. In the letter, she mentioned their wedding in Scotland. That's how Horace found out.'

'I'll admit that I'm guessing this part, Tom,' Clarice said gravely, 'but I believe that you took her to Horace, and he killed her.'

'She was such an innocent, lovely girl,' Tom gabbled. 'She convinced me to take her; she believed Horace would be thrilled at being a grandfather. But she wasn't stupid, and some maternal instinct stopped her bringing the child. She believed Roland would be there, trusting that he'd told Horace they were married.' Tom stopped speaking, struggling with the memory, his hands twisting together again. 'Horace went mad, completely lost it.

She was such a tiny little thing . . . he was a big man.' His voice dropped to a whisper. 'One punch, just one, and she was dead.' He looked at Laura. 'It's why I never got close to hitting your mother, no matter how far she pushed me.'

'Where did he bury her?' Rick asked.

Tom looked across at Jack, still speaking in the low whisper. 'He fed her to his pigs.'

Laura made a sharp sound before putting her hands over her mouth.

'He told me that he hadn't fed the boars for the two days prior to our visit and they were starving. I realised then that his killing Maggie wasn't a sudden fit of rage; he'd planned it. It was why I told Roland I would never manage the piggery.'

'And her son, the boy?' said Clarice.

'He told me to kill the child.'

'But you didn't?'

'No, of course not. I couldn't – I would never do that. We hid him, left him with Paula's parents in Norfolk. My father . . .' Tom looked at Roland, '*our* father followed us there because he knew I'd never kill the boy, and when he couldn't find him, he drove away in a rage. We heard about the accident the next day.'

'That was the day he died?' Roland asked.

Tom nodded.

'My God, you bloody bastard!' Roland, suddenly alive, staggered to his feet waving his arms. 'You're responsible for the death of my father. And then you moved back here, with your brood, to help manage the place.'

Tom didn't respond.

'That's rather twisted logic, considering what we've just heard.' It was Rick, his voice icy.

Roland gaped at him for a moment, then, looking around, appeared to become aware of the chilly expressions of the staff and police officers.

'Years later,' Clarice spoke directly to Roland, 'Sharon, who was then known as Rose, turned up to blackmail you. It was after Aunt Peggy died. Rose found the marriage certificate and the ring when she was clearing the house. She blackmailed you because she thought you were a bigamist, still married to her sister; she didn't know that Maggie was long dead. The framed map of Scotland was where the marriage certificate was hidden. Pete Smith had worked it out. He took it from the vicarage.'

'Complete cow,' Roland hissed. '*More, more, more*... She wanted to take the clothes from my back – but I didn't kill her.'

'So,' Clarice said, looking at Jack then to Tom, 'you kept Maggie's boy as your own.'

Vita gave a strange throaty gasp. The silence became heavy.

'You're mine?' Roland looked at Jack as if seeing him for the first time. 'You're Maggie's – mine and hers?'

Jack shrugged his shoulders, looking confused. 'Dad?' he said to Tom.

'Yes,' Tom said. 'The reason I didn't give you up was because I felt I owed it to Maggie. I hadn't realised that my father intended to kill her and you. And my half-brother Roland was a child himself, stupid, immature ... Look at him.' He pointed at Harry. 'That's how you might have turned out. I grew to love you as my own, but in reality you're Roland's legitimate son and heir.' He turned to Harry with a sarcastic smile. 'You are only the spare – the second son.'

Harry stood still, his eyes on Jack.

'Why did Mum not want to come clean after Horace died?' Laura asked. 'To tell everyone who Jack was?'

Tom looked at his daughter, confused, as if he was unsure himself. Or fearful of saying something that might hurt her.

'At first she said it was too soon after his death. She said someone might think it wasn't an accident. I think it was partly about control; she had me where she wanted. Then she said that Roland would kill himself soon enough with the booze – it was then that she would make her move.'

'Who killed her?' Jack directed his question to Rick. 'I thought of her as my mother – who killed Mum?'

There was a movement, and all heads turned to follow Rick and Clarice's gaze towards Harry. While their attention had been focused on Tom, he had bent to reach behind the chair next to the fireplace. Standing erect again, he held the side-by-side shotgun that Clarice had seen him with on the day of the shoot.

'Harry!' Vita stood up, her voice shrill. 'Put that down now; don't do anything silly.'

'Your mother's right,' Roland said in a voice that quavered.

'Shut up, shut up, shut up!' Harry screamed the words, looking from his mother to his father, the cry as from a trapped and wounded animal. 'They know, you silly bitch.' He flung the words at his mother. 'And you, my father, what are you but weak . . . useless. It's all your fault.'

'Harry.' Rick spoke in a calm but commanding voice. 'You're making it worse.'

'How can it be worse?' he spat. 'He told me after they found that woman Rose's body that she'd been milking him for over two years. He paid her, the weak, stupid, gutless man.'

'Harry . . .' Roland's voice was pleading.

'Then the other one turns up – slimy Pete and his thick wife – and guess what?' Harry swung the gun back and forth as he talked. 'The stupid bugger was only going to pay them as well!'

His eyes swivelled back and forth around the room, almost revelling in the attention. He looked, thought Clarice, completely insane.

'So yes – surprise – I did try to shoot the filthy blackmailer, but he scarpered and I got the wife. And then what happened?' He looked at Jack. 'That woman, the one I thought was your mother, told me: *want to know something really funny? Guess what, you're only the second son. Your father was married to someone before your mother – Jack was his firstborn.*'

'Harry.' Vita appealed to him. 'She was a bitch, you shouldn't have found out that way. I didn't know, I couldn't protect you.'

'She'd worked it out, Ma, she knew I'd shot the thick cow!'

'Please put the gun down, Harry,' Vita pleaded.

'She said,' he carried on talking, ignoring her appeal, 'that it was so funny, Jack would have all this,' he waved the barrels of the gun in a circle, 'and she would take Lady Muck's place – you, Ma, she meant you – while I would be in prison for the shooting. She laughed outright, laughed in my face.'

Vita stepped forward.

'Stay there!' He screamed the words before swinging the gun towards Jack. 'Guess what, she was wrong! If I don't get it, I'm bloody well going to make certain you won't.'

He aimed the gun at the centre of Jack's chest and pulled the trigger.

# Chapter 33

'How did you know the gun wasn't loaded?' Ginny asked Rick. She, Jack, Tom and Laura, together with Clarice, remained, in various degrees of shock and exhaustion, in the sunlit sitting room. After Harry's arrest, Roland and Vita had insisted they go with him to Lincoln police station. Daisy had read him his rights, but he'd been non-compliant and belligerent, having to be brought to the ground by Rob before he could be cuffed and taken away. Roland had phoned his solicitor, demanding that he meet them at the station immediately. Other staff members had been told that they would be needed later, to make statements.

As she'd watched Harry, kicking and screaming, being part carried, part dragged outside to the police van, the thought had come to Clarice that if he had returned to St Andrews to take his final year as planned, he would not have become embroiled in events unfolding at Winterby Hall.

'Clarice had told me she'd seen Harry take the gun from behind the chair on Thursday when the shoot was on,' Rick said. 'When we spoke on the phone this morning, she reminded me about it, but she didn't need to. I'd told my sergeant to search the room before we all went in there. Daisy had removed the cartridges before putting the gun back. Clarice also suggested that we shouldn't let Tom and Jack out of our sight.'

The two men turned to look at her.

'For reasons,' Rick continued, 'that became obvious.'

The six sat, all but Rick with a coffee cup in hand, in the semblance of a circle, Ginny, Jack and Tom on the sofa and the rest on chairs that had been brought together. The coffee, to Clarice, tasted muddy, as if it had been made too long ago, with a heavy hand; but her senses were all over the place – it might, she thought, actually be OK.

Tom looked worn out and fragile, as if emptied of every possible emotion. He had stopped playing with his fingers, sitting unmoving, hunched and pale. Clarice was aware that Rick would have to arrest him; because he'd known about Maggie's murder and not reported it, he was an accessory. And keeping Jack as his own son would have required registering his birth illegally.

Clarice felt cold – the fire, left unattended, had died. She was distracted by the winter sunshine coming through blinds that had not been pulled all the way up, falling in broken lines to show a fine dust on polished tables. The cleaning routine set by the late Paula Lyme had included the dusting of this room every morning at 7 a.m.

'There is one thing I want to know,' Laura said. They all turned to look at her. 'From what's been said about Harry discovering that Rose was blackmailing his father, he found out *after* Rose was dead ... so did Roland kill Rose?'

Rick and Clarice looked at one another. 'Can I tell them?' Clarice asked.

'Just the basics,' he said.

'No,' said Clarice, 'it wasn't Roland. We believe it was a man called Bill Whittle.'

'The man who was taken in by the police after Rose's body was found, right back at the beginning!' Laura said.

Clarice nodded.

'I'm afraid that's all we can tell you; it's still part of an ongoing investigation,' Rick cut in, 'but his name and the arrests will be public knowledge later today. The details are going to be given out to the press in time for the six o'clock news.'

The door opened and Daisy stepped in. 'We need you, sir,' she said to Rick.

'How did you find out?' Tom spoke as soon as Rick had left the room.

'About what?' Clarice asked.

'That my wife,' he spoke softly, looking downcast, 'was knocking me around.'

'Dad.' Laura moved to put her hands over her father's.

'It's all right, Laura,' he said, 'the secret's out.'

Clarice felt Tom's embarrassment. He was a man who understood dignity. That everyone knew he had been abused by his wife would be a source of personal humiliation.

'It was bits of things I picked up,' she said. 'You always had injuries; nobody could be that accident prone. Then there was Paula's controlling behaviour and her temper, and also the obvious family difficulties. I thought, in conversations that I had with Laura and Jack, that it's very often the things people don't say, rather than what they do, that are a giveaway. Despite the tough front you try to put up, you are a thoroughly kind and decent person.'

'That's not going to help me much now, is it?' Tom lifted

his eyes to meet hers. 'I know I'm going to be arrested for not reporting a murder, and then there's the disposal of poor Maggie's body.' His face contorted as if he was trying to control his emotions.

'That must have been an awful thing to live with,' Clarice said gently.

'Be honest, Dad,' Jack urged. 'Tell the truth and you might not get a prison sentence.'

Laura began to cry again.

'And just to set the record straight, it *was* Walter who scratched me, not Paula,' Tom said, looking at his daughter.

'I'm sorry, Dad. I thought it was Mum.' Laura reached out to take his hand.

The room's earlier tension had evaporated, replaced by a dream-like sense of unreality. Clarice imagined Jack trying to adjust to his new circumstances. His real mother was dead, as was the woman he'd imagined to be his mother. The man he knew as his father was in fact his uncle, and his sister was his cousin. And Harry, his half-brother, had intended to kill him.

'Can I ask you a question, Tom?' she said.

Tom looked at her, waiting.

'I realise Roland knew nothing at the time about your father asking you to bring Maggie to meet him for a reconciliation. So ... when did he find out Maggie was dead?'

'I told him when he came home after our father's accident.'

Clarice nodded.

'He'd believed Maggie had been staying with her aunt. He would never have understood why she had felt unable to tell Peggy what was really going on. She had nowhere else to go when I took her in. Roland said that it was a case of one piece of bad news and one good: that although Horace was dead, the good news was that he could now go and find his wife. *Find*, that was the word he actually used. As if he had put her down somewhere, like a misplaced object, and he just needed to go and get her. I had been wobbling, on the point of telling him about Jack, and then I thought no. I owed it to Maggie to protect her boy.'

'Did he suggest going to the police?' Clarice asked. 'When he knew Horace had murdered Maggie?'

'No, no, definitely not.' Tom gave a derisory snort. 'It was *done*, no point in sullying our father's reputation or the Fayrepoynt name. And I was aware that if it came out, then so would Jack's real parentage. I found it infuriating, after living my life as the family bastard, that Jack would not be able to become the rightful heir, but at least I had the satisfaction of being his father.' He looked at Jack. 'I know I'm not your real dad, but I am so proud of the person you've become.'

Jack managed a weak smile of acknowledgement.

'I was given a photograph by a friend of Auntie Peggy,' Clarice said. 'It showed you in the background. Sharon was in the photograph too. Did you know her back then, through Maggie?'

'Not really,' Tom said. 'I only met her that one time. She had gone to the aunt to ask for money. She had also asked Maggie to help get her a job at Snarebrook Hall; she wanted her to put a good word in with my mother, as the housekeeper.'

'Did Maggie do that?'

'No, she told me that although her sister had work experience in a lovely house in Hertfordshire, she had been dismissed for stealing. I told her my mother would find that out because she would want a reference. The next time I met Sharon, she was calling herself Rose and had contacted Roland. She had sent him a photocopy of his marriage certificate with the words *We need to talk* scrawled on the back.'

'You met her with Roland?'

'Yes, though after that first time, he insisted I had to see her on my own. I would meet her at a lay-by near Lincoln and hand over the cash.'

'And Pete Smith?' Clarice asked.

'No, Roland had told Harry by then about the money he'd paid to Rose – foolishly in my opinion, given Harry's volatile nature. When Pete got in touch, Roland met him with Harry. Pete wanted a large amount, a one-off, he said – ha!' Tom rolled his eyes. 'Until it ran out and he came back for more.'

'But Roland did agree to pay him?' Clarice asked.

'Yes, he got the money and Harry insisted he'd meet with Pete to pass it on.' Tom paused. 'Pete turned up with his wife, and you know the rest.'

When he had stopped speaking, a quietness entered the small gathering, each one of them considering what had happened.

'It's strange that the unravelling wasn't anything to do with the Fayrepoynt family,' Ginny said thoughtfully. 'It was that man whose wife was cheated in some swindle who brought it all out. If he hadn't killed Rose, Roland would still be paying her, Harry would still be the legitimate heir, Jack and I might, in time, have moved away from Winterby and everything would have gone on as normal.'

'No it wouldn't, you mustn't think like that,' Tom said. 'Do you really believe Paula would have allowed Jack to move away? It's what kept her going; she fed on it – the belief that one day she would oust Vita and be the mistress here. It was her dream, her life's work. She would have bided her time, and she would have poisoned your relationship.' He looked from Jack to Ginny. 'Remember what she did to Laura. Paula had to have her own way and she wouldn't share – that included her family. I tried to warn Roland, to get him to control Harry. I knew that if he pushed Paula too hard, it'd end badly.'

They looked at one another.

'In a way, it's a relief,' Tom continued. 'Although it's terrible that Paula has been killed, and the other two, the sisters, I'm glad the truth is out about Maggie's death. I feel a heavy weight has been lifted from me.'

'You really did care about Maggie,' Clarice said.

'I loved her.' Tom's words dropped into the surreal pool, the strange new reality that had been created by the events of the last few hours. 'I've never felt envy towards Roland apart from about Maggie. I've often wished that she'd been *my* wife, not his.'

'Did Paula know?' Clarice said, recognising shock flickering fleetingly across Laura's face.

'Yes, I never said anything but she sensed it. Another thing to hate me for.'

There was the sound of footsteps on the flags outside, and Rick came back into the room, followed by Daisy.

'I'm sorry, Tom,' he said, walking over to the huddled group, 'but my sergeant is going to have to formally arrest you and read you your rights.'

Before Clarice left, she was asked to give a formal statement to Meghan. She remembered how kind the young constable had been to her earlier in the day – it felt like decades ago now.

Afterwards, Meghan said she'd take her home. Gazing out silently at the undulating countryside, Clarice thought about how deeply distressed Vita must be, and the sudden and dramatic change in her circumstances. She thought too about their lost friendship. After Harry's arrest, Clarice had stepped out into the hall, watching Roland go, stiff-legged like a sleepwalker, to telephone his solicitor. As she turned back to rejoin the others, Vita had come from behind, moving around her to block her way, still burning with anger.

'You ridiculous interfering bitch!' The words were spat out.

'Vita!' Clarice stepped back. She could no longer see the beautiful woman she had known, only a hollow, poisoned shell, spewing venom.

'You've dragged my boy into this whole damn mess and he didn't deserve it. You really have *no* idea of the importance of family.'

'You're being irrational,' Clarice said calmly. 'How could Harry murdering two people be down to me?'

'If you hadn't gone poking your nose into affairs that had nothing to do with you, my son wouldn't have been driven to take such drastic action.'

'But what about Maggie? Roland married her and Horace murdered the poor girl.'

'You're being sentimental about a common little tart, a girl on the make! To bring a family like the Fayrepoynts to its knees because of her is utterly preposterous.'

'I can't believe what you're saying,' Clarice said.

'Well believe it – and if you think my boy is going to go to prison, and that one of the servants is going to take Roland's title, think again.' Vita took a step back, her eyes raking Clarice.

'Who are you?' She spoke quietly now. 'Someone who couldn't even hang onto that piece of rough.' Her eyes flicked to Rick on the other side of the hall, then back again to Clarice. 'Trash from some *sarf* London council estate.' She contorted the word to mimic Rick's accent, looking at Clarice with disdain before sweeping away.

Clarice had rejoined the others in the sitting room in a daze. Vita's assertion that her son, despite having murdered two people, could not be blamed was, she thought, not just about unconditional love, it was also about entitlement. She was right in one sense. Clarice didn't understand the belief that being part of a grand family sanctioned their doing as they wished, without consideration for others. And a refusal to take responsibility for the consequences of their actions.

# Chapter 34

Before leaving Winterby Hall, Rick had suggested Clarice ask Bob and Sandra if she might stay with them for the night. Georgie had also phoned offering her a bed, in part, Clarice thought, from kindness, but also, she realised, to pump her about what had been going on. She had declined both suggestions. She would have to adjust eventually to what had happened in the house. Putting it off for a night only meant having to face it tomorrow.

Once home, she had found that the sofa in the sitting room had been pulled out to convert it into a temporary bed with sheets, pillows and a duvet. When the police had finished their work and departed, Bob had cleaned up thoroughly, expunging any remaining evidence of the presence of Pete Smith and his death. The duvet from her bed had been taken by the police, as had the T-shirt she had been wearing last night; the broken door had been boarded up.

Lying on the temporary bed, boxed in by Blue and Jazz, with Micky on top and the cats flopping on the floor, she had feigned sleep. The door opened occasionally. She knew Sandra was looking in on her. But what Clarice needed, for a few hours, was her own space, without the need to talk.

Later, they watched the news together on both the regional and national television networks, Clarice propped up on the sofa bed with a cup of vegetable soup in her hands.

'All right, darlin'?' Sandra had asked for the umpteenth time. She had been in the kitchen making sandwiches for her and Bob and feeding the animals. On hearing the beginning of the news, she joined Clarice on the bed, with Bob sitting in the nearby armchair. Clarice smiled absent-mindedly to acknowledge Sandra's presence before concentrating on the news report.

There was huge media interest, especially with regard to Harry. A camera shot had captured Vita leaving Lincoln police station and getting into the back of a car to be driven away. She was alone. Had Roland not been released on bail? Clarice wondered. He and Tom had both known that Horace had killed Maggie. Tom had been arrested for withholding evidence and assisting an offender; the charge would be the same for Roland.

'She don't look a happy bunny,' Sandra commented without taking her eyes from the screen. 'And where's his lordship?' she added, voicing Clarice's thoughts.

The presenter went back to talking about the arrest of Bill Whittle. He had been charged with the murder of Sharon Cocker, aka Rose Miller. Sharon's sister Jacqueline had also been murdered, and both of their bodies had been found near to Winterby Hall, the home of Lord and Lady Fayrepoynt. Peter Smith, the husband of Jackie, had died of a fall less than twenty-four hours earlier. Although his death was thought to have been accidental, it was currently under investigation, the newsreader informed them.

'At least they didn't mention you, darlin',' Sandra said.

'Shh,' Clarice and Bob hissed.

The police now had evidence, the presenter continued, that the third sister, Margaret May Cocker, had also been murdered. It was thought she had died over thirty years ago. There would be no arrest for her murder, as the police believed the person responsible was now dead.

'But someone saw Rose after Bill went over to her house,' Sandra puzzled, looking more like her usual self now, complete with lipstick.

'I know what you're going to say, Sandra,' Clarice cut in. 'That all the cars were checked for forensics – his wife's, son's and daughter-in-law's, as well as his own. So how could it be him?'

Sandra nodded.

'I followed a flatbed truck on my way to Norfolk yesterday. It was watching the seed dust come through the back flaps and the plastic seed bags bouncing up and down that made me realise it was him. It all fell into place; something just clicked. When Bill was interviewed, Rick didn't know he did occasional work driving trucks. It was Ernie Jones who told me that Bill would fill in if he was busy. It was cash in hand, so being cautious, Bill kept quiet about it. Following the truck, I started to think about Ernie bagging up his seeds. If Bill could get access to one of Ernie's trucks, he could have used it to move Rose's body.'

'How many trucks does Ernie have?' asked Bob.

'Three. He's a creature of habit – the trucks are parked in the same place every day and the keys put on the same hooks. They're not used every day out of season. I left a text message for Rick when I arrived home in the early hours from Norfolk. I suggested that as there was a five-day window in which Rose could have been killed, might it be possible that it had happened *after* that first encounter, when Bill had gone, full of fury, to the vicarage. She died on one of her regular walking routes into Castlewick. If he had worked out her routines, he only had to wait, and then, once he had killed her, move her body.'

'It sounds pretty premeditated,' Sandra said.

'I believe it was,' Clarice said, 'and he attacked her from the front because he wanted her to know it was him. All that bitterness carried over the years from a prostitute who stole from him was used up on Rose because she'd done the same.'

'Jean was adamant it wasn't Bill,' Sandra said. 'It'll be a terrible shock for her.'

'At the CAW charity event, Jean laboured the point that she and Bill never told lies and how honest her husband is. But I know that they both lied. I can't help wondering if she might have had an inkling it was him.'

'Has Rick found anything definite?' Bob asked.

'He said that the team have been checking for forensic evidence in the trucks. No matter how thoroughly Bill tried to clean up, if Rose's body was there, they'll find evidence. And they've searched the skip that holds the discarded and damaged seed bags and found one bag with traces of blood, which has gone for analysis. Fortunately that skip only gets emptied when it's full, and out of season that's not very often. My own thought was that Bill might have put the plastic bag over Rose's head, thinking her to be dead. He didn't want her blood all over the truck. But she wasn't dead. She was asphyxiated in the truck, breathing in the seed dust while she was dying.

'Oh, horrible,' Sandra said, shuddering.

'She picked on the wrong bloke,' Bob said. 'Thieving all her life, maybe it had to happen. It's just strange how it unravelled the whole sorry tale about Maggie's death and the blackmail.'

'Ginny made the same point,' Clarice nodded, sipping her soup.

'But when Pete Smith told you it was "the bastard" who killed Jackie,' Sandra asked quizzically, 'how did you know he meant Harry? Why didn't you think it was Tom?'

'Because Pete couldn't have known about Tom being a bastard. But he did have Roland and Maggie's marriage certificate and he knew it was a big deal. He didn't actually know Maggie was dead, though I believe he suspected it. But if Vita and Roland had married and she was still alive, Harry would be illegitimate, so to Pete, he *was* a bastard.'

'But Maggie *was* already dead when Roland married Vita. Both Roland and Tom knew that. So he was a widower and his marriage to Vita was legitimate.'

'You're right,' Clarice said. 'But knowing how Maggie had died, Roland could hardly challenge Rose and say he wouldn't pay. I have to say, apart from the murders, I've been more preoccupied by the humiliation Roland has brought down on Vita – she's had her world ripped apart. The marriage between Roland and Maggie was legal, so Jack, not Harry, is the heir to the Fayrepoynt estate and, one day, the title.'

'I've always said that you're too kind, darlin',' Sandra said. 'If the situation were different, and it was you with problems, Lady Vita wouldn't give a donkey's backside about you.'

'Maybe not,' Clarice said. She didn't intend to tell them about her last encounter with Vita.

A few hours later, with Clarice under orders to stay put with her glass of red wine, Bob took Blue and Jazz around the garden whilst Sandra did a slow walk with Micky. After a while, Clarice heard doors slamming and the dogs yelping gleefully.

'Look who we've found outside,' Sandra said as she came back in, followed first by Bob, then by Rick with Blue glued to his side carrying a squashed tennis ball.

'Hello, you,' Clarice said, surprised.

'Hello, you,' he echoed with his half-smile.

'We're going now, darlin'.' Sandra went to give Clarice a hug, followed by Bob.

Clarice looked from one to the other. 'Thank you, both. I couldn't have got through today without you.'

Bob, who hated sentimentality, looked embarrassed, Sandra tearful as they said goodbye to the dogs.

'Did you cook up a plan with Sandra and Bob to come over?' Clarice asked when Rick had returned after seeing them to their car. She noticed that on his way back, while passing through the kitchen, he had lost his jacket and acquired a glass that, judging by its colour, contained whisky.

He shrugged his shoulders in response before removing his shoes and going to pick up two cushions from an armchair. He placed them on the sofa bed next to her pillows before reclining next to her. 'Cheers!' He lifted the whisky glass.

'Cheers!' She raised her own half-filled glass.

'Are you planning to sleep here tonight?' She nodded towards his glass.

'If you insist on being impossibly stubborn by not going to friends for the night, I've got no choice,' he said. 'If you kick me out, I'll just have to phone for a cab.'

'It's your turn,' she said. 'Unless you've had enough for one day.'

He looked questioningly at her.

'Spill.'

He held his poker face, not replying.

'There's a whole dish of black olives in the fridge,' Clarice said, knowing that he would be unable to resist.

'Now you're talking,' he said. He returned with the dish, which he balanced on his stomach.

'You're remarkably perky, DI Beech,' she said, 'considering you were up all last night.'

'And you are remarkably together after your ordeal,' he said. 'Most people who'd been through what you had would still be a pile of blubber.'

'I'll take that as a compliment.' She lifted her glass again.

His face became set in a serious mode. 'Vita completely lost it at the station. Full-on histrionics: the murders were everyone's fault but Harry's.'

'I imagine that includes me.'

'I wasn't actually going to tell you that,' he said, 'but your name did come up.'

Clarice nodded.

'She's living in another century,' he said, 'when being part of a family like the Fayrepoynts meant something else. Such as not being answerable for their behaviour. It's what she's taught Harry. She told me that I was trash from a council estate.'

'Yes, she said that to me.'

'About me?' He looked indignant. 'Cheeky bitch!'

'And that you were my bit of rough.' Clarice decided not to add Vita's comment about her not being able to hang onto him.

Rick roared with laughter.

'How was Harry?' Clarice asked.

His laughter stopped immediately. 'Sobbing like a two-year-old.'

'Bet he has a really hot solicitor.'

Rick nodded. 'Not hot enough to get him bail, though. Prison will be hell for Harry.'

'What about Tom and Roland?'

'You know that Tom was charged. Roland was too. He knew about Maggie's murder and how their father had disposed of her remains. They both got bail. Neither of them is charged with murder and I can't see either trying to run and hide.'

'And Bill Whittle?'

He looked at her whilst chomping on an olive. 'You got it right. Once he was told that we had evidence, he gave it up.'

'He confessed?'

Rick nodded. 'Was it just following the seed truck that switched you away from thinking it was Tom? I could see where you were going with that: that Tom had a fall after a fight in his office with Rose, and then asphyxiated her with the carrier bag used by Paula for her bread-making, containing flour and seed dust.'

'It had too many flaws,' Clarice said. 'Firstly, Tom would never have taken her to his office, because all the staff would have seen her. And then how, having killed her, would he have been able to move the body from the house to a car, with a broken arm, again without being seen?' She paused for a moment. 'It was in part watching the fine spray from the truck. The seeds Paula might have put in her bread would have started off whole; they wouldn't have been fine enough. Whereas an empty seed bag would have only the very fine remains, which was what Rose inhaled with her dying breath.'

'And?'

'And no matter how much the evidence pointed to Tom, I just couldn't bring myself to believe it was him. Bill Whittle wasn't just killing Rose; he was also killing the prostitute who stole from him forty years ago. You said how much it had irked him that she walked away with his money while he had a police record. All those years of carrying that bitterness, and then Rose stole from him and laughed when he told her he wanted the money back.'

'The most interesting part of his confession,' Rick said, 'was that he had taken Rose's bag with the keys to the vicarage and ransacked the place looking for money.'

'But he didn't take it,' Clarice said puzzled. 'The money and jewellery were still there!'

'He admitted to taking *exactly* two thousand pounds, which he found hidden in the wardrobe. The money that he said belonged to him and his wife.'

'So was he making a moral statement? That it was OK to be a murderer but not a thief?' Clarice pondered aloud.

'Bizarre!' Rick said. He got up and went into the kitchen with the empty olive dish, returning with two bottles, one of whisky and the other half filled with red wine. He paused to fill Clarice's glass before topping up his own with another generous dram.

'I could make you something to eat,' Clarice said.

'No,' he shook his head, 'I've been picking all day.' He raised his glass. 'This is what I need.'

Clarice's smiled response was non-committal.

'Now it's your turn,' he said.

'You know everything. I told you this morning.'

'Tell me about Linda Bates. And in detail about Pete Smith – I know that's in your statement, but we didn't really have time to talk properly earlier.'

Over the next hour, Clarice told him about her meeting with Mrs Freeman and the news that Linda had died, her encounter with Mike and Helen, and every small, horrible detail of what had gone on with Pete Smith.

He carried on drinking, but listened closely, hanging on every word. She didn't want him to become angry, or overpower her with sadness and regret at what she had been through, and she felt he sensed this.

When she had finished telling him about Pete Smith, she moved on to Walter. The role of the old three-legged cat was still a mystery. 'Did you find anyone Walter might have cadged a lift from to the Hanging Barn?' she asked.

'Nope, nobody who'd own up to it,' he said. 'Perhaps he walked there and, finding a ready source of meat, decided to stay.'

'Plausible,' she said. 'But I still think he got into a car. Maybe someone stopped there to relieve themselves and he jumped out, or they stopped because they'd spotted him and booted him out.'

'We'll never know,' he said; then, changing the subject: 'Have you heard about Rob and Lucy?' He drained the last drops from the whisky bottle into his glass.

'Are they an item?'

'What a very old-fashioned expression,' he laughed. 'I knew about them before you – a first!'

'Well actually . . .'

Later, when she'd explained how she had been ahead of him on that score, she thought that as well as looking worn out and tired, he also now looked blotto.

'OK,' she said, 'so where would you like to sleep? The bed is made up in the spare room.'

'I'm fine here,' he slurred, putting down his glass and sliding downwards.

'I'll fetch you a duvet,' she said, getting up.

'Won't you share yours?'

'No,' she said. 'I haven't forgotten the duvet thief; you can have one of your own.'

Coming back with the blue double duvet, she asked, 'Are you going to work in those clothes tomorrow?'

'I don't see why not.' He looked down blankly, pulling at the collar of his shirt.

'Take them off then,' she said. 'Don't sleep in them.'

He looked at her, trying to concentrate. 'You do say the nicest things, Mrs Beech.'

'Are you flirting with me?' she asked as she helped him unbutton his shirt and trousers.

'I might be.'

The comment might have been flattering if the eyes trying to focus on her hadn't been so alcohol-infused. As he rolled on his side, tugging off his socks, Clarice pulled down his underpants.

'You're trying to take advantage of me,' he chortled gruffly.

'Think I'd be onto a loser if I were,' she laughed, dropping the pants to the floor before walking around to her own side.

'I'm glad we're friends,' he muttered. 'You always were my best mate.'

By the time she had changed into another T-shirt to replace the one taken by the police, and got into her side of the bed, she could hear Rick snoring.

*Best mate*, she thought before she fell asleep. Not bad, but not exactly what she'd had in mind.

# Chapter 35

Clarice awoke to a feeling of confusion, to find that Jazz had jumped on her with wet, icy-cold paws. She sat up, hearing the front door closing, and felt a blast of cold air like an unwelcome visitor. Blue ran in, followed by Ena with her slow grace and her usual sly sideways glance on entering a room.

'Good, you're awake,' Rick boomed.

He was, thought Clarice, his usual noisy morning self. She had missed his company over the last six months, but not his early-morning exuberance and loudness.

'Look who's been walking the garden boundaries with us.' He glanced towards Ena. 'Our own local heroine.'

'I'll make some coffee.' Clarice spoke as she rose from the makeshift bed.

'Don't worry, I did it before I took the beasties around the garden.'

'It's been raining.' Both dogs were wet underneath, chests, legs and paws. And the room, which already had a seedy morning-after smell of sleep and alcohol, had taken on the added odour of wet dog fur.

'It's rained in the night, but it's stopped now. I'll get us a coffee.' He lifted his duvet to shake it.

'How long have you been up?'

'Long enough to shower, walk the dogs and put the coffee on,' he said, exploring the duvet further.

'What have you lost?' Clarice asked.

'Her-humm.' He cleared his throat jestingly. 'My underpants. Apart from my bum being cold, I can't go to work without underwear.'

'Why ever not?' Clarice said, deadpan.

Rick pulled a comical face of pretend shock while continuing to shake the duvet and scan the nearby floor.

'Do you think someone might have taken them?' They both looked at Blue, who wagged her tail with feigned innocence. 'However did I manage to take my clothes off?' he continued. 'I usually sleep fully dressed after a skinful ... not that I get plastered that often.'

'You didn't,' Clarice said.

'Ah.' He stopped searching.

'You've still got clothes in the spare room. The chest of drawers,' Clarice said. 'There are several items of underwear for sir to choose from.'

'Are there?' He sounded taken aback. 'I assumed you would have binned any clothes I'd left behind – it's been six months.'

'It's not up to me to throw away your stuff, and anyway, I didn't know if you might come back – one day.' The words were out.

Rick stood immobile, a range of confused emotions passing across his face.

'It was good of you to stay over, to be concerned for me,' she added lamely.

'I'll get the coffee,' he said.

He brought it to her while she was pulling a large sweater over the T-shirt. Putting the mug down on the hearth in front of the remains of the burnt-out fire, he pointed upward, before leaving the room. She realised that he was going upstairs to find the underwear.

'Successful mission,' he said on his return, giving a sheepish grin.

Clarice sensed a sadness in him, as if he had somehow collapsed within himself, folding up into something small. It was similar to what she'd perceived in him after she'd asked him if he were still living at the same address.

'Will you be OK?' he asked.

She nodded, looking at the clock. It was 6.30. 'Don't you want some breakfast?'

'No thanks, I'll have something in the canteen. I want to be in by seven. It's going to be another very long day.' He paused. 'Can I come back later?'

'Yes, of course.' She smiled.

He didn't return her smile, but came forward to kiss her cheek. 'We'll talk this evening, then.'

After he had gone, she realised that in his haste to leave, he had not poured himself a coffee.

Later, Sandra phoned to ask if Clarice would like her and Bob to come over. Clarice knew that they had a long-standing arrangement to see their daughter Michelle for a family birthday lunch, and despite Sandra's protestations that they could put if off, she insisted they honour the arrangement.

Around 9 a.m., she received concerned calls from Jonathan, then Georgie, and then one from Laura to ask if she might come over later that morning.

After the flurry of phone calls, she went upstairs. It was only the second time since the night of the attack that she had been up there. Rushing to bringing clothes she might want and the duvet for Rick, she had steeled herself not to look around or think.

She saw now that Sandra had remade the bed in her room, with everything clean and looking different from that night. Sitting on the edge of the bed, she couldn't help wondering what might have happened had it not been for Ena . . .

Apart from the wind against the windows, it was completely silent. She forced herself to lie down on the bed, to stretch out and watch through the window the deranged movement of the branches of the willow, caught in the strong gusts. Although devoid of its summer costume, she imagined the life the tree supported; the birds and insects. She remembered her mother resting on a different bed in this very room. Her slow decline. Her spirit doggedly clinging onto life as her body weakened, failing her. She decided that she would sleep in here again tonight.

When she heard a car pulling in, she assumed it must be Laura arriving early. Getting up, she realised she no longer felt panic and fear at the sound of a car engine. Pete Smith was dead – he could no longer harm her.

The dogs barked ceaselessly as she went downstairs and opened the door to Inspector Chris Cane.

'Hello, Clarice,' he said. 'I was passing and thought I'd call by. I hope it's not inconvenient.'

He spoke as he moved his bulky frame through the door, his eyes everywhere.

'Would you like a tea or a coffee?' she said.

'Normally I never say no,' he said, 'but I've got to be

somewhere else in ten minutes. I was driving on Long Road and thought that if I called now, it'd save me a trip tomorrow.'

Micky had come into the kitchen to stand behind Blue and Jazz. While they wagged their tails, the little mongrel hung back, watching Cane suspiciously.

'That's the dog I've come to see.' He held up some paperwork. 'He looks fine to me; has Jonathan seen him recently?'

'He has an appointment tomorrow afternoon,' Clarice said, 'but Jonathan has told me that it will be at least a couple of months before he's back to normal.'

'That's usual for a cruciate problem,' Cane said as he moved across the kitchen to the table. 'And you've got troubles of your own.' He pointed to her crutches.

She nodded.

'I've heard from the people that Micky and the other dog were removed from.'

'They're still being prosecuted?' Clarice asked.

'Yes,' he said, 'but they've signed Micky over to us.'

'That's great.'

'So what do you want to do? Will you keep him to re-home, or do you want to put him into one of our kennels when space comes up?'

'I'll hang onto him,' Clarice said. She was aware that returning the dog to a busy kennel would undo all her work in confidence-building. And she wanted to ensure that he'd have the best home possible, where his quiet charm might be appreciated.

'OK. Jonathan can put his visit tomorrow on our tab, and then he's over to you after that. I just need you to sign the paperwork accepting him.' Cane lowered his large posterior onto a pine chair, which let out a groan of protest.

Clarice took the pen offered and scrawled her name.

The inspector tore away the top sheet to give it to her. 'He's all yours.'

As he tucked the pen back into his jacket pocket, Blue came to him with a present, dropping the brown cloth into his lap.

'Is that for me?'

'She's got a lot of Lab in her, loves to carry things around,' Clarice said.

'Don't think they're my size,' Cane said in a sardonic voice as he held up the tan-coloured pair of men's underpants.

'So that's where they got to.' Clarice spoke coolly, hoping it covered her awkwardness.

There was a moment of silence, then Cane looked up from under his heavy eyebrows. 'I don't blame you, Clarice. You've been on your own a while now; inevitable that you're going to find yourself a boyfriend.'

'I beg your pardon?' Clarice was horrified by his presumption.

'Sorry, I didn't mean to put my foot in it,' he continued calmly, his voice patronising, 'but I speak as I find.' He looked around the room. 'All this to sell, the house and everything else.'

'What!' She fought to control her outrage.

'Well, you have to split everything these days fifty-fifty. I know it was your mum's house, but your ex-husband is entitled to his half.'

Clarice had the impression that he was working out the value of the property. 'Don't you have to be somewhere?' She moved towards the door.

'Yes, I do.' He rose from the chair without a hint of embarrassment. 'Don't take offence,' he added, as if she were in the wrong.

'I already have.' She glowered at him. 'And not that it's any of your business, but the underpants belong to my husband. I ripped them off his tight little arse last night.'

He paused half in and half out of the door, his mouth falling open.

'Goodbye,' she said, and as he stepped forward, she closed the door behind him.

'Cheeky bugger,' she said out loud, but immediately regretted that she had allowed him to push her into losing her temper.

When Laura arrived an hour later, Clarice's anger had abated. She'd tell Sandra and Bob about the encounter tomorrow and they'd laugh together about it.

Seated in the kitchen with Laura, she realised that her run-in with Chris Cane was nothing in comparison to her friend's problems. She listened while Laura told her about her father's desperate state of mind.

'He's deeply upset about Mum, despite how badly she behaved towards him. It's obvious that whatever he might say to the contrary, he still really cared for her.'

'I believe that it's quite complicated why those who are being abused continue to stay,' Clarice said. 'Whatever their relationship was, he'll be grieving.'

Laura sat with her head in her hands, as if thinking. 'Vita's gone,' she said after a moment.

'Gone where?'

'To the London house. Roland told Dad that she said she'll keep in touch with Harry's position through the solicitor. She's still saying he should be allowed out on bail.'

'I can't see that happening!'

'No, but she's gone a bit gaga. She believes that he was

provoked and the most he can be charged with will be manslaughter.'

'Twice!'

Laura nodded, and Clarice could see she was close to tears.

'At least Tom and Roland are still speaking.'

'They weren't until Vita went away, but I guess now she's gone, he's got no one else.'

'They are half-brothers and they've been through so much,' Clarice said, 'with the secrets they've kept all these years.'

Laura nodded and seemed to pull herself back from weeping. 'There is one thing, the reason that I came over.' She sounded awkward.

'What is it, Laura?'

'Vita told Tom that he had to get rid of *that cat*.'

'Walter?'

Laura nodded. 'I'm sorry, but Dad said that Vita and Roland have both become very odd after what's happened. Roland keeps saying *if that's what Vita wants*, as if by bending to her every whim he can put things right between them. Dad said that he'd look after Walter, that Roland didn't need to worry about him, but Roland said that if Vita wanted him gone, then he must go.'

'Yes, I see it could be awkward.'

'Dad said that it's spite, that Vita wants to get at you, Clarice. And he doesn't trust Roland because – and I don't need to tell you this – he loves blasting away at living things with a gun. Walter was meant to be Vita's. Roland doesn't even like cats.'

'So where is Walter now?' Clarice asked.

'In a cat carrier on the back seat of my car.'

*

323

An hour later, after Laura's departure, Clarice sat with Walter in the large room at the end of the barn. He wouldn't like staying in, but he could manage here for a few days. If she let him out, he would be terrorised by Ena, who, while accepting the cats in the house, would not tolerate one not known to her in the garden area, her territory. Tomorrow Clarice would phone around to find a new home for Walter, where he could come and go, being fed and cared for, but with a barn or outhouse as his safe territory.

She walked, fed and watered the animals, and when she had finished for the day, she went to stand outside, watching as the blackness crept in to enclose her and listening to the sound of the wind, its cold biting against her skin. She had a sudden hankering for a cigar: having given up smoking the long, slim cheroots over ten years earlier, the yearning took her by surprise.

In the evening, in the living room, Blue and Jazz pressed on either side of her on the sofa and Micky lay in what was now his regular spot on the hearthrug. The log fire blazed and she sipped from a glass of red wine. As Dave Brubeck played 'Take Five' for the third time, a little after nine, the delighted yelps of the dogs signalled Rick's arrival.

He came in looking tired and tense. 'Hello, you,' he said tentatively.

'Come in,' she said. 'Do you want a drink?'

'A coffee,' he said. 'I don't think I can turn up three days on the trot in the same clothes.'

'I made a pot before you arrived; go and help yourself.'

He went into the kitchen, coming back with a mug to sit in what had been his regular armchair.

'You got the sofa back up,' he observed.

'Yes, I managed it. How's it been today?'

'More of the same, really,' he said. 'What about you?'

'Not great, what with one thing and another.' She spoke in a detached, matter-of-fact tone.

'Are you OK?'

'Yes and no . . .'

'Tell me.' He leaned towards her.

She explained about Walter's return.

'I'm sorry,' he said, 'but I'm not surprised, are you?'

'No,' she said, before telling him about the visit from the inspector.

'Cheeky bugger.' He spat the words out. 'What's our private life got to do with him? Vile man.'

'I believe you're a good friend of his daughter, Sarah,' she said, watching for his reaction.

'No.' He was emphatic. 'Who told you that?'

'I can't quite remember.' Clarice's eyes were mischievous.

'Bet it was Daisy,' he laughed.

Clarice filled him in on Sarah's appearance and odd behaviour at the charity event.

He grimaced. 'It sounds like she was checking you out. I have never at any time encouraged her.'

'I know you haven't; quite the opposite, Daisy did tell me that.'

'Good on Daisy,' he said. 'She told me that you wouldn't agree to her suggesting you no longer cared about me . . . It gave me hope.'

Clarice remembered the smug look Daisy had given her.

'Sarah's old man did me a favour,' Rick said. 'It's sure to get out that Blue presented him with my discarded underwear.'

Blue, hearing her name and their laughter, thumped her tail up and down on the floor happily.

Rick stared down into his coffee. When Clarice did not speak, he asked, 'What else?'

She didn't respond until he looked up, their eyes connecting. 'You said that Daisy's words gave you hope?'

'Ah.'

She smiled at his awkward response. 'Yes, ah indeed.' It was her turn to wait, and when he continued not to speak, she asked, 'Is there someone else in your life? I know it's not Sarah, but have you met someone?'

'No.' His response was firm. 'Why ever would you say that?'

'It's been six months; we've not been a couple . . . you're a free man.'

'Is that what you believe?'

'I don't know what to believe. The time apart wasn't easy, and being with you again has had its upsides.' Clarice lifted her hands in a gesture of exasperation.

'Apart from the murders, attempted murders and dead bodies.' He kept his expression deadpan.

'Yes, apart from those.'

'But . . .' he said.

'You know.' As they stared at one another, she wondered if he'd had the same fears.

'Yes.' His smile held sadness.

'I've felt that we've got on well and made a connection,' she said, 'and then . . . you back away from me.'

He nodded. 'I've been feeling the same with you. It's like we've been moving in parallel lines, side by side but never touching. Do you think our relationship could be the same? Could we be as we once were?'

'No.' She spoke slowly. 'That was then, and this is now; we're different people.'

'But I still love you, Clarice, and it hurts like hell when I don't see you.'

'Me too.' Her voice was gentle. 'I've missed you so much.'

'I didn't know,' he said, 'if you could ever forgive me for leaving, and if we did get back together whether anything would have changed.'

'Your bloody job and my bloody cats,' she smiled. 'Our splitting up was as much my fault as yours, and yes, it will have changed, but what's to say that it might not be for the better? If nothing else, we'll be more tolerant.' She paused. 'I thought that you might want me just as a friend.'

'Of course I want you as a friend, and I will always be your best friend, but I want more than friendship. The truth is that I was frightened to make a move, frightened of your rejection. And would you want me to move back in?'

'Is that what *you* want?' she asked.

'I'm not sure.'

'Me neither.'

Rick stared at her, his mouth slightly open.

'So,' he said, 'I love you, and you love me, and neither of us wants a divorce.'

'But,' she picked up his thread of thought, 'we don't want to live together.'

'Yet,' he added.

'Yet,' she echoed. 'So . . . we're both thinking the same.'

'We always did,' he said. He stood up as he was speaking. 'Let me get the wine and top up your glass.' As he walked past, he gently caressed her hair with his fingertips before bending down to kiss her lips. 'I feel as if a huge weight has lifted.'

'Me too,' she said. Then: 'Are you getting a glass for yourself?'

'Yup.'

'Shall I book you a taxi?'

'I think not.' His smile was tender.

'That's what I hoped you'd say.'

# Acknowledgements

A huge thank-you to my agent Anne Williams, without whose support this novel would not have been possible. Also to Krystyna Green, and all at Constable/Little, Brown.

My thanks to good friends for always being there for me, and for the long lunches, kitchen suppers, yoga, dog-walking, weekends away, evenings in the pub and regular telephone calls. To my animal welfare allies, who share the concern for those who do not have a voice.

Thanks to my Faber writing buddies, for their support and encouragement. Also to my fellow book lovers at the book club, with whom I enjoy long, lazy lunches and chats about books.

Thanks to Lincolnshire Police, who were helpful with information concerning procedures: INSP Ed Delderfield, DI Jim Hodgeson, DS Tina Kennedy, DI Jon Shields, DC Glenn Wright (retired), DC Debra Charlesworth and DC Maria Horner and DC Nicholas Jones.

A big thank-you to Nigel Turner, a partner in Allen, Briggs and Turner veterinary practice, for his advice, and also for the care and support of the vast number of animals – my own and animal welfare cases – over more than fifteen years.

Thank you, for his professional skills, to photographer David Hart. Also to John Snowdon – friend, fellow dog-lover and ceramicist/potter – for his advice.

A big thank-you to Stephen, who is both my dearest friend and brother, for all the splendid days and evenings in the UK and abroad sharing whisky, memories and laughter.

The final thank-you is to Ted, my husband and soulmate for almost forty years, who always encouraged me to follow my dreams. Still with me in joyful memory.